THE EDGE OF FOREVER

J. SAMAN

Cover Design: Danielle Leigh

Editing: Gina J. Re-edited

Chapter One

ARIA

"I can't go on," Margot moans. "Just leave me here. Save yourselves. This will only end one way." I'd say my friend here is being dramatic, but considering her head is now pressed against the side of the wood bar, eyes closed and hand lingering next to the now empty shot glass she just finished off, I know she's not. Because she's right. This will only end one way.

With her facedown in the toilet.

"I told you not to take that last shot," Rina chastises with a disapproving scowl on her face. She puffs out a breath, her hand going to her lean hips.

Margot manages to flip Rina off, but that's all she's got left in her.

I sigh, silently cursing our other friend, Halle, for leaving early and leaving us with a drunk Margot to clean up. I turn to Rina.

Time to get serious.

I raise my hands, curling one into a fist and positioning it above my other hand that is open, palm facing up. "You ready?"

Rina nods. Brushing her long dirty-blonde hair over her shoulders so it doesn't detract from her focus, she rolls her neck, cracking it once. Then she pivots to face me head-on. Getting her game face on, she mimics my position. She nods her head again, this one a signal that we should start.

"Rock, paper, scissors, shoot," we say in unison before throwing out our best offering. I go with paper and she hits me with rock.

"Ha." I grin, giving her a hip bump. "Have fun with drunk Joe over here."

"Hey," Margot objects to my pet name for her, but she doesn't really have the energy to do much else. "I resent that."

"You also resemble it, babe. Keep this up and it's intervention time."

Margot doesn't respond.

"Best two out of three?" Rina begs with wide big puppy dog eyes. That shit never works on me, so I don't know why she bothers.

"Nice try, dollface. But I had this distinct honor last time, and it took me two weeks to get the smell of vomit out of my car. Plus, I didn't drive tonight so…," I trail off with a shrug.

"Fine," she concedes her loss with grace. "But we really need to put a cap on Margot's shots. I mean, if the girl can't handle her liquor—"

"I swear, this is the last time," Margot slurs out, attempting to raise her head off the wood of the bar and not getting all that far.

"You always say that, sweetie." I squeeze her shoulder. "But for real, next time, we're putting you on a limit. Think of your liver."

"Seriously," Rina agrees. "You're a nurse. You know better."

Margot offers up a weak shrug, her brown hair is, well, it's everywhere. Probably stuck to the beer encrusted bar top. Even the people sitting next to her have shifted to give her a wider berth.

"Didn't you outgrow this madness in college?" I ask.

Margot is finally able to raise her head, her eyes opening into tiny bloodshot slits. She shakes her head and then winces. "I went to an all-girls Christian college. It was worse than my all-girls Christian high school. No men. No alcohol. I might as well have been in a convent. I think I've still kissed more girls than I have boys. I know I've had sex with more and I am most definitely not a lesbian."

Rina and I exchange looks of horror. "How did we miss this?" I ask.

"No idea," she replies. "How many men have you had sex with?" Rina asks, turning back to Margot.

"Five. And they were all awful. Especially the guy last night." Ah. So now the shots make sense. "Tiny dicks that couldn't last more than a couple of minutes. The women were actually better. Sort of made me wish I batted for the vagina squad."

"That's quite possibly the saddest thing I've ever heard."

"Ditto." We both stare down at our poor friend, Margot. In truth, we've only known her about a year and we've never talked much about college, so that's probably how we missed it, but still. I feel like that's something we should have known right off the bat. "Have you at least had an orgasm?" She nods, but her expression is grim. And then it hits me. "Holy shit. You've never had one by a member of the opposite sex."

She shakes her head this time and I think I might pass out. That's how distressing this news is.

"Next time we go out, you're staying sober and we're getting you a guy. Someone hot. Someone who knows how to work his fingers, and mouth, and dick." That's Rina, and she's clearly taking this situation as seriously as I am. "We did it for Halle and we can do it for you too."

But Margot just shakes her head at us again. "I'm done with one-night stands."

Okay. I guess I can understand that. I don't ride that train myself. Then again, I was in a relationship up until six months ago for over a year and a half. It's how I met these two lovely ladies and Halle who ditched early to go home to her hot man. And sex was not why we broke up.

"Fine then. We'll find you a hot doc." Rina looks to me for encouragement.

"Yes. Definitely." And then something occurs to me. "You can have Drew." I get raised eyebrows for that. Apparently, offering up your ex-boyfriend to your friend is a no-no. "Okay, maybe not Drew. But someone hot. Someone sexy."

"Sounds good," she mumbles. "Discussing my miserable excuse

for a sex life has been awesome and all, but can someone take me home now. The room is starting to spin."

Shit. Margot is a puker. "Um, yeah. Maybe you should get her out of here?"

Just as the words leave my mouth, Margot lurches, her shoulders jerking forward. Both Rina and I spring into action, hauling our petite friend off the stool and dragging her outside without so much as a good night or a see ya later.

At least she's getting it out now instead of in Rina's car.

Which basically means I get stuck with the tab, but I don't really mind. Money isn't an issue for me and it was a fun night, despite Margot's propensity for drunken oblivion. Signaling the bartender, I ask to settle up before I make my way home.

I'm so exhausted all I can think about is my bed.

I sat, holed up in my house all day painting. It was productive but after a day of that, I needed to unwind some. Or a lot in this case because I wasn't loving what I was creating.

My phone chimes in with a text and once I notice it's from Drew, my ex, I ignore it. I don't even pay attention to what he sent me. The last text was about how much he missed me. So not helpful for the whole getting over him thing. The previous text was about a cool-ass case he had in the emergency room that actually made my stomach turn. Before that, it was about a dream he had about me. It's been going on over the last few months, and lately they're coming in with more frequency than they used to.

And really, he's the one who ended it, so I don't exactly feel the need to text him back. I've been hoping he'd get the message that I don't want to talk to him, but it doesn't seem as though he is.

Whatever his game is with me, I don't like it.

My feet carry me east for more blocks than I care to think about before I bang a right onto Dartmouth, hopping up the steps to the brownstone I own.

Unlocking my door, I toss my keys onto the entryway table, lock everything back up tight and then head immediately upstairs. My teeth brushed, I strip down into my panties and then climb into bed with a loud, grateful groan.

My eyes close and they stay that way until a blaringly loud noise startles me awake.

I jolt upright, but I cannot figure out what that sound was. I'm foggy, disoriented, and for the briefest of moments, I have no idea where I am. My eyes zip around the interminable darkness, my muddled senses taking in the scent of snow when I spot the barely open window. I'm home, in my bed, and I left the window open. In January. Again. Ugh!

The sound that woke me starts again, loud and unforgiving.

My head whips over, locating my ringing phone lighting up my nightstand. Heavy, uncoordinated limbs slow me down as I scramble across the bed to answer it. Glancing at my alarm clock, I notice it's 12:43. No one ever calls you at this hour with good news, and my mind immediately flickers to my parents as a mild dose of panic crawls up my spine.

My thoughts are almost confirmed before I pick up the phone as I catch the Boston area code attached to a number I do not recognize. I swipe my finger across the phone. "Hello?" I answer hesitantly, praying that maybe it's just a wrong number.

The gravelly sound of someone clearing their throat fills my ear. "Is this Miss Aria Davenport?" a very male voice says with the studious air of professionalism.

"Yes," I answer reflexively, but my heart is exploding in my chest as I lean back against the fabric of my headboard, drawing my knees up to my chest like they'll somehow protect me from the bad news I know is yet to come.

He clears his throat again. "Aria," he starts, using my first name. "My name is Doctor Tim James." He pauses, and my mind is swimming, trying to place a name I'm nearly positive I've never heard before. And then I realize what he led with, *Doctor*. "I'm a doctor at Massachusetts General Hospital in Boston." Drew works at MGH. So do Rina and Margot. "I'm sorry to call you, but you're listed as Joshua Brown's emergency contact and healthcare proxy."

"What?" I practically shriek, my hand flying up to my mouth. "Josh?" Disbelief and a fresh wave of terror fills me. "Is he…" I can't even finish that thought or sentence. I just can't.

"Mr. Brown is alive."

Relief floods through me but just as quickly recedes, because I'm still getting this call, which means something is terribly wrong.

"He was brought into the emergency department, suffering from several injuries including a fractured fibula, three fractured ribs, as well as other internal injuries that we're going to need to surgically explore. He also has a severe contusion to the right side of his head—"

"What the hell are you saying?" I snap, interrupting his medical rant. None of this means anything to me. This man might as well be speaking Russian for all the sense he's making. "Is he okay?"

"He suffered a head trauma that resulted in pressure and swelling on his brain as well as the other injuries I mentioned."

"Oh God, no. Josh." My chin drops to my chest as my hand slides up to cover my eyes. Tears leak out despite my best attempts at reining them in.

"The surgical team is about to wheel him to the OR now to repair the internal injuries he sustained. His broken leg will not require surgery, just setting."

I shake my head. I can't handle this. I. Cannot. Handle. This. "What happened?"

"I'm sorry, I don't know the specifics. I just needed to make you aware. But if you're able, you should come. He may need someone here to make medical decisions for him."

"Uh. Okay." I shake my head, wiping furiously at my eyes. "I'll be there soon."

Then he hangs up. That's it. But I don't really have the mental capacity at the moment to think too deeply on that. Flipping on the lights, I squint against the brightness before riffling through my drawers for something to wear. I dig out a black long sleeve thermal and a pair of jeans, put my hair up in a messy bun, grab my phone, and I'm out my door in less than ten minutes.

Without my coat.

Shit.

But it's too late to go back as the Uber is pulling right up and

I'm in too much of a hurry to get to the hospital or care all that much about freezing. Coats can wait. Josh cannot.

Once I get inside the enticingly warm car, I call Tyler, Josh's boyfriend. I spoke to Josh two days ago, and he was most definitely still with Tyler. I want details and I want them now. The phone rings three times before his groggy, sleep-filled voice fills my ear.

"What the hell, Aria?"

"Tyler," I clip out. "Have you talked to Josh?"

Silence. I'm greeted with freaking silence and I'm about to lose my mind.

"No. Not since last night." He's confused. "We had a late dinner and a drink and then we called it a night. I have an eight a.m. client I'm supposed to meet…" He trails off as silence once again ensues and I can't find my voice to fill it. "What's going on?"

"A doctor from MGH called me." I swallow hard, staring sightlessly out the windshield of the car. "Tyler, Josh was in an accident or something. I don't know the details, but he's really messed up. They're taking him into surgery."

"What?! Surgery? No. That's impossible."

"I don't know anything, Tyler. I'm sitting in the back of an Uber on my way to MGH, but you need to get your ass over to the hospital now."

"Shit." He's silent, but I hear rustling in the background, so I assume he's getting out of bed. "I'm on my way. Fuck," he growls, anxiety leaching from his voice. "I'm on my way. I'll call you when I get there." He's frantic. Good thing he lives down the street from the hospital.

"Take a breath, Tyler. I don't want to get a call about you next."

He takes that breath, but then he starts to gulp, and I wonder if he's holding back tears. "I feel so…I can't stand this."

"I know. Just get to him and I'll be there as soon as I can."

"Right. Talk soon, honey."

"Talk soon."

Slipping my phone into my purse, I lean back in the seat. The driver is silent, and I'm not even afforded the luxury of awful background music to distract me from my thoughts. One question continues to torture me.

What happened?

Because Josh is a strong guy. A big guy. But he's also a gay guy. A gay guy who has been in more fights because of his sexuality than I can count. And since the doctor didn't mention a car accident, I'm going with worst-case scenarios here. Josh was attacked.

Chapter Two

ARIA

Fear cripples me, setting my skin on edge and making my stomach roll. Josh has to be all right. There is no alternative. The longer I sit here, riding through the snow-slick streets with nothing but my toxic thoughts to keep me company the more insane I become. Just as the realization that he could actually die crosses my mind, the phone that has been glued to my hand since I got the initial call, vibrates.

Tyler. Thank Christ.

"Hey."

"He's in rough shape, Aria. Real rough." Tyler sounds broken up. Like he's been crying. Maybe still is. "He's in surgery. I haven't even gotten to see him. They're fixing his spleen or something and they might have to open his goddamn skull."

"Jesus." I blow out a harsh breath as fresh tears burn my eyes anew. I will not fall apart. Not yet. "Did the doctor say what happened?"

"I spoke to a nurse and the police. They found Josh beaten behind the restaurant we went to last night." He lets out a strangled sound. "He walked me to my car, Aria, we kissed good night and then I left. I didn't make sure he got into his. I didn't make sure he drove off safely. What the hell is wrong with me?"

"This is not your fault, Tyler. It's not. And it could have easily been both of you and not just him having surgery. You two do this a million times over and Josh is a formidable man. You had no reason to consider he'd get *jumped*."

I hear him sniffle and my heart breaks. I know he's blaming himself. I'm sure I would too if I were him, but I meant what I said. It's not his fault and I don't blame him.

"The police are clueless." He chokes. "They have no idea who did this. They didn't take his wallet or his keys and from the way they described it, whoever did it, got him from behind. Clocked him over the head with something and then beat him while he was unconscious and bleeding."

I curse under my breath. My fist clenches in my lap, the other gripping my phone so tightly I'm shocked it's not cracking.

"Take a breath there, cowgirl." *Cowgirl.* Josh calls me cowgirl. "They're on it. Right now, we have to focus on Josh and pray they catch the person who did it. Breathe, Aria," he repeats when I fall silent and I know it's an attempt to get through to me. To calm me down. "Look. I have to go back in, but they're going to want to speak to you about his treatment options or whatever. That's what the nurse said."

"Do I need to speak to them now?"

"No. He's in good hands. They have all of his documentation on file about you being in charge of his medical decision-making. Good thing he's a lawyer and actually took care of all this stuff."

"Yeah," I whisper, because when Josh had me sign all those forms after his parents died, I never in a million years thought I'd have to use them. We end the call, my mind swirling in a never-ending vicious cycle.

It's taking entirely too long to reach the hospital. But the second the Uber stops, I jump out, sprinting inside the hospital. I find my way through the main floor over to the elevators. Sixty-two seconds later, the doors part on the surgical floor. A nurse wearing blue scrubs directs me to the waiting room where I find Tyler, sitting with this dark-haired head in his hands.

"It could have easily been both of you," I start the moment I enter the room, causing his head to lift and his dark eyes to find mine, "and not just him."

"The police have nothing," he chokes out as he stands up and hugs me with the type of ferocity that only people suffering a tragedy can share. "They were here for like a hot second, asked me five questions, and then left."

Anger and frustration war through me. I had a million questions for them and now they're not here. "Are they coming back?"

He shrugs. "Tomorrow, I think they said."

"Goddammit," I hiss. My fist clenches and I instantly release him. I need to walk, but all I end up doing is orbiting around the room.

Tyler puts his head back into his hands as he settles back down. "Sit, Aria," he scolds. "You're about to take off."

He's right. I need to calm down even though doing so feels impossible. I take a seat next to him, but only because my insides suddenly feel like they're lined with lead. Sinking into the unforgiving plastic of the chair, I drop my head back. My eyes stare unfocused up at the drop-ceiling for the longest time until someone says, "I'm looking for the family of Joshua Brown."

I might have fallen asleep. Tyler most definitely is when my head snaps to attention. My eyes find the round clock on the wall, and I see it's well into four in the morning. I feel like I've been awake for days and it's only been a few hours here. My eyes flutter over to a woman in navy blue scrubs with a soft smile on her severe face. You can tell this chick has been through the trenches and back.

"I'm Vanessa, Mr. Brown's nurse. He is ready for you."

Jolting upright, I grab Tyler's arm, shaking it. He rouses with a start, jumping out of his seat before he's ready and ends up staggering back a step before he rights his body and stares at the nurse in bewildered concern.

"How's he doing? Is he awake?" I spitfire and she motions with her head in the direction of the hall, indicating that we should follow.

The moment we reach the sterile hall, she says, "He's still unconscious, which is how they're going to keep him for at least the next few days to help with the swelling in his brain." *Swelling in his brain*! "He's stable. His vital signs are good and we're very hopeful."

"The surgery went well?"

"It did. They were able to repair his spleen without removing it as well as a few other injuries. One of the surgeons will be in to speak with you shortly."

"Thank you." I smile, letting her know how much I appreciate that.

But when we enter the small rectangular room faced with glass on three sides, shrouded in ugly curtains at the far end of the ICU, I freeze, taking in my friend.

My first thought? He looks like he's sleeping.

Then I get a second look and I notice the angry dark purple welts across the side of his face. The bandage on the left side of his forehead. The hideous blue and white gown and the white blanket that's covering him, pulled up to his chest. The tubes in his mouth and arms. The incessant beeping and hissing of machines on both sides of his lifeless body.

It's funny, the bed almost looks too small for his large body.

"Oh, Josh," I sob, wilting into the large chair next to his bed, unsure as to how I got there. My warm small hand covers his large ice-cold one.

I can't speak anymore.

I just sit here.

"His face," Tyler says, and for a moment, I forgot he was with me. I glance up and watch him touching the side of Josh's arm like he doesn't know where else is safe to go. Yeah. His face looks like shit. That will really piss Josh off when he wakes up. Almost as much as the gown they have him wearing. But really, I feel like the large bandage on his head and the tube in his mouth are more alarming than a few bruises. But what do I know?

"How…," I cry. "How could someone do this to him?"

Tyler's eyes cinch shut as his body shudders. He looks away. "He'll be fine," he says as much for himself as for me. And maybe for Josh too, because he certainly looks like he needs the encouragement.

"Yeah." It's all I can offer. Because right now, he doesn't look fine. He looks like the opposite of fine. He looks like someone mugged him. Only he wasn't mugged since nothing was taken.

Someone tried to kill him.

"I'm so glad you're here," Tyler says, drawing me out of my dark thoughts. He stares down on Josh's lifeless form with an expression I can't read. "He would be too. You always bring him such happiness and love." Tyler smiles adoringly at his partner before turning his gaze on me. "We were talking about you last night at dinner. Josh was telling me about how you used to go pool hopping."

I let out a small laugh, the half-smile lingering on my lips. "We had a pool, but I was never allowed in it after dark. Ridiculous really." I roll my eyes, remembering the odd things my parents were strict about. "It started as a dare, but when we did it a few times and didn't get caught, we became increasingly adventurous, going to other people's houses."

"I wish I had known him then." Tyler caresses the back of Josh's hand with his fingertips in one of the most loving and tender gestures I've ever witnessed.

"You know him now, and you're both so lucky to have each other."

He nods once. Blows out a breath. "I love him so much."

We fall silent for a few minutes, just watching our loved one, victims to our own thoughts and memories. But in my gut, I know, this is only the beginning.

***

"I don't think I've ever been so exhausted in my life," Tyler groans, following up his statement with a big yawn. Rising slowly out of the chair, he walks over to the window, looking at nothing. He's done that several times today and has increased the frequency in the last two hours.

"Go home," I offer, standing up and joining him at the window. Tyler shakes his head, but he doesn't respond. "I mean it. You've been here for like eighteen hours. Get some sleep tonight and in the morning, you'll come back and relieve me."

He sighs, and even though I know he doesn't like the idea of leaving Josh, I also know he's very tempted. After a long beat, he sighs again. This one heavier. Resigned. "You'll call me if anything changes?"

"Of course."

"Tomorrow I have a meeting I cannot move, but I'll be back here by ten at the latest."

"No rush. I'm good."

Tyler shakes his head, his nearly black hair all over the place from a day spent in the ICU and running his hands through it repeatedly. I can only imagine what I look like. Mercifully this place is lacking in mirrors other than the bathroom and that one is easy to ignore. He turns to me, a pained fogginess in his eyes as he pulls me in for a tight hug.

Tyler steps back, the saddest smile I've ever seen reluctantly pulling up the corners of his mouth. "When he wakes up and is no longer in this godforsaken hospital, it's time he gets over the casual shit. Life is motherfucking short."

I laugh and nod my head. "I agree."

"If the police show up again before I get back, I want details."

"Promise."

"Okay. I'm leaving then." I push him a bit and he chuckles, walking over to Josh. "I'll see you tomorrow, baby." Tyler bends down, kissing a part of Josh's face that isn't covered in bruises or hospital tape and then he's gone. And I don't know why, but I'm relieved to be alone with Josh. Part of me feels like it's always been him and me against the world, and though Tyler is, of course, entitled to be here, taking care of Josh is my responsibility.

I don't remember the last time I had anything to eat, but I can't seem to make myself leave. I've sat in this room, doing nothing but watching my friend sleep. It's been the longest, and most excruciatingly emotional, day of my life and I'm not just talking about the hours.

Moving back across the room, I drop myself into the chair that has housed my ass for the last few hours. They brought me a recliner. And a blanket and pillow because I told them I would not leave. I've tried to sleep, but I can't get my eyes to close. I feel like if I shut them, even for a second, he could be gone.

The only noise occupying the room is the overly exaggerated hissing of his breathing as oxygen forces itself in and out of his lungs through the tube down his throat. It should be comforting. It should serve as a reminder that he's alive.

But I find no comfort in the sound.

I find only emptiness and longing. I can't begin to comprehend how this lifeless, bruised and battered form is my friend. It looks nothing like him.

Maybe that's what I'm struggling with the most.

"Josh," I start, standing back up and staring down at him as I twist my back, my hands intertwined as I stretch them up toward the ceiling, "it's been a very long time since we've had a sleepover together, my friend. This is not how I saw our next get-together going. No champagne. No calorie-laden munchies. I can't even pass you a joint, though I'd bet they're giving you the good stuff to make you pain-free."

Twisting back in the other direction, I jump, my arms dropping to my chest as a small frightened gasp escapes my lips.

Someone is standing in the doorway, leaning against the metal frame watching me.

Our eyes lock.

My breath catches in my chest.

Because there is no possible way I'm seeing who I think I'm seeing.

Chapter Three

ARIA

My eyes blink. Focus. Then blink again.

No. Just *no*.

My lungs burn from lack of oxygen. My cheeks heat and my stomach flutters with nervous butterflies as I squint, trying to confirm what my body seems to already know.

What my body remembers.

"No way," I whisper aloud.

A slow easy smile curls up the corners of his mouth, his pale green eyes turning from incredulous to astounded to possibly amused. We stare at each other for a moment, unable to drag our eyes away. He tilts his head to the side, his smile turning lopsided as some of his hair flops over his forehead.

My heart.

Holy crap, it's out of control.

I forgot how gorgeous he is. How devastating that smile is.

Visions of the last time I saw him flash unbidden into my brain. I can't stop them, and the faster the images come, the hotter my face and body grow.

His face above mine. Our naked bodies pressed together, limbs intertwined. The sounds he made as he came inside of me. The way I stared into him as I came.

Holy shit. I cannot believe this moment.

And hell, there are so many more moments than our last. I want to revel in them. Sit in a bath with a glass of wine and relive each one, one at a time like I'm stealing back what has been taken from me.

Ever so slowly, he stalks across the room in my direction with a purpose I cannot ignore.

And then I realize where I am. And then I realize what he's wearing. Scrubs.

I blink again. Admiring his chest and then his legs and then his shoes and then back up to his face.

Because suddenly he's standing before me, so goddamn tall and beautiful as he says, "Aria Davenport."

"Weston Kincaid."

What are the freaking odds? Ten years and a lifetime in between and now here I am. Staring up into the eyes of the man who was my first… everything. The man who shattered my adolescent, lovesick heart into pieces when he left.

His sandy hair, the perfect combination of blond and brown, is shorter on the sides than the last time I saw him, but still long enough on top that I can run my fingers through it. Instead of being the familiar disheveled mess, it's well-kempt and stylish.

Green eyes twinkle, even against the harsh fluorescent lighting this place boasts, as his grin broadens, no doubt at my bewildered expression. His jawline is smooth, angular, chiseled, ending with that damn dimple in his chin that I always loved so much.

He's taller than I remember. Definitely more built. There is no hiding his broad chest, arms, and shoulders, even beneath his ugly scrubs. Gone is the physique of the boy from my memories and in its place, is that of a man's. A sexy man's, and that thought is not doing me any favors right now. Especially considering who this man that is patiently staring at me is.

My stomach does a dip and then a swoosh and then it rolls over, playing dead.

His smile is huge before he envelops me in his massive arms. I don't remember this many muscles. And I would have. He was naked, after all. But he most certainly smelled this good. That I remember very clearly. Even the hint of hospital and antiseptic cannot hide it. Sandalwood. Citrus. Weston Kincaid.

It's like coming home.

He pulls back, cupping my face with his strong warm hands, his eyes devouring me, before he remembers that we haven't seen each other in a decade and that this sort of personal contact is considered socially odd. Especially given our surroundings and this situation.

His hands drop to his sides, but he continues his inspection of me.

My face. My body. Everywhere.

"I can't believe my eyes," he says with a small incredulous chuckle. God, his voice. It's smooth and deep and rolls over me like a fine wine or rich chocolate. The sort you only take out on special occasions because it's just that decadent. "It's been so long since I've seen you."

"Ten years," I reply instantly and leave it at that because I don't want to tell him I just calculated that it's technically been ten years, five months, eight days, and twelve hours. I think that might freak him out a bit.

"Yeah." He smiles a smile that tells me he's also picturing our last encounter in his head. And if I thought I was blushing before, I clearly had no idea what that term meant. "Ten years."

His eyes do another sweep and I feel them everywhere they move as if he were physically touching me. The heat radiating from his body surrounds me. Wraps me up in lost nights and adolescent mischief. In forbidden kisses and stolen glances.

"You look amazing. All grown-up. How've you been?"

I frown, hating the way he said that. *All grown-up.* Like I was a child the last time he saw me. No one needs that reminder from the man who took their virginity. Granted, he is almost three years older than me, but I was eighteen when he saw me last. So…not a child.

I don't answer his question. I'm not sure I want him to know. Not sure if he's earned the right.

There's too much history between us, and evidently, I hold a grudge. Even after a decade.

"You're a doctor here?" I cringe at the stupidity of my question. Of course, he's a doctor here. I can see his freaking ID badge and he's wearing goddamn scrubs. But I'm just too...rattled. Slightly keyed up. This man has always had a way of discomposing me like no one else.

His smile slips, his warmth slipping into cooler waters. "I'm one of Josh's doctors, actually," he explains. Wes's eyes drift to Josh, before returning to mine. "I was in the ER when he was brought in and I'm the one who performed the surgery on him early this morning."

"Oh." I don't know what to say to that. I'm still in shock. I never thought I'd see Wes again. Not sure if I wanted to by this point in my life. The time for that was so long ago. I don't know how to make sense of this. Of him. "Wow, okay then."

I remember my brother, Brecken, telling me years ago that Wes was in medical school at Stanford. That was the last time Brecken mentioned him to me. Or maybe it was the last time I actively listened to anything that had to do with Weston Kincaid.

I had no idea he was back in Mass.

"Do you have any questions for me about his care or treatment plan? I'm the surgical fellow on right now."

"Right," I say, swallowing hard before I clear away...everything. "Dr. Franklin said the surgery went well." He nods. "And that you're monitoring the pressure in his brain closely." Another nod. "That if everything improves the way you're hoping it will then you'll lighten his sedation in the next day or two."

"That's correct," he answers with the most clinical and indifferent tone I think I've ever heard. "He's doing well after the surgery, and so far, his ICP or intracranial pressure is holding at an acceptable level. Neurology is following that closely and they're hoping that with the medications they're giving him, it will continue to go down. For now, I will be monitoring his abdominal wounds. I repaired his spleen, but there was a small abrasion to his bowel as well as a large contusion to his liver. Neither required repair in the

OR at the time, but we're going to watch him closely. His internal injuries were severe. As you can see." He waves a hand over to Josh. "Orthopedics casted his leg fracture and thankfully that won't require surgery."

I nod, swallowing thickly, exhausted and overwhelmed with so many things that they're threatening to consume me. Sucking in a deep breath, I say, "Thank you, Dr. Kincaid."

He scowls slightly, but I'm not really sure why. The way he's speaking to me does not oblige first names. At least not in his direction.

"If you need anything, just have the nurse page me."

He turns to leave, and I want to fold in on myself from the pressure surrounding me.

"How long have you been living here?" I blurt out before I can stop myself.

"For about a year."

Wow. That…hurts. A year. In this hospital. In the hospital I've spent time in since my friends work here. Since Drew works here. And I never saw him. Never ran into him.

Until tonight.

"Do you live here? In Boston, I mean?"

"Yes. For almost two and a half years now."

"I didn't know," he says, and I force myself to meet his eyes again as he turns back around with an indecipherable expression. "Your brother never mentioned it."

"You still speak to Brecken?"

He shrugs a shoulder.

"Not much anymore," he admits. "Just a text or an email here and there. But when I told him I was coming to Boston to finish my residency, he didn't say anything about you living here." Wes gives me an impish grin, the devil dancing around his light eyes in a way that makes my stomach surge with butterflies. "I wonder why that is? You think he's still trying to keep me away from you?"

I have to laugh at that, because looking back, it almost seems ridiculous now. "Maybe," I muse. Brecken lives in New York now, but we're still pretty close. Always have been even though he's two years older than me.

My girlfriends never objected to hanging out with my older brother and his friends. Couldn't blame them on that one, most of his friends were hot. And my brother and his friends never objected to hanging out with my overly eager pretty friends. So it worked. A little too well, I think, since I know for a fact my brother slept with at least one friend of mine.

But Brecken doesn't know about my history with Wes.

I certainly never told him, and I know Wes didn't either. Our desire was sequestered to dark corners and private hideaways like a dirty secret. Forever his best friend's little sister by the light of day. Untouchable.

"Breck always had a lot of threats for his friends where I was concerned."

Wes nods. Laughs a little. Turns his body so it faces me fully as his heated gaze sweeps…everywhere, sending the violent sparks of a flash fire searing through me.

He knows our lie. All that we hid.

"I believe he threatened to cut off our arms if we ever touched you."

"I believe you're correct on that one." *And we both know you didn't listen.*

He pivots on his heels and begins to head back out again. My eyes close and then a loud yawn slips past my lips before I can tamper it.

"Are you staying here tonight?" he asks, rolling his head back over his shoulder to find me once more.

"Yes. I was told that's okay."

"It is," he replies quickly. "But those recliners are brutal. I've slept on them a time or twenty. If your place is far, you can always crash at mine." He smirks playfully when my eyes widen, realizing how that offer sounded. "I wouldn't be there. I work a lot."

I can't help my smile. Wes isn't flirting, at least not much, but what he's offering me, given the situation we find ourselves in, is beyond anything I ever expected.

I may not have had the same impact on him that he had on me all those years ago, but sleeping at his place, surrounded in his things, is probably the worst thing I can do for myself.

"Thank you, Wes. That is unbelievably generous of you, but I don't live far and I'm not ready to leave him yet."

He stares at me for a long moment and I don't know if I want him to stay or go. Speak to me with delicious innuendo covered in meaningless formality or never look at me again.

He was once the wrecker of my heart. The destroyer of my resolve. And I can't decide if I should smack him or kiss him for that dominance.

"Have the nurse page me if you need anything," he repeats.

"I will. Thanks."

He turns back to the door and starts to walk out, only to pause again on the threshold with his back to me. He blows out a breath. Like he's as exhausted as I am.

Like he's having the same inner battle I am.

"I'm glad you're here." My breath catches before he adds, "Josh is going to need you."

Then he leaves me like he was never there.

Only he was.

I can still feel him.

When I close my eyes, I can still see him. And when I breathe in, I can still smell the remnants of his woodsy cologne.

I drop into my recliner, drawing the blanket over my body, all the way up to my chin, demanding its comfort.

"Goddammit, Josh," I grouse, blustering out an incredulous laugh. "Weston Fucking Kincaid is your doctor and we can't even talk about that. You're going to freak out when you realize he had his hands inside your body and you slept through the whole thing." I puff out some air and sink back, my eyes closing. "Seeing him is a nightmare. How will I ever get through unscathed with him as your doctor?"

Chapter Four

ARIA

Past

THE HUMID AUGUST heat is stifling as I open the unwilling glass doors of my high school. Cold air blasts across my face and exposed arms and legs, causing gooseflesh to erupt across my skin. The school is still fairly quiet. Most of the students won't be here for at least another twenty minutes, but I like to get here early.

I like the quiet of the morning. The peace before the rush. The calm before the storm.

Reaching into my messenger bag that's positioned against my hip, I pull out my neatly folded schedule. I don't really need to look at it. I've got it memorized, but it gives my eyes a place to go in the hopes that Dr. Hamburg, who is walking briskly in my direction, will ignore me if I look busy. He does. But it's possible he didn't notice me. He's typically lost to his own purpose.

My first-period class is AP English. A waste of my time considering I've already read every single book on the list. I'm a sophomore this year, but really, I'm already taking all senior-level courses. School, unfortunately, bores me to tears. My schedule consists of AP

English. AP Physics. AP Calculus. Art expression—who knows what the hell that is–two independent studies, one creative writing, the other music.

At least I'm done with my day before two.

Nothing to complain about there, other than the fact that my father will try to get me to help out in his office.

Business and earning money are two of his favorite things, outside of his family, and he's hoping I'll change my winsome ways and adopt his serious inclination.

I won't.

I hate business and money is a necessity. Art is my passion. Art is what I live for. Music isn't so bad either.

"Hey, cowgirl," a familiar voice calls out from behind me. I spin around, a little startled, to find Josh here so early. The second my eyes land on him, I burst out laughing. "What?" He smiles brightly. "You don't like?" His hand waves down the front of his clothes like he's on display before he does a twirl.

I shake my head, unable to contain my grin. "No. I love. You're a statement within a statement."

And he is. He's wearing a green Silversun Pickups concert shirt, black and white pin striped shorts with splashes of blue and green on them made to look like paint and red high-top Converse. Josh has the height and physique of a football player and is definitely easy on the eyes with short, perfectly-styled light, almost platinum, blond hair and big beaming blue eyes.

Too bad he's gay.

"I know, right?" His smile turns mischievous as he walks up to me, looping his arm through mine before using his other hand to yank the elastic from my low ponytail. "No." He wags the thing in front of my face like it offends him personally. "Just no, Aria. You have beautiful hair. You need to stop trying to hide it. Curly is sexy."

I snort, rolling my eyes and snatch the elastic back from him, sliding it on my wrist instead of back in my hair. I'll have to wait until he's no longer around to do that. I can feel the frizz starting to make its way into my curls. Fucking August. "Frizz is not."

"So." He leans down into me as my head only comes up to his shoulder. "How does the third to last first day feel?"

"The same as the fourth to the last did last year." I smirk cheekily up at him.

"At least we have English together. After that, I think we're both on our own until the dreaded lunch time." His voice drops ominously as he says that, giving off an exaggerated shudder. "I don't get why you have to be an overachiever with all of those AP classes. It's not even like you plan on going to college, anyway."

"Shhhh…," I hiss dramatically at him, my eyes scanning the halls that are progressively becoming more congested with students. "My father has spies everywhere. They'll hear you."

He laughs, rolling his eyes at me.

"Are you actually planning on doing your homework this year or just going to continue to get by on good looks and charm?"

"We don't all have your brains, sweets," he claims. "Some of us have to use the limited resources we were blessed with."

I let out a derisive scoff because Josh is nothing if not smart. The guy doesn't study. Barely does his homework and yet somehow manages to get almost straight As.

We round the hall where our class is located, the linoleum floors polished to a sheen for the first day, the pervasive scent of high school grossness barely detectable. Neither of us use a locker to store our books. My excuse is that my locker is all the way across the school down by the gymnasium, which means it would take me an extra ten minutes to get down there and back.

And I'm lazy.

It's easier to carry everything on me. Josh's excuse? Last year he got his head bashed into it by an upperclassman. That upper-classman also called him a faggot, warning that he better not catch Josh in the locker room. Asshole.

In truth, Josh puts himself out there.

And I admire his bravery and courage, but it makes some of the regulars uncomfortable. He's grown a lot since that incident last year. So now his size helps to diminish some of it. I mean, it's not always wise to pick on a guy who's six-foot-two and a hundred and eighty pounds of muscle. Now and then a few of the football and baseball players get together and try to gang up on him.

A lot of it is stupid, ignorant name-calling, but every once in a while, it leads to more.

It never seems to affect him. At least not for very long. It doesn't stop him from being himself and that alone is one of the many things I love about him. He doesn't let others dictate who he should be.

The halls are starting to fill up as the metal clang of lockers opening and slamming shut mixes in with the excited chatter of students on the first day. I spot my brother, Brecken, and a few of his friends laughing, all smiles and delight. And why shouldn't they be? They're seniors. Top of the pecking order with limitless possibilities set ahead of them.

The buzz is in the air and you can't help but breathe in some of that energy for yourself. I don't mind school. I don't mind the kids or the drama or the scene. It's all a lot of fun if you take it for what it is and keep your nose out of it.

"You don't think Mrs. Hayes is going to give us assigned seats, do you?" Josh asks, leaning up against the wall next to our class room, his eyes scanning, casting from person to person, occasionally throwing a what's up head bob to someone he knows.

I face him, my back pressing into the side of the lockers, one of my sandaled feet sliding up to rest against it. I stare down at my nails, picking at the chipped black polish I wasn't in the mood to touch up last night. "Nah. She's pretty cool. I think she'll let us pick."

"God, I hope so. Last year I got stuck next to Simon in biology and that guy is totally against deodorant or something, because damn, that smell was pungent." I snort out a laugh. "And in chemistry, I got stuck next to Brady."

He doesn't have to elaborate for me on that one. "That genius was taking a freshman chemistry class?" I ask sarcastically. "Hopefully, this year, you'll get stuck with me. I always use deodorant and pride myself on not being a half-brained homophobic fuckwit."

"Yes. But it will take every ounce of control I have not to do you over." He shakes his head, eyeing my outfit.

"Leave it be," I bark, running a self-conscious hand down my hair, checking its frizz factor. It's almost at a seven. I can feel it. I grab the elastic from my wrist, twisting my hair into some kind of a knot and then secure it in place.

Josh groans like I'm killing him, but he'll just have to get over it. "Your hair is so beautiful, cowgirl. Especially when it's down. Thick, dark, and don't get me started on those curls. But you could at least try wearing another color other than black or white."

I shrug. "Black and white are not technically colors."

"Such a bitch." He winks, and I shrug again, this time with a playful smile. This is obviously not the first time we've had this argument. And while I love color on canvas, it's just not my thing on me. So yeah, I wear a lot of black. Makes accessorizing easy.

"Who's a bitch?" A heavy male voice booms beside us. "You talking about yourself again, Brown?" My eyes lock on Connor Shaw, the brawny defensive lineman and all around douchetard. He personifies misogyny and bigotry, bringing both to a whole new level.

"Definitely not, Shaw." Josh smirks, pushing off from the wall to show off his full height. Connor is about four inches shorter than Josh, but probably weighs the same, as a large majority of that weight is concentrated in Connor's bulbous abdomen. His oily face and hair give him a perpetual sheen, which highlights his ever-present pig-like snout.

I like to imagine that Connor Shaw is just misunderstood.

Insecure to the point where he finds it easier to divert the attention away from himself. He's the type of guy who likes to be the class clown. Who gets his rocks off by making others feel small. He's popular, and people, including my brother, find him amusing. But really, he's nothing more than a bully. A bully with a vicious streak that has been known to go beyond verbal altercations.

"Oh, scary guy, huh?" Connor ridicules with a mock shudder. "Don't chip a nail there, *sweetheart*."

Or maybe he's just a priapic douchebag. My eyes widen and my breath catches. Certainly, there is no way this will end without getting physical. The last thing Josh needs is to get suspended from school.

Shit.

But Josh just laughs, loud and cackling. Garnering the attention of a few curious onlookers as they walk by. "I always knew you were in the closet, Shaw. I just had no idea you liked *me*." He shakes his head, pointing to his chest. "Sorry, babe, stupid and ugly really aren't my type."

Connor slams into Josh with the side of his shoulder. Hard. Josh doesn't move, and he doesn't make a sound, but it had to hurt. Connor steps back and then glances over at me, like he just now noticed me standing here mere feet away. A shit-eating grin spreads malevolently across his round face, making him resemble The Joker from *Batman*.

He reaches out, grasping my arm and tugging me until my chest is against his. The action surprises me, my breath lodging in my lungs. I struggle, twisting my arm back and forth, and pushing off him with my other, but he's got a firm grip on me. "Let me go, asshole."

"Hey, Aria," he half-yells so everyone—and I do mean everyone—around us turns to watch, "I know you want me, but you really can't jump my bones at school, babe."

The kingdom naturally laughs with their jester, ha, ha, and Connor gets what he was after. Making himself look funny while embarrassing me.

"I bet this is the closest a woman has ever gotten to you," I say in a saccharine sweet voice, a venomous smirk on my lips. "We all know no one would willingly go near you." I yank my hand away from him, shoving with all my might against his chest so he'll give me space. He laughs harder, because he's just *so* funny.

"Oh, honey, don't be like that. We both know the gay kid isn't giving you what you need."

"Douchebag," I snap. Josh steps forward, encroaching on Connor like he's about to start something. And you can feel it. The rise in temperature. The tension building to that point-of-no-return crescendo. "He's not worth it," I remind Josh.

"Doesn't mean I won't enjoy kicking his fat ass."

"Would love to see you try, buttercup," Connor sneers.

I open my mouth to try and end this, when someone from behind me growls, "Back off, man." Weston Kincaid brushes between Josh—who looks like it's taking every ounce of restraint not to smash Connor into a pile of pulp—and Connor, slapping a hard hand on his shoulder and physically jerking him back a step.

Connor's eyes narrow, but he does as his captain instructs, taking another small, measured step back. Gotta love football hierarchy. "I was just having a little fun with my girl, Aria, here." I fold my arms across my chest, staring Connor down.

"And I said back off," Wes clips with a bit more force, his eyes skirting mine.

I've known Wes since I was eight years old. Since he moved in next door and became fast friends with my brother. Since his parents moved in next door and became fast friends with mine. Since I developed a very early crush on the boy next door. On my brother's best friend. Since the first time he smiled at me with that dimple in his chin and those green eyes that pulverize me every single time I look at them.

And for most of that time, he's blatantly ignored me. Been completely and utterly indifferent towards me. I was his best friend's little sister and nothing more.

The invisible little girl.

Then, something changed over the summer. He found me sitting up on the roof of my house one night, staring at the stars, and we talked. *For hours*. I didn't think much of it that first night. Told myself it didn't mean anything. But then he came back the next night and the one after that and so on. He came back every night and spent hours talking with me under the summer stars on my rooftop. It was magical. Romantic. Otherworldly.

And yet, I've forced my brain away from all that. He's still Wes and I'm still Aria. Distant ships in the night. I believed we had grown to be friends. Hoped it could be more. Especially when he'd touch me in small ways.

An almost kiss, I know it.

But since football started two weeks ago, he hasn't come by. Our nights stopped as suddenly as they began. When he's around Brecken and his friends, he reverts to ignoring me entirely. It makes me wonder if I've read more into those nights than he did. He's older. Popular. Gorgeous. Smart. Funny and generally perfect in every way. He can—and often does—have any girl he wants.

And I'm fifteen.

"Come on, Connor. Leave them alone. She's Breck's little sister."

Little sister. I hate that he just referred to me as that. Especially when that's the last thing I want him to see me as.

I haven't moved a muscle during this entire exchange, but suddenly, as Wes's green eyes descend upon me, I wish I could slink off. He's looking at me like he's never seen me before. Like he doesn't know who I am. Like we haven't spent countless hours together. Just the two of us. Like he hasn't held my hand or brushed his body against mine in a way that could only be construed as deliberate.

"Since when do you care if I mess with Breck's sister? Or this asshole for that matter?" Connor juts his thumb in Josh's direction.

"I care. And I said cut it out." His eyes leave my face as he says this, and I try to pretend that his words didn't cut me. "No need to start shit in the halls. A fight is not worth a suspension."

Connor bristles a little before trying to laugh it off. "Always the perfect captain. Whatever. Fuck it. I gotta run to class." He slaps Wes on the back before turning to Josh. "See ya at lunch, cocksucker," he sneers. "Until later, Aria. I don't think we're quite finished yet."

I glare at him and he stalks off, leaving Wes standing here in front of us, consumed with an awkward silence I don't feel the need to fill. Probably because I'm too hurt and pissed off at him to say anything. But really, what did I expect?

I'm Breck's little sister, right?

Josh on the other hand? He tends not to let things go.

"You've got some shit taste in friends there, Wes. Next time you want to be the hero, don't bother. You're just as bad as he is."

"How do you figure that?"

"Guilty by association."

The door to our class swings open before Wes can respond. Josh reaches out, grasping my forearm and tugging me out of the way of the swinging door I barely saw coming. We enter the room like that, arm in arm. It's a relief. I feel like I would have lost a piece of myself if I had been made to go in alone. I don't want to feel like this. I don't want to hurt over the guy who doesn't remember I'm alive. Who casts me aside without a second thought.

Who reminds me that I deserve better.

The classrooms smells and looks exactly the way it did last year. Cleaning products, dry erase markers, and recycled air fills the space surrounding the short two-person tables stacked into organized rows and columns.

"Check the chart," Mrs. Hayes calls out and a collective groan rumbles through the room. Josh throws me an aggravated sideways glance over his shoulder before we walk up to the desk to do as we're instructed. "I've arranged the names randomly and I will not hear any complaining about the assignments."

My eyes scroll over the names on the chart and find myself sitting next to none other than Weston Kincaid. Of course, I am. I inwardly begrudge karma for being an ironic bitch before patting Josh on the shoulder. Making my way across the room towards the bank of windows and my assigned seat, which is located in the third row, inside chair. Josh is two rows ahead and dead center, his least favorite spot.

If this is any indication for the coming year, I think we're both screwed.

I toss my bag onto the floor between the wall and my chair with a thud, after placing my notebook and pen on the table in front of me. I feel the table shift and the chair to my right scratches against the linoleum as Wes takes his seat. He's tall. Much taller than I am, and since there is very little room for him to push his chair back, he slides the table in front of us forward to accommodate his size.

The table is at an odd angle now and I find I have to scooch up a couple of times in order to meet the writing surface. Wes chuckles under his breath, which I'm sure is somehow directed at me. "Sorry," he mutters sheepishly, leaning in a little so I can hear him. "It's not easy for me to fit in here."

"No. I imagine it's not." My eyes follow a path over his dark gray shirt that clings desperately to his large biceps, past his broad shoulders and up to his face. A thin layer of sandy stubble lines his perfectly angled jaw, giving the appearance that he was too lazy to shave today. His longish hair has the I-just-rolled-out-of-bed-and-I-need-a-haircut look to it. He's exactly the same as he was the last time I saw him two weeks ago. Funny how you can go from being so close with someone to virtual strangers in such a short amount of time.

"How was the rest of your summer?" He's still speaking quietly, even though class hasn't started yet and everyone else isn't bothering to check the volume of their voices. He's not even glancing in my direction and I have to believe it's so others won't notice him engaging me in conversation.

"Awesome." My tone does not indicate that anything is awesome. Not the rest of my summer. Not this conversation. Not the fact that he's sitting beside me and smells so good I want to close my eyes and take a deep breath.

But then he shifts to face me and my breath hitches in the back of my throat. He's looking at me. For real this time. His eyes rake over my hair, my eyes, the freckles scattered across the bridge of my nose and upper cheeks. My lips. They linger there for a moment and I wonder if he's remembering that almost kiss. The one where his face tilted to mine and mine tilted to his and our lips barely brushed as he moved at the last moment and kissed my forehead instead. That kiss wasn't so bad, but it wasn't the one I was hoping for.

Being fifteen sucks.

"I'm sorry about what happened in the hall," he whispers,

leaning farther into me. I'm quietly stunned. "I just didn't like the things he was doing and saying to you, and I had to stop it. Shaw isn't my friend. We play football together and he's friends with people I'm friends with. That's it."

"Hi, Wes," a very perky female purrs from behind us. Wes's eyes instantly flash away from mine in favor of Lindsay Prescott. The head cheerleader. He twists his body halfway around in his seat to talk to her, and I hate that I'm jealous.

I don't like the way this makes me feel.

They chat and flirt and swap stories about their summers while I focus my attention on the front of the room, counting the seconds between bells. I can make it through fifty-two minutes a day sitting next to Weston Kincaid. I can. But the moment the bell rings and Mrs. Hayes calls the class to attention and he turns around to face the front of the room again, his hand brushes mine. And then his foot brushes mine.

And then he leans in and whispers so only I can hear, "Being close to you like this all year is going to be hell."

My thoughts exactly.

Chapter Five

WES

Present Day

I RECOGNIZED Joshua Brown almost instantly. Even with his face all busted up. But for some reason, it didn't fully click into place until I heard someone say his name. Then I found myself moving just a bit faster. Scrubbing in with a bit more vigor. There was an attending in the OR as well as an intern, so when I walked in and the scrub nurse gowned and gloved me up, all I could do was listen to them speak.

This was not being done laparoscopically, which didn't really surprise me given the extent of Josh's injuries. But I hated that the attending let the intern make the initial incision. I hated the way they were speaking about Josh like he wasn't a person I knew once upon a time, but a body for which to learn and practice on.

And I get it.

That's how it is in this room.

This is a teaching hospital and doctors need to learn so they don't kill people. So they continue to fix the next guy who gets wheeled in here. And disconnecting the physical body that needs fixing from the emotion of it being a person is essential.

I was and am no different.

But, in truth, I hated it more for my sake than Josh's.

Because Joshua Brown made me think of Aria. That's how he's forever been associated in my mind and it was like I was working on him for her. For the girl I haven't seen in ten years since she crawled out my window that last time. For the girl who still makes my chest ache when I think about her, even all these years later.

Then when I went to check on him, hours later and at the start of a new shift, there she was. Like the universe was fucking with me and felt the need to conjure her up. Like it was saying wake up, asshole, and rediscover everything you've been missing.

Everything you let get away a few too many times.

She was an apparition. A mirage. Even more beautiful than I remember her being.

I have thought about her over the years.

At first, right after I left for college, it was constant. She was young, and we had that night and it felt...I don't know, special. Like a long time coming. Like she and I were always supposed to happen. I liked that I was the guy who took her virginity. That whenever anyone asked her about that in the future, her thoughts would automatically stray to me.

And when my life fell apart, she was there. In the periphery. Where I needed her to be. Even if it's not where I *wanted* her to be.

Two years later, when she was no longer sixteen and I was no longer eighteen, I finally went back home. I was twenty, and she was eighteen, and it all felt different. It no longer reeked of tragedy and loss, but of do-overs and second chances. At least that's what my mother was going for, even if I couldn't fully swallow that bitter pill.

Seeing Aria was just something I couldn't help but do. I never needed anyone to explain to me how forbidden she was. I knew she was off-limits. That hadn't changed in our years apart. It might have even been more pronounced, given the perfection of our ages and imperfection of our situations.

I was all wrong for then. I was always all wrong for her.

But I needed something bright to wash down all the dark. I needed her. And no one else.

It was a dick move in retrospect. I hadn't spoken to her in two years, and I was planning on leaving again the next day. As soon as possible really.

I shouldn't have done it.

I can't call her a mistake, because she never will be to me. But if I could go back, I would do everything differently with her. I'd fix all the wrongs I caused.

She told me she'd deal with me leaving again. She told me she had gotten through those two years without a hitch. That hurt. Mostly because my life felt like one big hitch and she was a large part of that.

She just wanted the memory, she said. To have our first time not be our only time. Aria was always about her moments. "That's all we get," she'd say to me as we'd sneak out together and stare at the stars from her roof or hide in her treehouse. "Just a series of moments. And if we're lucky, we'll have more amazing ones than sad ones."

I agreed, and we went into it that last time with our eyes open and our hearts closed. But were they really closed?

Mine certainly never was.

When I left home for Princeton, I figured I'd come back for breaks and see her. But life inevitably has a way of taking your plans and crapping all over them. My mom was still living in the house I had lived in the majority of my life with both my parents and I just couldn't face it. And I wasn't ready for Aria to be part of my world yet. Wasn't capable of giving her what she deserved. Everything.

The entirety of my four years at Princeton felt like they revolved around her. Well, my dad too, but that was different. After college, everything changed. My life took on a different course. It wasn't the one I had hoped for, not entirely anyway, and I forced myself to think of Aria less when our paths never realigned. Typically, only in passing or if I spoke to or saw her brother, Brecken. But every now and then, during some particularly dark moments or late nights, I'd relive our time together. I'd smile, wondering about the girl life seemed to enjoy keeping away from me.

Until today.

Until Joshua Brown ended up on my table.

It was the unexpected that quickly morphed into a holy shit moment. A true genuine one because I saw her a full second before she saw me, and even though I was inconceivably shocked that it was, in fact, her, I also couldn't look away. And that part had nothing to do with my shock.

Her hair is just as I remember it, long, thick, wild dark curls. Her eyes are still that same sparkling blue that reminds me of the summer sky. Her smile is still big and bright and breathtaking. But everything else is different. Her cheeks have thinned out, having lost the remnants of adolescent baby fat. Her body is most definitely that of a woman's, with fuller tits and a small narrow waist that slopes into her curvy hips and gorgeous ass.

She's the perfect combination of familiar and new. Of expected and unexpected. She's everything I ever wanted, but could never have.

I have no idea what Brecken has told her about me over the years. He and I really don't speak often anymore and rarely about Aria. I never asked about her after she left New York. I never wanted to know. I felt too much, too guilty to ask her brother anything more, and guys don't typically discuss their little sisters when they're catching up with old friends. I have no idea what she knows of my life, but considering the fact that she didn't have any idea I was living and working here, I doubt it's much.

If only I had known she was living here sooner.

My eyes close as my forearm rests against my bleary eyes. I should try and sleep while I have a few moments respite, but I cannot get Aria out of my head. I cannot stop smiling. I wonder if she hates me. I'd hate me if I were her. I mean, I fucked her twice and left immediately after both times. If that doesn't scream asshole, I don't know what does.

My phone vibrates in my pocket and I groan out loud. Sliding my phone out, I check it and see that it's a text page from Vanessa,

Josh's nurse. ***Abdomen on Joshua Brown is distended and firm. Please come to evaluate.***

A post-surgical abdomen can be both of those things, but Vanessa has been doing this long enough to tell the difference between nothing and something. So I pull my tired ass up and make my way back to the surgical ICU. Vanessa is already there when I arrive, and Aria is sitting up in her chair, watching vigilantly, her eyes focused on Josh's body that is now only covered by his gown.

"You should probably wait outside," I tell her. Her head swivels in my direction as if my voice startled her, and then she shakes her head no. It's an adamant, fuck you if you even try and get me to leave, no. I'm assuming she already said the same thing to the nurse who does not look happy to have an audience. "Seriously, Aria. You don't need to see this."

"I'm not leaving."

I know better than most that arguing with her will get me nowhere. I move to stand in front of her, an attempt to block her view, and surprisingly, she lets me do that. She doesn't want to leave him, but she doesn't want to see this either. I pull up his gown and appreciate that his abdomen is exactly the way Vanessa described it. I palpate around and note it's warmer and a hell of a lot firmer than it should be. "Is he febrile?"

"One hundred point six."

"How's his BP?"

"Stable. One twenty-two over sixty-four. Heart rate is slightly tachy at one thirteen."

I nod, and when I listen with my stethoscope, no bowel sounds. *Shit.*

"What are you doing?" Aria questions softly, as if she's afraid to interrupt, but has to know.

"We're just examining him," I reply equally as soft. "Yes, he's definitely distended," I say delicately to Vanessa who's at my side. "I want a stat abdominal CT, and someone needs to call down to the OR to have them prep it. My guess is his bowel perfed."

Vanessa nods. Picking up the phone attached to her hip, she dials a number before she begins to speak to someone on the other end. A few moments later she says, "Transport is on their way and both CT and the OR have been alerted."

"Great. Thanks." Nothing better than a nurse who knows her shit and is on top of her game. I turn to leave. The CT will take only a few minutes to get done and I need to get down to the OR. I do not want an intern on this. I know we explored the bowel, but that contusion–

"Dr. Kincaid," Aria cuts in loud enough to pull me back as she takes a step in my direction, effectively cutting off my escape. The nurse steps around us and politely excuses herself from the room. "What the hell is going on?"

Her blue eyes are on fire and I wonder if she was trying to get my attention before now. "His abdomen is distended and firm. He's also slightly febrile. I'm guessing it's a perforation of his bowel, or possibly his splenic repair opened. But I'm not positive and I don't want to open him up again until I know what we're dealing with. I'm sending him down for a stat CT and then I'll probably end up doing surgery on him again."

She shoves me. Hard. I step back, more out of shock than anything else, despite the fact that she put some effort into it. "God-dammit," she yells, pushing me again. "Speak fucking English to me! I don't know if you hate me or what. But please," she begins to crumple as her adrenaline ebbs, her expression tortured with heartache and defeat, "just talk to me. I'll call you Dr. Kincaid. I'll only speak to you about Josh. Just," she sniffles back her tears, "tell me what's going on so I understand. He's my best friend in the world. I can't lose him."

Christ… this girl.

"Okay," I say softly, reaching out to brush some of her hair from her face, wanting to touch her, but realizing how that might not be the right thing to do. I don't deserve to touch her, I remind myself. My hand drops immediately as I regain my equilibrium. There are so many things in that small heartbroken speech I want to address, but now really isn't the time. "That area on his bowel? The one I mentioned to you earlier?" She nods. "I think there might be a cut on it that's bleeding and leaking things into his body that are making him sick. I'm going to get a CAT scan to confirm it and make sure I know where to go in, but I'm going to do surgery on him within the next hour."

"I…is…" She sucks in a shuddered breath before blowing it out slowly, desperately trying to contain herself. "Is he going to be okay?"

"I'll do everything I can for him, Aria." My hand squeezes her upper arm as my eyes find hers. "I promise you, I will."

"Will someone update me?"

"I'll make sure they do."

She tries for a smile, but not much happens as she stares up at me with watery eyes. "I'm sorry I pushed you. I just got really frustrated with this whole situation. I'm scared, and I haven't slept in a really long time, and nothing is making sense to me even if it should."

"I understand." And I do. I know her well enough to know how she works. "Hell, I deserved it and worse from you."

"Probably. If you were any other doctor, I don't think I would have done that," she muses more to herself than to me. She shakes her head slowly, a wry half-grin on her face like she can't believe she pushed me.

I don't care in the slightest. I actually love that I can still emotionally charge her up. "When we're alone like this, you can call me Wes."

"Okay," she whispers, and I release her, heading for the door.

But before I go, I turn back to her. "I definitely don't hate you," I say, pausing on the threshold of the door. "I never have. Honestly, I always assumed it was the reverse. I wouldn't have blamed you for it either."

She lets out a humorless laugh, wiping at her tears. "I don't hate you either. Maybe I should have, but I never did. So now that we got that out of the way, can you go and save my friend's life?"

"Sure." I give her a wink and then I'm gone. Briskly walking through the ICU before I hit the hall and make my way to the OR.

I'll admit, coming back to Boston wasn't my first choice. Even if the hospitals are some of the best in the world. My mom got remarried to an incredible man who incidentally had a pretty severe heart attack shortly before I picked my fellowship. I applied for the one here because it's not too far from them and I wanted to be close now that they need me, and I didn't have to live in that house again.

And secretly, I think I had always hoped she'd come back. Or maybe that's just how it feels now when I look at her. I was crazy about Aria Davenport for most of my life and then I was gone. Two years later, I came back, only to leave her again like the coward I was.

This feels like that do-over. Like that second chance.

A second chance I'm suddenly very interested in exploring.

Chapter Six

ARIA

I'm floating. How the hell am I floating? I'm pressed up against a warm, strong body that smells strongly of antiseptic soap and a woodsy cologne that is oddly familiar. My eyes blink open. "What are you doing?" I rasp out. My throat is so dry I feel like I've swallowed sand and washed it down with cotton balls.

"I'm carrying you over to the reclining chair," Wes says with an amused smirk playing on the corner of his lips, his green eyes full of mischief. "You looked really uncomfortable slouched over his bed, and the nurses had trouble getting Josh back into it after his surgery with you draped over it."

"You could have woken me up, and I would have walked."

"Where would be the fun in that?" He sets me down gently, laying me back and picking up a white blanket from the foot of the bed. He unfolds it, covering me with its heat. It feels so freaking good I can't even find the will to complain again.

"How is he?" I ask, my head snapping over to the bed. I have no idea what time it is. I feel like I'm in an alternate reality. Day and night no longer exist. How did I not wake up when they put him back in? Jesus, I must have really been out. He looks exactly as he did before they wheeled him out.

"Good. Better. He had a small tear in his bowel that was leaking, but I was able to repair it. The bruise to his liver is improving, and the laceration to his spleen that I fixed is holding perfectly."

I blow out the breath I didn't even realize I was holding, scrubbing my hands up and down my face as I swallow back my tears. I don't want to cry in front of Wes again, but I'm so overwhelmed with everything I'm finding it nearly impossible to hold back my emotions. The perpetual pendulum of life and death feels like it's swinging back and forth around me. The day/night continuum mixed with too little sleep isn't doing me any favors either.

"The swelling in his brain went up a bit during the surgery. That's pretty common, and we were able to control it with medications. I believe neurology plans on keeping him sedated a bit longer."

A humorless laugh passes my lips. "This is so surreal. I still can't comprehend how any of this happened."

"Do the police have any leads?"

I shake my head. "I didn't speak with them. Tyler did. They're supposed to come back at some point tomorrow, I think." I check my watch and sigh because it's after three in the morning. "Christ, it is tomorrow. Anyway, I'm hoping they have some answers."

Wes nods, but he doesn't offer anything more, and this is just getting awkward. There are so many things unsaid. And so many years in between. I have questions I've always wanted answers to. He might even have the same for me. The way we parted, ended, was...well, it was brutal. At least for me. There were times when my adolescent heart felt like it was going to shrivel up and die. I have no idea if it was that way for him, but considering I never heard from him again, I doubt it.

Yeah, maybe I should have hated him.

I knew the first time he left that he was going to leave and that would be it. I expected it. It still hurt. It more than hurt. But then he came back two years later, and I couldn't help myself. My feelings for him hadn't changed a bit. They might have been stronger if that's even possible.

I wanted to be with him.

Even when he told me he was leaving again the next morning. He was sweet and tender and looked at me with what I believed resembled love. He warned me, but I couldn't find it in myself to believe him. Or maybe I just didn't want to stop. I wanted that memory. I just didn't realize what it would be like after. Him leaving again didn't mean I didn't expect more. I did. He made me believe it was there, right on the cusp. Just a couple of years away. In the years that followed, I realized that illusion was of my own making.

He's standing over me, and I wish I didn't remember everything the way I do. I wish some of that had dissipated with time. "You look different," I say before I can help it.

"So do you."

"I see you got what you wanted."

His eyebrows furrow before his expression hardens. "How do you mean?"

"You're a doctor."

He nods, but he doesn't follow that up with anything else. Even though there is a library of unspoken words flashing across his face. He doesn't ask what happened to me. What I've done all these years in between.

But he wants to.

"Thank you," I start, but my throat feels like it's closing up on me and I have to clear it, "for taking care of Josh."

His eyes focus in on mine, an internal battle warring inside him.

"Taking care of Josh is my job," he starts slowly, calculating, like he's measuring my reaction to his words. "He was my patient when he was first admitted, and he's still my patient now. He will continue to be as long as he's on the surgical service."

"Right. Of course."

I turn away from him, gazing over to my friend and hoping that Wes will take the hint and leave. I have too much hurt inside of me right now to tack on an old heartbreak. Josh in a fucking coma after being beaten practically to death and having two surgeries within twenty-four hours is a lot to take on. And now Wes. It's just too much.

His hand runs through my hair, and I shrug him off. He doesn't get to touch me right now. "Aria."

"Shut up, Wes. You don't get to use that tone with me. I'm not a child anymore." He shifts in closer, his body heat against me though he's not touching me. But his proximity is also my total undoing. My chin trembles, my nose and eyes burn as I try desperately to rein back my tears.

I feel him kneel down until his face is close to mine. "Josh is my patient, Aria, and I take my job very seriously." I turn back to him. There is something in his voice that compels me to. "But seeing you again…," he trails off, his eyes searching mine. "Is it too much if I say I've thought about you over the years? Wondered about you." My breath hitches as his fingers come up, tracing the lines of my cheek until they're diving through my hair, cupping the back of my head. I feel like I'm flying. The way he's staring into me makes me feel weightless. "I know it's been a long time, and I fucked up a hundred different ways with you. But looking at you now, it doesn't feel like any time has past, does it?"

I shake my head, unable to verbalize just what this is.

His eyes dance about my face and he swallows, regret creasing the corners of his eyes and turning his lips down into a frown. "It feels like you just climbed out of my bedroom window."

"It does." His thoughts echo mine from just a few hours ago. My voice is quiet, the sound getting absorbed into the din of Josh's machines and hospital doings. His head dips down to catch my words, his face inches from mine now. It's too much. I can't stand it. I have no idea how to react to it.

"I can't believe I'm seeing you again after all this time."

I swallow so hard. He has no idea. He was my first everything. Including my first love. I've since compared every single man to him. Including Drew. Who also works in this hospital as a doctor. They probably know each other. I bet they do. Drew works in the emergency department and Wes is a trauma surgeon. That thought twists my stomach for some reason.

My eyes trail along the muscles of his arms. The sleeve of his scrub top looks like it could tear any moment. "You're bigger than I remember," I comment and then instantly cringe. Me and my mouth. I swear, it's like it goes on total disconnect from my brain whenever I get nervous. He laughs, dropping his forehead to mine. And even though this should probably be considered weird or out of place, it's not. It feels like the most natural thing in the world. Probably because he's done it dozens of times before.

I should pull away. I should stop this.

"Aria," he whispers against me, his sweet breath tickling my lips. "Am I making you nervous?"

I both love and hate that he remembers my little quirk. But then again, I couldn't shut up before he gave me that first ever kiss on my roof. Or while he was undressing me that first time months after that. And definitely not when he was first inside me.

"Yes," I admit ruefully. "You always have."

"In a bad way?" *Like he doesn't know.*

"In a good way. In a fun way."

"A fun way." He smirks, testing the words. "Is that all I am to you?"

"Well." I laugh bitterly because I can't help it. "Considering I haven't seen you in a freaking decade, I can't say what you are to me. Stop flirting with me, Dr. Kincaid."

He winces. "Okay. I'll give you that one. For now," he adds and I don't quite understand his meaning. Wes pulls back from me, standing up to his full height. He tilts his head, his hair flopping down across his forehead making him look so adorably boyish, reminding me of the teenager from my memories. "I have to go. But I'll be back to check on him later."

"Sure," I say, my voice suddenly thick with more freaking tears as I look over at Josh.

"I can't give you promises, Aria. But Josh looks good, all things considered, and I heard the neurologist saying that his exam went really well."

"Thank you." I smile at that. I need to pull myself together.

He throws me a wink before walking out of the room.

"Shit," I mutter, dropping my head back in the chair that lets out a squeak when my weight presses down. I have no idea what is happening here. "Joshua Brown. You better get your ass on the mend because shit is getting far too real for me here and I don't know what to do about it." No response. "Dammit, Josh, I need you. Who the hell else can I talk to about this?" Still nothing. "You're going to shit a whale when you do wake up and I tell you that not only is Weston Kincaid the person who did surgery on you twice, but he's flirting with me. That has to be what that was. And I hate it. I really do. It's horrible. And he sucks at it," I tack on as I adjust in my recliner so I'm sitting up a little more, facing him.

I need my friend to wake up.

I need his sarcastic, cutting remarks.

"Josh, you need to wake up and smack me upside the head. Do you remember how bad Wes is for me? What happened between us? This is bad, my friend. Bad, bad, bad."

Because nothing about Wes is easy. But it's time. It's been far too long. I have to face the demons of my past so I can move forward. Isn't that what people always say? You can't outrun your past. Even when they've hurt you time and time again.

Awesome.

That doesn't mean I want to walk right back into the lion's den either. I don't want to give in to him the way I find myself already doing. I don't want to tell him what his leaving did to me all those years ago. I don't want to get my heart broken again. I feel like that's all I ever do and Wes happens to be the cause of two out of the three.

Maturational wisdom does not protect against emotional stupidity.

Weston Kincaid needs to keep his distance. So if he wants to be amicable and friendly, fantastic. I can do that. But anything else? No. I won't do that to myself again.

"I'm not gonna tell him, Josh." The only response I get is the swoosh of air in and out of his lungs through that damn tube. "There's really nothing to tell anymore, anyway. I was a young girl who fell for the wrong guy. Besides, I'm done with him. Promise. Okay?" I feel so stupid talking to him like this. "Okay." I sag back into my chair, resting my head on the slightly softer plastic and pull the blanket up over my shoulders, curling my body under it.

My eyes close and I breathe in deeply.

I hate this place. I hate Josh being beaten into a coma. I hate that we don't know who did it and that they're still out there. I hate that Weston Kincaid flirted with me.

And I hate that I liked flirting with him back. That won't happen again.

Chapter Seven

ARIA

"Wake up, sleeping beauty," a soft voice sings close to my ear. I stir, moving awkwardly, my neck and upper back stiff as hell. "I brought you food."

I grin. "It better be something fattening. And fried. I haven't eaten anything fried in so long."

"I believe that," Tyler says with a chuckle. I open my eyes, blinking against the harsh hospital lights. I wonder how long I actually slept for. It doesn't feel like very long going by the headache I'm sporting. "Come on, Aria. Get your ass up. You need to eat. You're wasting away."

I snort out in a very unladylike way. "You're a godsend." I roll over, sitting up and rotating my head, trying to alleviate some of my stiffness. Tyler is looking at me with a smile that lights up his cleanly shaven, freshly showered face. "I feel bad for all womankind." I shake my head at him, laughing. "It's just so unfair that men who look as good as you do are gay."

He laughs too. "I tried women. Weren't for me."

"Me either," I muse, and his eyebrows hit his hairline. I can only shrug. Then my eyes spot his hand. "What the hell happened?"

Tyler glances down at his right hand that is now swollen, and purple, and oozing. Was it like that before? I can't recall. "I punched a wall."

"You punched a *wall*?"

He nods, sheepishly. "I was just so…angry. So frustrated. I lost it. So I punched the wall."

"With your *fist*?"

Another sheepish nod.

"Well, keep it under wraps, counselor." Tyler forces a grin but it doesn't quite meet his eyes. "Is it broken?"

"I don't think so. It looks worse than it feels."

"I hate this," I whisper, tears well in my eyes for what feels like the umpteenth time. I'm pissed at myself for them. Much the way Tyler was helplessly pissed off and punched his wall. I'm not from the criers.

"It's the worst," he agrees, cupping my face with his large, uninjured hand. "How long can you stay?"

"As long as I need to. I was supposed to be in New York for a gallery exhibit. But whatever, my PA, Lydia, is there. My art can wait." Actually, I'm sort of freaking out about that. This opening is big. It means everything for my career and I really should be there.

He laughs. "Or not. Aren't trauma and tragedy the stuff art is made of?"

"Something like that." I smile humorlessly. "What time is it?" I glance toward the window and notice it's dark and pouring rain.

"It's just about seven. I thought I'd come by and see how he is before I have to go into the office for a bit." He frowns, and I know this must upset him. "I spoke to the nurse who said it was a very long night." I nod. "But he's doing better now? They did another surgery?" Another nod as I sit up, wiping away a night spent sitting in a chair, flirting with a once upon a time lover, and watching Josh sleep.

"They did. I have no way of determining if he's better, though. I go on whatever they tell me."

"Why don't you go grab yourself a shower and a change of clothes. Take a break. You've been here for like thirty hours and you look rough."

"Thanks," I reply dryly. "I want to be here when the police come."

He makes a *pfft* noise. "They're not coming back until later."

"Probably not." I sigh, leaning forward and touching Josh's ice-cold hand. I'm hoping that temperature means his fever is gone. I would text Rina and Margot, but I know both of them have to work, and I don't want to worry them. Especially at the start of their shifts.

I stand up, twisting my stiff muscles as I do. Nothing is helping here. I feel like shit. I really could use a shower and some food and some more sleep.

"Okay, I'll go shower. But I'm coming back."

"That a threat or a promise?" Tyler asks, taking a bite of whatever he's eating. And even though I haven't had anything to eat in forever, the idea of a shower is more favorable.

"A promise. Because I'm going. I feel like a used-up tissue, and I need to change my clothes and shower off too many hours here."

"Sounds like a plan." He's laughing at me now. Probably because I'm mindlessly rambling and repeating myself.

I walk over to him, dropping a kiss on his forehead. "You'll call if anything changes?"

He nods, taking another bite of his food. I snatch a piece of potato off his plate and he shoos me away. "Of course, honey. Now go. You stink."

I swat at his shoulder but do as I'm told. I kiss Josh goodbye, promising to be back, and then I'm out the door. I even forget my fattening breakfast in my haste, but I don't care. I can find something later. Food is at the bottom of my list.

But coffee isn't, and maybe a blueberry muffin because suddenly my stomach is growling out its discontent. Walking along the first floor, I try to find the coffee shop that's somewhere around here when I spot him. Drew. My ex. I stand frozen in the middle of the busy corridor. People coming and moving around me as they go. He's laughing with another doctor, the two of them talking about God knows what. We're friendly enough. For exes. Well, let me amend that. *He's* friendly with *me*. He still texts and calls, and I do not reciprocate.

I was always under the assumption that when you end a relationship with someone you've been with for a year and a half, it's over. You don't become buddy-buddy with someone you claimed to have loved. At least that's always been my thinking on it.

I don't know. I just know that I need sleep because my overly emotional brain doesn't feel like it's making much sense right now. I don't have the energy to deal with him right now. His head starts to move in my direction, his gray eyes following its path, and before he can see me, I turn to my left and bolt toward the exit. I don't even know what part of the hospital I'm in, but I do not care. An exit is an exit.

Until I step outside.

It's raining. Like a full-on Texas-sized storm to the point where water is running down the sides of the streets in rivers. I took an Uber here. I was in a rush and a mess and didn't want to drive only to have to try to find a lot or garage. But it's not even seven in the morning and I don't see anything anywhere that would be helpful.

Except the street all the way down past a garage on my right. And then I spot a cab go flying by. Then another one. Sucking in a rush of air, I duck my head down to the ground and start to run out into the monsoon. Icy cold rain pelts me, soaking my hair and clothes instantly, because I don't have a coat on. Fucking fantastic. Now that I'm running toward the street, I don't see any other cabs going by. That actually makes me pause, to look back at the exit I just vacated. I should go back in and order an Uber.

Water runs down my face, obscuring my vision, but just as I spin back around, I slam into someone and fall backward to the ground, landing on my ass with a hard, wet splat.

"I'm so sorry," the person who knocked me down says, reaching for my arm to help me. They hoist me up effortlessly and as I wipe the matted hair out of my face and clear my eyes, I see it's Wes. Of course, it's Wes. Why would it be any of the other people who come and go from this hospital? "What the hell are you doing out here in this weather?" he snaps, his tone morphing from apologetic to accusatory.

"I'm looking for a stupid cab, and then I realized that I'd probably be better off taking an Uber," I yell back, staring straight up into his dark face. He's soaking wet, same as me. Except he's smart enough to be wearing a coat whereas I forgot mine in my haste last night. "What the hell is your excuse?"

"Mine?" he barks out, incredulous. "I was running to get to the garage when the person I was behind suddenly stopped moving and I plowed into her. And it had to be you. Of all people, only you'd run out into a rainstorm without a coat or a plan."

"Then go," I scream, my voice getting louder, competing with the sound of the rain pounding against the pavement. "I'm not stopping you."

"Goddammit, Aria." He stares down at me in indecision, licking his lips as water drips into his mouth. "You're soaking wet and shivering." He pulls off his jacket, throwing it over my shoulders. It's enticingly warm and mostly dry inside.

It smells like him. Like cologne and rain and something so wonderfully male and recognizable that I sob out before I can stop it. It smells like unfulfilled dreams. Like nights spent awake painting and writing and singing and remembering. Like longing and aching and deep-seated hurt. Like a lost love I haven't allowed myself to dwell on in a very long time.

It's all piling up on me suddenly.

Josh and Wes and even goddamn Drew. But right now, all I see is Wes.

"Are you hurt?" he asks, clearly confused by my sudden onslaught of emotion.

But I can't help it. I'm overtaken with an agonizing fear and pain and nostalgia that is so strong I shudder violently.

"Oh baby, come here. Don't cry." His arms wrap around me, drawing me into his chest. I try to pull away, but he tightens his grip. "Stop fighting me and let me hold you." He presses me in closer. "I'm sorry," he whispers into my hair, resting my head against his soaking wet chest. His light blue scrub top is plastered to his body, showing off every perfect line of his cut chest and abdomen. And without his coat, he's soaked through, same as me.

My breath burns as I inhale, desperately trying to pull air into my shredded lungs.

I can't get control.

I'm clinging to him like my life depends on it, because, at this moment, I am absolutely positive it does. That if I let go, I'll drown in this. His strong body cocoons me in a warmth so intense I gasp with it. His hands are in my hair, his lips press to my forehead as he holds me to him. He doesn't rush me, surprisingly enough, given the inhospitable weather we're entrenched in.

He just waits me out until I'm back together.

"Are you ready?" he asks gently, cupping my cheek in his large hand. I nod, and he smiles. "Come on," he says before grabbing my arm and tugging on me to move. "We'll drown out here." I let out a derisive snort at his choice of words. I meant it figuratively, and he means it literally, and I think the truth is somewhere in between.

"Where are we going?" I ask, my voice barely carrying over the sound of the fat icy droplets as they hit the ground.

"I'm taking you to my car and then I'm driving you wherever you were going." I start to pull back, but once again his grip tightens, and he tugs me harder as he throws me a sidelong glare. "For once in your life, don't argue with me."

My mouth opens but just as quickly shuts. What are my alternatives? I'm soaked, freezing, and have no quick way of getting home.

I let him lead me into the garage, relieved that I'm no longer out in the rain that now feels like it's freezing my body to the core. We walk up a ramp and then down to his Jeep. The same Jeep he got his senior year when he turned eighteen. His father bought it for him after a really big football game that he personally won. I think that was one of the best moments of his life. At least back then. I remember spending a lot of hidden time with Wes in this car. A lot of heated making out.

I can't help but smirk when I see it, even if the memories are laced with despair for his loss. I never in a million years thought he'd still have this thing. Especially since it's over twelve years old. "Don't they pay you anything, Doctor?"

Wes pauses as he unlocks my door, his eyes meet mine and I see him trying to hide his smile the same way I am. "I'm a fellow." He shrugs like that explains it, but I don't think that's why. Wes loved this car when we were teenagers and I bet he still loves it today. I wonder if he kept it all these years because of his father. I wonder if he still thinks of him when he gets in it.

I can only shake my head as I wring out the excess water from my hair, creating a puddle on the ground beside me. I'm completely frozen through. And even though I'm reluctant to part with it, I start to shrug out of his coat, but he shakes his head, holding up a hand to stop me. "Keep it on. It's freezing and you're soaked."

"So are you."

"I'm fine. I want you to wear it."

"So if I got into your car in my soaking wet jeans?"

He chuckles, our intense moment from earlier gone. I feel like I should be embarrassed by what happened, but I can't find that emotion anywhere. I'm so many things right now, but embarrassed isn't one of them. "I'm getting you a towel from the trunk."

Thank God, because I'm shivering my ass off.

I follow him to the back of his car as he swings open the door, and sure enough, he's still a freaking boy scout. Towels, blankets, full water bottles, and a first aid kit. There are even extra clothes. All of them in their proper place of course. He hands me a towel and as I wrap the soft cotton around my sodden body, Wes reaches behind his neck and tugs his wet scrubs top over his head.

Holy sweet baby Jesus eating ice cream. It's been way too long since I've seen this man without a shirt on, but his chest is everything it used to be and so much more. *So* much more. The first things I notice are his shoulder and back muscles, probably because those are what's facing me as he tosses his soaked shirt into his trunk and grabs his own towel. I can't pull my eyes away from the way his muscles move and stretch as he dries himself.

Am I drooling? I think I actually might be.

When he's done with his back, he pauses, his towel covered hand gliding down the front of his abs. It's like I'm watching porn. Men don't look like Weston Kincaid in real life. His pecs have a light covering of blond hair, but his abs are bare and toned and look as if they're cut from stone, all the way down to the V he has that disappears inside the black band of his boxers. He catches me staring at him, a crooked grin turning up the corner of his mouth as he throws on his dry long sleeve thermal shirt.

But then he stops and just…stares back at me. His eyes boring into mine, green to blue. My heart begins to pound in my chest as I think about the last time he looked at me like this.

Like he wants to devour me all over again.

A shaky breath rushes out past my lips as I stare back at him. His hand reaches for me but I shake my head, stepping back, and he quickly drops it.

"We should go," I tell him, keeping my voice strong and even. I swallow hard and turn on the heel of my squeaky Vans and get into his car.

Because in that moment, I wanted him toss me into the back of his Boy Scout trunk and fuck me senseless. And that is *not* the way I should be thinking when it comes to this man.

The good doctor is hazardous to my health.

He wordlessly gets in, starting up his car. Fucking country music comes blaring out of his speakers, snapping me out of my world of tortured memories and wet panties.

"Where am I taking you?" he asks as he turns up the heat to full blast, pointing the vents in my direction.

Fucking considerate bastard. Give me your flaws, Wes. I need them to remember why you're the worst idea in the history of ideas.

"My place," I say and then sigh. He doesn't know where I live. He didn't even know I was living in Boston until he saw me. I give him my address and fall silent. He backs us out of the spot, navigating through the garage and out into the rain that is still coming down, though not as hard as before. "Do you know where that is?"

A nod. That's all I get and I can only hope that means that our moment of friendliness is over. Leaning my head against the window, I close my eyes before they reopen again at the sound of his voice. "What happened to Josh's parents?"

"Car accident," I reply softly. "Two years ago."

"You're all he has then."

I can't tell what he means by that, so I don't respond. I'm not sure if I need to. Instead, I close my eyes again, too tired to try to fill the silence with getting to know you again crap. The car stops fifteen minutes later, and my eyes flitter open, noticing that the rain has pretty much stopped as well.

Sitting up, I unbuckle my seatbelt and then move to open the door, but Wes's voice stops me once again. "I read an article about you once. In *The New York Times*. About your art. About what you were doing with your life." He's not looking at me. He's staring sightlessly out the windshield. My breath lodges in my throat and my hand is stuck to the latch of the door. The windshield wipers squeak against the glass as they swoosh back and forth, wiping away the remnants of the icy rain. "It was my senior year of college. I was finishing up. Applying for medical schools." He turns to look at me now, searing a path through me with his intensity. "Some here in Boston. Some out west. Some in New York. All over really. I had gotten into Harvard and Stanford and was waiting on Columbia and NYU. I was planning on Columbia even though I had always thought about Stanford."

"Why were you planning on Columbia?" I ask before I can stop my curiosity from getting the best of me, my voice barely a whisper.

His expression turns sad. Introspective. "I thought I had more time. It had been years and I knew all the mistakes I made with that. So many mistakes, Aria." His eyes bleed sincerity into mine. "I thought New York would be the answer. The fix. But when I read that article, I realized I was too late. I had run out of time."

He gives a half-hearted shrug, his expression a combination of broken and impassive. A look that only makes sense on Wes. One he's perfected. Like he's fighting a battle with showing any emotion and losing the war.

"I was so happy for you that you were going to London. That you were living your dream. That it was all just getting started for you. I was also so unbelievably angry with myself. And wrecked with jealousy over the world that was getting you when I wasn't because I fucked up. So I chose Stanford instead of Columbia."

I shake my head, my eyebrows furrowing at his tone. I can't tell how he feels about this admission. And I have absolutely no idea what to say in response. Is he suggesting he was thinking of attending Columbia because of me? Because he thought I was going to stay in New York indefinitely, waiting on him?

I remember the article he's talking about. I have it saved somewhere because when *The New York Times* writes an article about you, you keep it. Well, if it's good and this one was.

I was moving from New York to London. I hit it big in a short amount of time. I was fortunate enough to never ensure the life of a struggling artist. My mom's contacts in the art world and my dad's in the business world thrust me quickly into the spotlight. I had an offer from a prestigious gallery in London. They had commissioned me to give them twelve paintings, and I thought living there would be an adventure. I spoke about that in the article.

But I was in New York for two years before that.

Two. Years.

And yeah, Wes was still in college. So was Brecken, who was in New York, and they were friends. And I knew Wes had been through a lot.

But he never came for me.

I had hoped he would. That maybe we would have crossed paths during a visit. Or he'd hear I was there and come see me.

Neither of those things happened, and after the first year, I stopped waiting on the guy who was never coming back for me. On the guy who never took the risk on me.

I should feel some semblance of relief or elation or something at the fact that he's telling me he considered moving to New York for me. That I wasn't as forgotten or discarded as I felt.

I believe that's what that little speech was about.

But I don't feel any of those things. Instead, it angers me. He never paid any attention. He let time go. He lived his life and followed his dreams and plans and thought I would be there, patiently waiting for him when he was ready.

I don't work that way.

And maybe if he had come sooner, things would have turned out differently. But maybe not.

"Lost time is never found again," I say, quoting Benjamin Franklin. I remove his towel and his coat from my body and hop out of the car. "Thanks for the ride, Wes. And for saving Josh's life."

I smile at that thought and then jog up the stone steps of my building. I don't turn around to see if Wes is still there when I unlock my door. And I try really hard not to listen for the sound of his car pulling away. But the moment the door shuts behind me, and I'm standing in the foyer, I do look. Because even though I was trying not to listen, I was.

He's still there, staring straight out his windshield, his hands gripping the upper column of the steering wheel. He appears lost in thought and I wonder what he was expecting me to say or do at his confession.

For a beat of a second, I'm tempted to go back out there. But I don't and I won't. Some things are better left in the past.

Chapter Eight

ARIA

My phone pings from my nightstand where it's plugged into the charger.

I have no idea how long I've been out. I didn't even mean to fall asleep. I just plopped down for a second while I put my clothes in the washing machine. It can't be all that long; my head is still pounding. Rolling over, I find my phone and stare at it for a moment, unsure of what I'm reading.

Why were you in my hospital this morning?

That's from Drew and I don't know what to say to that. I have zero interest in seeing him. I wish he would just accept the breakup he enacted and move on. But he hasn't. It's like he was wishing I would beg at his feet for him to reconsider or something. Not exactly my style. All he had to do was stay. Try a little harder with me. But he didn't, and that's on him.

Josh was badly hurt and is in the hospital.

I get the message bubble almost instantly.

Your Josh? Is he kidding me with that? **Is he all right? Where is he?**

The ICU.

Which one, Aria. There are several here.

Fucking asshole.

SICU.

My phone rings and I let out a loud groan. Why can't exes just leave you be? "What?" I snap into the phone, in no mood to play games. Drew is an emergency room attending. When I met him two years ago, he was still a resident working crazy hours and very much in love with me. It happened so quickly. He approached me at a bar I was at with friends, asked if he could buy me a drink and that was all it took for me to fall for him.

I'm not even joking.

We talked all night. He walked me home because I was living close to that bar at the time and kissed me good night.

When he called the next day for a date, I said yes immediately. I didn't even try to play it cool. He was tall and smart and sexy and made me feel things I hadn't felt since Wes left my life. I figured if he could do all that within a few hours of meeting him, then maybe he was my future. And he was. For a year and a half, he was my everything.

The reason I bought a place in Boston. The reason I stayed. The reason I gave up so much of myself for his long hours.

Then something began to shift. It was slow. It started with little arguments about the amount of time I was spending with my art. I would disappear for days at a time, lost in my work, and he didn't like that. He worked long hours too and expected me to drop everything the moment he surfaced for air.

I didn't. No, I don't save lives, but my work is my life and I wasn't about to give that up. Not for anyone.

Eventually, it progressed to the point where he told me he couldn't be with someone who was more committed to themselves than to him. And even though I believed that to be incredibly unfair and wholly hypocritical, I understood. Well, sort of. He ended things with me, explaining that it shouldn't be so hard to be together.

"What happened? Is he okay?"

"He was attacked."

"Damn. I'm so sorry, babe." My eyes cinch shut. I hate that he called me babe. I never exactly enjoyed that term of endearment, but that's not what has me cringing right now. "I'll go check on him as soon as I can. Who's his doctor?"

I hesitate, biting my lip nervously. Why, I have no idea. "Weston Kincaid."

"Oh," Drew says with an approving note. "Yeah. He's very good. One of the best surgeons we have in trauma."

That's actually about as glowing as it gets from Drew, and I feel relieved that not only does he have no idea who Wes is to me but that he said that.

"Right. Thanks. I need to go." And then I hang up. Because I don't want to talk to Drew. I have no idea what he's doing with me but none of it is good.

Rolling out of bed, I shuffle my way into the bathroom to shower. I catch a glimpse of my reflection and quickly turn away. I look like something out of *The Walking Dead* and I don't feel much better. My shower is one of those that has a million different sprayers, and this makes me smile. I can be such a prima donna when I want to be. Doesn't bother me in the slightest.

Especially when I step into the practically scalding water that is spraying every part of my body. It's heaven and I find myself standing here in the cascade for longer than I should. I know I need to get my ass in gear and get back to the hospital.

I wash my hair and body and force myself to get out. As I enter my bedroom, a towel wrapped around my chest, my eyes fall upon my laptop that's resting on my desk. I really should check my emails. I have that gallery opening I told Tyler about going on in New York. Lydia, my PA is there, but I have no idea how it's doing. If I'm selling anything or if it's tanking. The owner is going to be level five pissed at me for not being there. Especially for opening night. That's a big deal. A real big deal. Newspapers and magazines and celebrities and tons of photographs.

But really, how could I leave? Josh comes first. Family before work.

I stare at my laptop for another moment and decide I can't

handle that right now. If I start in on work, I'll never get out of here. I'll get sucked into the vortex. I sigh out my regret and guilt and towel off. I throw on clothes, remembering my coat this time as I head out the door.

The Uber I ordered pulls up just as my feet hit the sidewalk. Another fifteen minutes later, I'm walking back into Josh's hospital room. Tyler is sitting in one of the chairs, his feet propped up on the edge of Josh's hospital bed a legal notepad in his lap.

My mouth opens in apology, but my voice gets caught in my throat. "I thought you were a righty," I say, noting how he's writing with his left hand. His non-injured hand at that.

He glances up, his dark eyes smiling. "I'm ambidextrous," he replies and then holds up his injured hand. "Good thing."

I nod, kissing Josh on the forehead and then dropping down into the recliner on the other side of the bed. "How's that feeling?"

He shrugs. "Not bad actually. Not that I would complain." And then his eyes scroll over to Josh.

"How's he doing?"

"Better, I think," he says with a small smile. "They said the swelling in his brain has improved and if it continues to do so, they'll reduce his sedation in the next day or so."

I smile. Like so goddamn big. "That's great," I exclaim.

Tyler nods, almost absently, his bleary eyes focused on his partner. "Yeah," he murmurs slowly before he shifts his anguished gaze on me. "I don't know what I would do if he didn't pull through."

I stare soberly, but just as I open my mouth, the nurse pops her head in. "You must be Aria?" She's a pretty young nurse with fire red hair. All of these nurses, especially this redhead, makes me miss my friends. I need to call them. Halle, my resident redhead BFF, will cut a bitch when she finds out about Josh and the fact that I waited so long to tell her.

"I am."

"You're back," she states, and really, I wasn't gone *that* long. Just a couple of hours.

"And cleaner," I add with a cheeky grin.

She laughs lightly. "The police are out in the waiting room. They'd like to speak to both of you."

Tyler's face grows pale as he stands up slowly, his hand reaching over to touch Josh's. I stand up too, sucking in a deep breath. "Here's hoping they have some answers."

Tyler nods, unable to meet my eyes, as he leans down and kisses Josh's cheek. "I'll be back," he whispers to him and my heart squeezes. It warms me that Josh has that with someone. But I still can't help but feel that old longing when I see Tyler with Josh.

Tyler and I exit Josh's room together, both stoically quiet as we leave the confines of the ICU and walk down the hall to the waiting room. It's a good size room with blue-and cream-colored chairs and benches. There's a flat-screen affixed to the wall in the corner playing daytime soaps and the large bank of windows allows for the streaming afternoon sun to gleam in.

There are two men sitting across from the windows, both dressed in dark pants and button-down shirts. Both toting guns and badges on their waist. They stand in tandem when they hear us approach, and I watch as they take me in, likely wondering exactly who I am in all of this.

"Miss Davenport?" the bald guy with dark eyes asks. "I'm Detective O'Brien. This is my partner, Detective Marcedes."

Tyler stands up straight next to me. "Like the car."

"Only spelled differently," he says, his thick black hair brushed back off his face. He's younger than Detective O'Brien. Not that it matters really, but the look he gives me is different. More appreciative. Maybe it's the lack of a wedding band adorning his finger that makes the difference.

"We're pleased to finally meet you, Miss Davenport." That's O'Brien, and he appears warm and genuine. I like this in my law enforcement. And he's searching for my friend's assailant, so I think I like him instantly. I cross the room and shake his large hand.

"You as well," I reply before turning to Marcedes and shaking his hand. "Nice to meet you."

He nods, blushing, and it makes me grin. "I've followed your career," Marcedes says, and now I realize that's why he's blushing around me. "You're a very talented artist."

"Thank you," I exclaim with a pleased smile. I don't typically meet many men in law enforcement who follow the art world. I'm taken aback in the best possible way. "That's very kind of you to say."

Tyler sits down in a chair in front of the window, crossing his legs at the knee. He doesn't shake their hand. He simply greets them with a universal, "Detectives." It makes me scowl for some reason. The two detectives sit, and the four of us stare at each other for a quiet moment, until finally O'Brien is done with his mental interrogation.

"Miss Davenport," he starts. "Where were you the night Joshua Brown was attacked?"

"I was out with friends at S-Bar and then I walked home and went to bed."

"When was the last time you saw him prior to the attack?"

"Um…two, maybe three days before, I think. We had lunch at a restaurant on Boylston and then he had to get back to work."

"Did he mention anything to you at the time about any problems or issues he was having?"

I shake my head. "No. We talked about our normal stuff."

"Did he appear scared or agitated?"

"No. He was Josh."

"Can you think of anyone that would want to hurt Joshua Brown?"

I shake my head again, growing aggravated with myself. I've wracked my brain around that very same question since I found out that he was attacked, and I've come up empty. Sure, he's a gay guy but being openly gay isn't all that big of a deal anymore. He's also a successful lawyer. And not a sleazy lawyer at that. He does corporate tax law, so I can't imagine things get real angry and heated in that world. Or maybe they do and I'm just ignorant.

"No," I say, blowing out a breath as I lean back in my seat. "He's never mentioned anything to me and he would have. We've been best friends our whole lives. The only thing I can think of is that maybe someone saw Tyler and Josh together and didn't like it."

"Are you referring to the two gentlemen who approached their table that night?"

I scrunch my eyebrows together. "What men?"

I glance over to Tyler who blanches. "I'm sorry. I thought I mentioned them to you." He runs a hand through his dark hair as I stare him down. "I'm just so out of sorts with everything." He drops his face into his hands and sighs out like this is all just too much, and he's way past exhausted. "They were old friends of Josh's, though I think calling them friends is a stretch considering one of them called us faggots," he says with disdain.

"What?" I practically shriek. "Who were they?"

"I don't know their last names. Josh called them Connor and Brady. They didn't stick around long. They said their hellos and a few other choice things and then Josh told them to leave. They did, but I don't know if they left the restaurant or not."

"You're kidding me," I gasp, my hand covering my mouth before I turn back to the detectives. "Did they do this?"

"You know these two men?" Marcedes surmises.

"Yes. I know them." I click my tongue. "We went to high school together, and they were horrible to Josh then. I can't believe this." I stand up, pacing over to a gap in the chairs in front of the window, needing the movement because I'm about to jump out of my skin.

O'Brien holds up a hand. "Before this gets out of hand, we're on top it. We've already spoken with both them."

"And?"

"And I'm not at liberty to discuss an ongoing investigation. But I can tell you that neither are under arrest at the moment. Let's move on. What happened to your hand, Mr. Adams?" he asks Tyler, and I pause my pacing, my attention now focused on Tyler.

"I uh...," Tyler pauses, staring down at his hand. "I punched a wall after I left here the other night."

"Do you typically have a problem with your anger?"

"That's not what this is. I was upset about Josh being in the hospital, and I lost it on a wall. You can come to my house and look at it if you'd like. You saw me the other night when Josh was first brought in. I shook your hands then."

"That's not what we asked you," Marcedes says coolly.

"No," Tyler answers, locking eyes with both detectives. "I do not have a problem with my anger."

O'Brien nods, turning back to me. "And you're the one in charge of all of Joshua Brown's affairs? His estate?"

"Yes," I reply, avoiding the inclination to roll my eyes at that. Dropping back into one of the seats in a heap, I frown instead. Give me a break. Like I care about his money. If they know who I am, they know money doesn't have its standard weight with me. Even if my parents weren't wealthy themselves, I do very well with my art. "His parents died in a car accident about two years back. We're family to each other. He had me sign a bunch of papers that put me in control of things in the event of his demise or if he's incapacitated. And before you even ask, I couldn't care less about his money. I have no idea what he has and what he doesn't."

"We understand, and I hope you understand that we have to ask."

I give them a tight nod. "Can you tell me what happened?"

"As far as we can conclude, Joshua Brown exited the restaurant using the back entrance. He was in the small parking lot there when he was attacked from behind with a heavy blunt object to the left side of his skull, indicating a left-handed assailant. After that, he was repeatedly kicked or punched in the abdomen before the assailant fled the scene. He was not robbed. Nothing was taken. There were no witnesses as far as we've discovered, and there are no cameras on that side of the building."

My hand covers my mouth, stifling my sob, as Detective O'Brien gives me a clinical explanation of Josh's attack. My stomach rolls, twisting and knotting up to the point where I double over. Bile climbs up the back of my throat that I quickly swallow down.

"Do you have any other questions for us?" I can only shake my head, unable to formulate words. Tyler stays silent. "Okay," O'Brien says. "I think we have enough for now. We'll update you when something develops."

I give them my phone number and then they leave. That's it. Short and not so sweet. I don't know what I was expecting, but I was absolutely hoping for more from the Boston Police Department on this. I mean, how can someone be beaten nearly to death and no one saw it? How can they not have any leads? Doesn't everyone have a goddamn phone at the ready to take videos? How were there no cameras?

And just what the fuck with this Brady and Connor stuff? I had no idea those two assholes were still in this state let alone in Boston. I turn to Tyler who still looks a little sick and say, "You need to tell me everything that happened with Brady and Connor."

He blows out a breath as if he's reluctant to, and I cannot figure this out. Because he has to know that he never mentioned them to me. And why not? "Josh and I were eating dinner and talking about stuff." He sighs, running that bad hand across his thigh and back again. "We were having a fight, okay? I didn't want to mention this, and I certainly don't want those cops to know, but we were fighting. I wanted him to move in with me and he didn't want to. Said he didn't want to give up his place. That it was too soon. Whatever. It wasn't a big deal. We've had this conversation before."

"Okay," I draw out the word.

He turns to me, but his eyes are locked on the wall behind me, lost in something I cannot see. "They must have spotted Josh because the next thing I knew, they were sitting with us. One scooted right in next to me and the other next to Josh even though neither of us invited them. Josh immediately laid into them. Asking them what they were doing sitting with us. The three of them went back and forth for a bit. Josh was teasing them, and they were taking the bait. I don't know. They called us a couple of faggots and then got up and left."

"That was it?"

He shrugs. "More or less. I mean, they didn't stay longer than five minutes. Josh and I finished our dinners and then left separately. I had an early meeting, and I think we were both still a little upset with the other."

"Do you think they did this to him?"

Tyler nods slowly, his eyes refocusing on the floor by my feet. "It seems like the most likely scenario. They were pretty hostile. Very verbally aggressive."

My thoughts instantly go to Wes. It makes me wonder if he's still friends with them. They were close in high school. One thing is for sure, there is a lot to figure out about the night Josh was attacked. And Weston Kincaid.

Chapter Nine

WES

Past

SMOKE BILLOWS out from the wet wood in the center of the pit, thick and heavy into the frigid night, filling the air with its sweet toxic scent. No one seems to mind it though as the steady flow of beer has everyone smiling and laughing with a double high. Our last football game was tonight. We won. I threw for over two hundred and fifty yards. Ran for over sixty. I had scouts there from half a dozen big-name football schools, all at the hands of my father.

Ivy League schools do not give scholarships for football. And those are precisely the schools I'm interested in. Princeton was not there. Harvard was not there. Neither was Yale. And when I mentioned to my father I was interested in Princeton over Alabama, he went nuts. What kind of father does that? Wants football over medicine for their son? Wants a state school over an Ivy League one?

Why can't I be good enough for him as I am?

My father did present me with a car. A Jeep. It's big and black and fucking awesome. Tonight, despite the football scouts, might be one of the best nights of my life.

Rough bark from the log I'm sitting on scratches through the thick material of my jeans, but it beats the hell out of sitting on the ground or standing all night, so I endure it. I've been here for a solid hour and I think I'm just about at my end for the evening. I came here with Brecken, Johnny, and a few of the other guys. It's always the same.

But tonight, Aria is here.

Somewhere. And so are her friends. I saw her talking and laughing with them earlier, but when Eli Ross started flirting with her, I turned away. Sophomore girls are in abundance and the junior and senior girls are making their displeasure known.

"Dude." Brady smacks me in the chest with the back of his hand. His drunk ass somehow found his way over to my side of the circle. I stand up to join him. "Tell me you're getting back together with Piper." My eyes fly over in her general direction, taking in the tall, thin, blonde cheerleader across the fire who's talking to a few of her friends. "She looks fucking hot in that dress." She does look hot. And cold as it's not even above freezing out here. "And she was talking about you. She told Keri that you two were getting close again."

I laugh, even though there really is nothing humorous about that. "Nah, man. Piper and I are definitely done. You can have at her if you want though."

"I just might, Wes. I just might." Both of us laugh again because that's what guys do. That's what's expected of me. "What about that neighbor of yours? Breck's sister." His tone is full of humor, but I know what he's doing. Despite that, I take the bait one hundred percent. My head snaps in his direction and my heart rate begins to increase.

I don't like people talking about Aria to me. Especially not people like Brady.

"What about her?" I ask cautiously.

"I heard you were talking to her at lunch today." I can only stare at him. "And I also heard you were making a move on her during class. You screwing her or what?"

"Don't be an asshole."

Right, like he's not being one already.

Brady continues his annoying laughter, shaking his head like he's on to me. "Oh no? Not into her? Fifteen too young for you?" he asks dubiously. "I bet she's a freak in bed. Those artsy types are wild, if you know what I mean."

My fists clench so tight, my knuckles are turning white. Pivoting to him, I stare him down with a gaze that promises a pain he's never experienced before. "Watch it, Brady," I clip out and that reaction just makes him laugh harder. I know I'm feeding him what he wants. I know I'm making this moment easier. But I can't stand him talking about Aria like that. It makes me fucking insane. "I mean it. Shut your mouth about her." *Or I'll knock your ass to the ground and watch you bleed.*

His posture rises slowly, his head angling toward me. He's smiling. Grinning. Loving every goddamn second of this.

"Hey, assholes," someone I cannot see calls out. "You dickheads up for truth or dare?"

I turn in the direction of Connor's voice, relieved he's interrupting this tense moment. Brady's eyes drag around the clearing until they spot someone standing behind him and then a slow devilish smile spreads across his lips. "Only if Miss Aria here plays," he calls back, not taking his eyes off Aria who happens to be standing not too far behind us with a few of her friends.

Did she hear us?

She shakes her head, waving him off. "I'm all set with that."

"Bring her over," Connor yells back, his voice carrying over the flames. Laughter ensues, and her cheeks brighten. One of her friends whispers something to the other and then one girl leans in and whispers something to Aria. She doesn't respond to whatever they're saying, but a half-second later, they walk off, leaving her all alone. I can't believe they just did that to her.

Brady's eyes light up at this as he marches over, wrapping his arm around her with an unrelenting grip. "Come on, Brady. Let me go. I'm not up for playing your asinine games."

"No way, honey pie. You're coming with me." Brady lifts her into his side, where she fits under his arm like a purse. "It'll be fun." He squeezes her body again, but it's not playful. It appears... playfully aggressive. "I'm sure a girl like you is dying for the chance to get dared into kissing one of us."

She snorts. "Your modesty is so becoming, Brady, but I think I'll have to pass on that tempting offer." She shoves into his side with all her might. "Now. Let. Me. Go."

But he doesn't. He just holds her tighter, practically dragging her in the direction of where everyone else has congregated. "Oh, don't be like that." He leans down, kissing the top of her head before laughing raucously. My heart rate begins to speed up, my vision growing as hazy as the smoke billowing from the wet wood.

"Let her go now, Brady," I bark, my voice rising.

"No way," Brady laughs, pulling her in closer and pinning me with a stare. "I'm enjoying watching her squirm way too much. Besides, she can play it off all she wants, but I know she's into me."

I step forward, back straight, head high, fists ready to pound him into the ground. She jabs her elbow into his flank, making him puff out air, before she pinches his side as hard as she can. He yelps out, adjusting her, spanking her ass hard and making everyone who is watching the show laugh.

"Stupid bitch," Brady mutters, looking like he's about to attack her for real.

"That's enough," I yell, getting right up in his face, unable to stand it a minute longer. Aria's eyes widen into cerulean circles. "I said let her go, and I mean it. You're hurting her and being a total dick." If he wasn't holding Aria as close as he is, he'd already be on the ground.

Brady stops in his tracks, pulling her just a bit closer to his side. He kisses her dark hair again and I feel any remaining blood drain from my hands. Sweat slicks the back of my neck even though the temperatures are arctic out here. My eyes blaze. His don't. He's still all about the game. It only makes me want to hurt him more.

"And what if I don't let your little girlfriend go, Wes? What do you plan to do about it?"

"Do you really want to find out?"

My tone is murderous as I stare him down. I feel a million pairs of eyes on me, but right now, Brady is all I see. Aria twists around, pinching his side again. He squirms, his eyes on mine as he releases his grip, dropping her. She hits the frozen ground on all fours and my fist flies without conscious thought, hitting him in the mouth.

He staggers back a step, shock in his eyes as he wipes a trickle of blood from his lip. But he doesn't advance or show any signs of retaliating.

Aria springs up to her feet. "Fuck you," she snaps, shoving Brady hard in the side. "Touch me like that again and I swear, you'll be lucky to have children one day."

Then she's gone. Stalking off into the darkness that surrounds the fire pit. She doesn't even spare me a cursory glance.

Brady laughs malevolently. "Careful there, Weston. You're going to be in trouble when her big brother finds out."

Everyone is silent, watching our exchange. I step forward, wanting to say too many things, but mindful of our audience.

"Try me, Brady. I fucking dare you."

After a strained moment, Brady relaxes his stiff posture. He knows better than to mess with me. I have four inches and twenty pounds of muscle on him. And now he knows I will kick his ass over her. There is no mistaking that.

"Whatever, bro. I was just messing around. She's hardly worth my effort."

"You better watch your fucking mouth," Brecken roars from behind me. I turn over my shoulder and catch him stalking toward us. "What the hell did you do to my sister, Brady?"

Brady laughs, that's all he seems capable of, but I wonder just how genuine his amusement is. "Relax, Breck. No harm, no foul. Your boy Wes here already came to her rescue."

Brecken looks at me for a moment and I shake my head, unable to control my ire. My jaw is clenched as tight as my fists and I want to pummel Brady into the frozen earth. I want to crush him into the nothing he is.

"Just leave her alone, Brady," Brecken says, all the edge having dissipated from his voice. "And if you don't, I'll let Wes here kill you." He throws his arm over Brady's shoulder and the two of them head off in the direction of Connor. I don't follow. I have zero interest in a game of truth or dare right now.

I spin around and find Aria staring at me, poised on the edge of the darkness. I run over to her without a second thought. "Are you okay?" I ask softly. No reply. "I'm sorry, Aria. I shouldn't have let it get that far."

She twists around, marching off into the frozen tall grasses that crunch beneath her feet. I follow her. She knows I'm following her, which is why she begins to talk. "You ignore me with the ease and grace of indifference in one minute and then freely come to my rescue the next. You talk to me when you believe no one is watching and then I no longer exist the moment eyes are on you." She shakes her head, her fire steadily climbing. "I'm not interested in your apologies, Wes. I handled Brady myself. You can go back to tending to your flock."

We're wading through the overgrown brush and tall grasses as she heads in the direction of the street. It's dark, the only light out here coming from the fire at my back, but after spending countless nights out here, I know my way. So does she.

"Aria, wait." I break into a jog and a few seconds later, I'm by her side once again.

"What do you want?" she bristles. "I'm not going back to play your stupid games."

I let out a long-suffering sigh. "I'm sorry, okay? I'm not here to bring you back. I just want to talk and maybe drive you home."

A small humorless laugh bubbles up out of her chest. "You want to talk to me? About what?"

Good question. What do I want to say to her? Nothing's changed in our situation. We continue in silence for a beat, weeding through the brush, blanketed in total darkness against the moonless sky. The only light at this point is the stars, and they offer nothing more than window dressing. They're quickly being consumed by thick clouds that promise snow.

"I've been a dick to you," I tell her quietly as we reach the outer edge of the field.

The road is ahead and then on the other side of that is where I parked my new Jeep. There is nothing around here except dirt and vacant land for miles. It's why we choose this area as our regular fire pit. The cops don't bother to come out here because no one wants to be the one to arrest any of the star athletes and be responsible for a loss.

In a town like this, high school sports are about all we've got in the way of entertainment.

"You have," she agrees. "But it's been that way for a long time so I don't think too much about it anymore."

She's lying. I can tell she's lying. The emotion in her voice betrays everything, and suddenly I feel sick at the way I've been treating her. I thought I was doing the right thing by her. She's too young and I'm too old. She's Breck's sister and I'm his best friend. I'm a senior and she's a sophomore. And I have…expectations on me that will inherently cause an issue if we ever became something real together.

"Aria, stop." I grab her arm, bringing her to a halt. She yanks her arm free of me, and I run a frustrated hand through my hair before staring up at the night sky. It's no help, and right now, I don't know what to do or what to say to her. "You have every right to be pissed at me. And I know you handled Brady on your own. I just didn't like him doing that with you, and I stepped in. The bastard had that hit coming for a long time though and I don't regret it. In truth, I don't like any of them touching you or talking about you."

"I don't care that you hit him, Wes. That's not why I'm so angry."

"Jesus, you really can't accept an apology, can you?"

"What exactly are you apologizing for?" She stares up into my dark face. I hate how tall I am compared to her. I want her face to be closer to mine.

"For everything," I whisper as I gaze down on her. "Whatever you need me to apologize for, that's what I'm doing."

"God." She laughs out. "That's the worst apology in the history of apologies. You were better off not saying anything."

I laugh. "Probably. As you know I'm not good at bearing my soul. But it's late and I'm sorry and I just want to make sure you get home safe."

"Huh. Okay. I'll let you drive me home in your new car."

Leaning down, I press my lips to her forehead before spinning her around and marching her through the grass like a child. I bring my mouth down, close to her ear, press my body directly behind hers, so she can feel me against her.

She shudders, and I smile so goddamn big, I can barely contain it. "It's a Jeep, Aria. Not a car. Big difference, baby. Big difference."

"Right. My mistake," she bites out sarcastically, and I know she's rolling her eyes at me, even if I can't see them. We both fall silent, mainly because I can't think of anything else somewhat intelligent to say after that shudder.

Because I can't figure it out and I don't know what to do. How do you stop wanting the one girl you should not want? The one girl you cannot have? The one girl you'd give anything to kiss.

Chapter Ten

WES

Past

IT JUST STARTED SNOWING. And it's only November. That should be an ominous sign of things to come considering it doesn't typically snow this early in the season, but it's not. It's beautiful. The first snow of the season always is.

I dropped Aria off at home. Well, I pulled into my driveway and she hopped out of my Jeep as fast as she could and ran into her house without a thank you or even looking back. She didn't even let me walk her to her door. I don't blame her, but it still sucks. Then again, I didn't exactly chase her. I assumed she wanted her space from me.

I have a lot of ground to make up with her, the problem is, I'm not sure I should.

The moment I crossed the threshold into my house, my father was there to greet me. Waiting up for me is not something he typically does and it made me grateful I only had one beer tonight. And when I asked him what was up, he marched over to me and threw his arms around my shoulders. It stunned me. My father is not an affectionate man. In fact, I can't remember the last time he hugged me before tonight.

"Auburn and Alabama are both extremely interested in recruiting you," he said, the excitement in his voice unmistakable. I swallowed down my guilt and anxiety. How could he not know?

"I've applied to some Ivy League schools," I said softly, hoping it would be an afterthought. It wasn't. His eyes turned to molten steel, fiery hot and painfully hard. He looked at me like I was the shit beneath his shoes. Like I was the most abhorrent thing he'd ever come across. All because I want something different for my life than what he wants for me.

"I will not pay for an Ivy League school, boy," he said sternly, his green eyes piercing into mine. I look like my father with a similar build. I think that only makes this harder for him to accept. "You will get a sports scholarship and you will play ball." It made me wish I had blown out my knee tonight. And that alone makes me hate him a little.

I shook my head. Because fuck him. I was not about to let him tell me how to live my life. "I don't care if you won't pay. I'll get an academic scholarship, and if I can't," I stood taller, straightening my spine and making sure my eyes were on his, "I'll take out loans."

His face turned puce. His eyes blazing. His back arched forward, encroaching into my personal space. The tip of his index finger jutted into my chest. Hard. "I can take back that Jeep I just gave you."

"It's registered to me." It kills me that he wanted to take that present back. That I had to point out that not so small detail.

"You're nothing but a disappointment to me. Do you know that?" He jabbed me again, and this time, I took a step back. The force of his words nearly knocked me over. "In ten years, when any chance of a football career is over, you'll regret your life. Your choices. Just the way I do."

Me. He regrets me.

That's what that little speech was about. And part of me wonders if I did follow his plan if he'd be happy with me. If I'd finally make him proud. The only light to ever touch his eyes is when I have a football in my hands and even then he's criticizing everything I do with it. I have no words for the pain I felt when he told me that. My entire life, I've done nothing but try to please him. To be the perfect son, part of the perfect family. At least that's how we're seen.

And now I'm hiding in my room. Thinking back over all that transpired tonight. If I should have bothered with telling him what I want. What I'm planning on doing with my life. That I'm slowly giving up on him and any hopes he'll see me as the man I am. As a man who knows what he wants out of life and is capable of getting it. I want to go to the best schools in the country. If I get in and go pre-med and do well, I'll have my pick of medical schools.

Plus, the schools I want are not too far away from here. And even though that shouldn't matter to me, it does. It's stupid, really. I know it is. Aria is young. Fifteen is young. I'm looking at colleges, and she's growing boobs. And shit, are they growing. But I can't get her out of my head. Years and years' worth of Aria consuming my thoughts is not something I can just shut off.

But tonight, at the field, something inside me changed.

And as I drove her home, any time her eyes caught mine, she'd immediately look away. She's mad at me. Again. It's this ongoing theme with us. She thinks I abandoned her. That I ignore her and callously brushed her aside once we went back to regular life.

But she's only mad because she likes me. Because she doesn't like that I keep my distance when we both know all we want is to do the opposite.

The snow is quiet and oh so white as it tumbles from the heavens in big fat flakes. The sky is dark but has a reddish hue against the snow as it falls. Sliding my bedroom window up, I slip out, my boots crunching into the thin layer of powder covering the frozen earth. I take a step forward and my eyes immediately go next door. First to the edge of the fence line and then up to the roof. It's become a reflex.

And more nights than not, she's not there.

At least not since it's become this cold. I haven't climbed up to her since the summer, but that doesn't mean I don't watch her from afar, hating myself for hoping she's up there waiting for me, as she stares at the sky.

But tonight? Tonight, she's there as I knew she would be, and I find myself opening the gate between our properties without a thought in my mind but her. She doesn't hear me, or if she does, she's pretending not to until I'm climbing up the tree that abuts this side of her roof. There is a flat spot in the middle of her house. It's actually directly below her bedroom, which is why she comes out here with some frequency.

The first time I found her there I was dragging Brecken into his bed after a night of too much alcohol and weed. He doesn't smoke often, but he had that night and he was beyond repair as a result. He was out before I even got him into his bed, and after positioning him on his side so if he threw up in his sleep he wouldn't die, I left the way I came. But when I crawled out his bedroom window, I caught a glimpse of Aria.

Her head was cast up, and I remember finding myself mesmerized by the long column of her neck. Who the hell is mesmerized by a neck? The thought made me smile at the time, but she was just so... God, she was breathtaking under the light of the full moon. I didn't hesitate climbing the rest of the way up that tree to join her instead of going back down and over to my house the way I should have.

I knew better.

That night was far from the first time I had thought about her. Had noticed her.

I climbed up with the intention of it being just that night. But when she asked me to return the following night, I did. All too willingly. With zero resistance or second thoughts. I did feel guilty for hiding it from Brecken, but in my mind, I convinced myself it was innocent. That I wasn't touching her or doing anything wrong. After all, we were just two friends talking on a roof.

That's how it went all summer.

I climbed up this tree and occasionally held her hand and listened to her talk. She told me stories about constellations. About her family. About herself. About her art. I'd talk too. About things

I'd never told anyone. Things I never wanted anyone to know about myself. About how neither my family nor I are as perfect as we're perceived.

She didn't judge me. She listened with rapt attention and sometimes leaned into me, resting her head on my shoulder. Sometimes she'd squeeze my hand. Sometimes, I'd just get a smile. I didn't care. I took anything and everything she was willing to give me.

I fell in love with Aria Davenport on top of her roof, under the stars.

I can't even pretend that I didn't.

So as I climb the tree now, knowing she's sitting in the snow, allowing it to fall around her, the breath in my chest feels a little heavier. Because I'm cold. And horny. And I hate my father. And I'm so hopelessly in love with my best friend's little sister, that I don't know how to stop it.

I'm a pretty special level of fucked when it comes to this girl.

"That better not be you," she warns as I approach. Her reproachful tone actually makes my steps falter.

"And if it is?"

She sighs. Her breath coming out in a shock of smoky fog. "Then you better kiss me, Weston Kincaid, because I've had it up to here with you and your games and you're interrupting my quiet snowfall."

"You want me to kiss you?" I'm smiling like crazy. My heart finally beating the way it feels like it should. For her. And all that anger and resentment and guilt I felt with my father seems to dissipate into nothing. It's just her and me and this snow on our roof.

"Yes. I do. I won't even pretend like I don't." She props herself up onto her elbows and finds me. She's wearing the most adorable baby pink snow hat with a large white pompom on top and her cheeks are red, and her blue eyes are so goddamn bright. "But more importantly, I know you want to. I saw it in your eyes tonight at the field. So really, I'm just doing you a favor."

A laugh stumbles its way from my chest along with the breath that had been lodged in there. Her head drops back, and I climb onto the patch of snow next to her. Turning onto my back, I stare up at the sky as white flakes fall upon us. "It's beautiful," I say reverently, almost to myself.

"It is. Which is why I'm here. But now you are, too, and I don't like it, Wes. You throw me off balance." I smile. I don't even laugh. She talks so much when she's nervous and her incessant babbling means I'm making her nervous. It's making me giddy. It's making me high. "But this snow," she continues. "It's so pretty. And white. And I want to paint how this moment feels." I grab my chest. "I'd use black and white, obviously. But a lot of deep burgundy and eggplant purple and charcoal gray and deep, deep navy blue. I want to paint the moment the flakes first start to fall as you're staring up at them and they feel like winter."

I roll over, and I kiss her. I pull her face to mine, and my cold lips press to hers, and I catch her gasp, and I swallow it down. I push my tongue into her mouth, and she lets me take the lead.

I kiss her.

Fuck all do I kiss her.

Like I've never kissed a girl before. Because I love this one. She makes me feel alive. On fire. Excited and calm. Restless and settled. She makes me feel everything I've always wanted to feel. Hell, she makes me feel *seen*.

She smiles against my lips. Aria is happy I took her requirement and made it my own. But that's not why I kissed her. I kissed her because I'm so tired of *not* kissing her.

Her mouth is warm despite the frigid temperatures, and she tastes spicy despite the sweetness of the air. My hand glides into her hair, which is cool and wet and silky soft. Her body rolls over onto mine, and I wrap my arm around her as I make out with Aria Davenport on the roof of her parents' house. Of my best friend's house. Ask me if I care. Because I do not. Not even a little.

She pulls back an inch or so, staring down at me, her eyes luminous as she smiles. "I knew it would be that good."

I push her face back down into mine and I kiss her again. I kiss her crazy. "Me too," I hum against her. "These lips are made for mine. Only mine."

She smiles, but it's more of a laugh. "Not possible, Wes. My lips will kiss others."

I shake my head against her, our noses brushing. "I want them to only kiss me."

"You kiss other girls."

I do kiss other girls. As recently as three nights ago. I was drinking at a party and Piper put her lips on mine. But even though Piper is eighteen and Aria is fifteen, her kisses do not compare. Aria kisses like a woman. And her body against mine might just be the best thing ever.

I just kissed Aria and I have no idea what it means. If anything. "I don't want other girls."

She kisses me again. Her body dropping onto mine fully until we're meshed together. One piece with nothing in between. Coats and clothes against each other, but our mouths are telling an entirely different story. My rock hard cock presses into her and I can't stop it as my hips thrust up to meet hers. I'm desperate. Aching.

"You don't want to only kiss me."

I shake my head and cinch my eyes shut because I took that too far. I push back against her, trying to stop her kisses, and then she rolls off me.

I feel her loss like someone just doused me in ice water in the middle of this storm. Snow falls down on my heated body, and I can only stare up at it as I breathe hard and loud and frustrated. I want her back. I want all of her yeses and none of her noes and I don't want her to say yes to anyone but me ever again. She's all I could ever want. She feels like the adventure of a lifetime and I want to be part of the ride.

But how can I be? She can't have my life and I can't have hers. At least not for several years. Maybe the way I love her will go away? Maybe it will dissipate with time and other women?

Maybe…

"When do you leave for college, Wes?"

I close my eyes again. I hate that question. It hurts. Not just for me, but for what it could mean for my family. "I don't know. It depends on where I go and what I do there. But not until at least the summer."

"It's too dark and snowy out tonight to see the constellations."

I blink up at the heavens and then twist over on the roof to face her. I like that she just changed the subject like that. It saves me from myself and my tormented thoughts.

"Do you remember how we used to watch the stars for hours on my roof?" she whispers, almost to herself, trying to find something that is not visible above us. I move toward her, but she doesn't dare look at me. I want her to look at me, but I don't at the same time. Instead, I turn back, searching for the incredible collage in the sky that is hidden behind the clouds and the snow.

I chuckle as if I haven't thought about that in months when really, it's been only minutes. "You'd spend hours telling me all the stories about the constellations."

She nods, still with her head raised, staring at a vastness I will never comprehend. I would listen to her with undiverted attention. That was around the time she got heavy into mythology. She liked Greek mythology the best. And the way she would speak about it? I couldn't not listen. All I wanted was for her to tell me more. She had me questioning things I thought I knew.

"*They lived like Gods with carefree heart, free and apart from trouble and pain,*" she recites effortlessly. *Free and apart from trouble and pain.* God, how I wish. I have no idea how she does that, but she does this all the time. I'm convinced she has a photographic memory, though she denies it.

"Who is that?"

"Hesiod. *The Golden Age of Man.*"

Shit, why do I make her so damn despondent? Everything about me is wrong with her. That kiss probably didn't help. Me or her. I don't know what I'm doing here with her.

"What does that mean, Aria?"

She lowers her head to stare at me finally. I'm so much taller, even lying down on the roof. I roll onto my side, angling my body over hers in this dark night. My eyes are cold and my mouth is set into a hard line. I'm desperate for anything but affected. She glares at me like she wants to hit me. Knock me over and throw me off balance—the way I do her—with all her frustration. Too late for that. This girl has me perpetually dodging landmines.

"Nothing, Wes. Just something to wish for."

I sigh and then shake my head at her, unsure of her meaning.

"I'm fine out here. I needed some time alone and since you took that from me earlier today." She shrugs, trying for nonchalance, "I'm trying to find it again now."

I did take it from her. I followed her outside at lunch and sat with her in the freezing fucking cold. I bothered her when she tried to listen to her music and I interfered when she wanted to write and draw. And I stepped in tonight too.

"It's not safe out here in the dark by yourself." My tone is annoyed, which makes her chuckle at the irony of that. How many nights have we lain out here together?

"Since when do you care about my safety?" she asks incredulously.

I rake a disappointed hand through my hair and then burn her with my stare. "Since when do I not?" I bark out, making absolutely no move to leave. I want to tell her that she's all I care about, but I keep my big mouth shut.

"Hateful to me as the Gates of Hades is that man who hides one thing in his heart and speaks another." She quotes Homer to me. I recognize it. I may not be as smart as Aria is, but I'm not an idiot either. I remember that quote on the board in my junior English class.

I laugh out humorlessly. "Is that what you think is going on here, Aria? That I'm hiding things in my heart for you while I say something else?" I move closer to her and it takes everything in her power not to move away from me. But she's not wrong. My question is practically rhetorical.

"No, Wes. I think you coming out here is laughable. I think you kissing me is a tease. Yet here you are." She tilts her head questioning. "I've wanted that kiss for so long."

"Me too," I reply honestly.

"But you won't do more than that with me."

"You're fifteen and I'm eighteen. It doesn't feel right."

She sighs and then she's back on top of me. "Then kiss me some more if that's all you're willing to give. But if you ever ignore me again, I'll never kiss you again."

"I'll never ignore you again."

And I mean it. Her kisses are everything. She's everything.

"Hateful to me as the Gates of Hades is that man who hides one thing in his heart and speaks another." She has no idea how close she is. Because I love her. Like nothing else. My young, sweet, brilliant, beautiful girl. And when she's a woman, I'm going to make her mine for good. But for now, I kiss her. Because she asked me to.

Chapter Eleven

WES

Present Day

THE DAY CREPT into night too quickly. I don't tend to mind night shifts. At least not while I'm working them. More traumas happen at night than during the day. The only thing I don't like is never seeing the sun. That's how it is in the winter. It makes me feel like a vampire. Especially when I'm around blood all day—or night in this case—long.

I pull into the garage and sigh, grasping the back of my neck and squeezing. It does nothing to release the tension. I shouldn't have told her I was thinking about New York for medical school. That angered her. I could see it. She gave me a where-were-you-for-the-two-years-I-was-there, look. But the simple answer for that is I wasn't in a position to be with her. I was in college. I was working my ass off.

I was a fucking mess.

And definitely not good enough for Aria Davenport.

I knew she was there. I avoided her. Because I appreciated that if I saw her, everything would change. I was in Princeton and she was in New York. I was in college and she was painting. I was a disaster, and she was perfect.

But the truth is, I fucked-up by not going to her. I fucked-up by assuming time would stand still for me while I got my shit together. I wanted to be in a position where I could commit to her. Where I could give her the world she deserved. At the very least, be in the same physical place, because I was already going to have to split my time between her and medical school.

So yeah, I fucked-up. I made more mistakes with that woman than I can even begin to count. So many regrets they weigh me down like an anchor.

Because she went to London before I could get to her. Before I could convince her to take a chance on me.

But now she's in Boston.

And I'm in Boston.

So maybe it's not too late to fix all my mistakes. I have another six months left on my fellowship and then I'll be a board-certified trauma surgeon.

I would be lying if I said I didn't love doing trauma surgery. I absolutely do. I save lives. It's all I've ever wanted to do, even if the path getting here wasn't what I imagined it would be. But I did it and I was complete in that. I didn't need anything else. I convinced myself of that. That my father's words were meaningless. That the girl I lost, wouldn't always feel lost.

But seeing Aria again makes me second-guess that.

I checked my messages and emails from home, so I go straight to the ER first and immediately spot the last person I thought I'd see. Connor Shaw is sitting on a gurney with a piece of blood-saturated gauze pressed to his forehead. A nurse is talking to him as I make my way over.

"Hey," I say, and his head raises up, his brown eyes meeting mine as he gives me a relieved half-smile. "What happened?"

He shrugs, his eyes skirting over to the nurse who is young and somewhat attractive. Evidently, he doesn't want her to know, so I snap on some gloves and tell her I've got it from here. The moment she's out of sight, he says, "I fell and smacked my forehead into the side of a brick building. Whatever," he scoffs with an edge to his voice. "It was a dumb fuck thing to do."

"It's going to need some stitches."

"I figured. Can you do them?"

"Yeah, I can do them. Have you been drinking?"

"No, Doctor, I haven't." He rolls his eyes at me. "I tripped over a two by four at a site I'm working. I was carrying something big and I didn't see it."

"On Sunday?"

He shrugs again. "I need to get it done. We don't all have doctors' hours."

"Funny."

Another half-shrug. "I thought so. Let's do this already."

I finish cleaning his wound, and luckily the nurse had everything set up already, so I just use what's here and get started. "It should only be a few. Any dizziness, nausea, vision changes, or headaches?"

"No, man. I'm fine. Really. It's just a cut." I nod, injecting the area around the wound with lidocaine. "Did you hear that the police interviewed me and Brady?"

I pause for a moment and meet his eyes. "Why?"

"Because we saw that kid we went to high school with, Josh Brown, at a pub the other night. Evidently, someone beat his ass." I continue to stare at him, the hairs on the back of my neck standing at attention. I can't tell him that Josh is here in this hospital. That I'm his doctor and that I know all about him getting his ass beat. "Him and his faggot boyfriend were there together." I raise an eyebrow, my mouth pinching into an angry scowl. He throws up his hands. "Sorry. I know. Whatever. I never liked that guy, and his boyfriend was a dick too."

"Well?" I ask, trying not to make my need for answers known.

"Well, what?" he clips with an overly defensive edge. "It wasn't us." *Then why can't he meet my eyes?*

"And?" I prompt when he falls silent. "What happened?"

He blows out a breath as I begin to stitch him up. "And Brady and I sat down and started talking some shit. I won't even deny that.

But then we left, man. They told us to fuck off, and we did. We didn't stick around, I swear."

I want to believe him. I genuinely do. I've known these guys a long time. As long as I've known Aria, even. I nod. I don't know what else to say. I don't know if I believe him or not and it's troubling me.

"Do you know how he was hurt?"

He stares at me. "No. The cops just said someone jumped him." He clears his throat. "How's he doing? He's here, right? That's what the cops said."

"He's rough, man. I can't get into specifics, but whoever did do this, nearly got what they were after." I glare at him, trying to read what I'm hoping I don't see.

"Jesus," he puffs out softly as he closes his eyes, his face falling. "It wasn't us, Wes. I don't like the guy, but I don't wish him dead, you know? I'd never hurt someone like that. Ever."

"I know," I say because I do. At least I think I do. He's still having trouble meeting my eyes and I'm not sure how honest he's being with me. "What do the police think?"

"They believed us, I guess." He shrugs a shoulder. "We went straight from that pub over to this girl's house in Cambridge. She was having a party close to where we live. We gave them some names of people who could vouch for us being there."

I forgot that Brady and Connor live only a couple of blocks away from each other. I don't see them all that often anymore, truth be told. Only once, maybe twice since I moved back.

I finish his stitches and bandage him up. I'm restless and uneasy. "Brady, tell me the truth. Did you do it?"

He looks up, directly into my eyes. "No. I didn't."

"Next time, keep your stupid mouth shut."

He nods. "Yeah. I need to work on that one." He laughs, and I awkwardly smile even though I find very little humor in the situation. *What if it was them?* What if he's lying right to my face? "Am I all set?"

"Yeah. Sit tight for a minute. I need to print out some discharge paperwork."

"Yes, Doctor Kincaid. But only if you bring me a lollipop."

I flip him off and walk over to the nearest computer. I had no clue that Brady and Connor were there that night. In truth, my job was to fix Josh up, not figure out who his attacker was. But now it's on my mind. Because someone did attack Josh. Someone very nearly killed him.

So the question is, who was mad enough at him to do that?

The moment I discharge Connor, my feet carry me directly up to Josh's room. It's automatic. I don't even challenge the action. I want to find out if the police came today. If they have any leads. I also really want to see Aria. I hate the way we left things earlier. But when I get there, I pause on the threshold of the door, staring in.

Aria is there, but so are three nurses. One is an ICU float nurse, one works in the ER. The last is someone I don't recognize, but her scrubs tell me she's in the field. They're laughing like they know Aria well and maybe Josh too. The copper redhead, whose name I don't know, touches Josh's hand in a way that goes beyond the professional. Just as I'm about to enter the room, I feel movement on my left.

Glancing over, I catch Andrew Albright, an emergency department attending. "Hey, man," he greets me with a smile and a slap on my back. Drew is a good guy, I guess. We're friendly, but I wouldn't call us friends.

"Hey," I respond back, surprised to see him up here in the SICU.

"I hear you saved Josh's life."

I blink at him, tilting my head in confusion. "How do you know Josh?"

He gives me a big broad smile and then juts his chin in the direction of the room. "My ex-girlfriend is his best friend."

I'm floored. "Your *ex*-girlfriend? You mean Aria?"

"That's her. Well, I doubt she'll stay my ex for long, if you know what I mean." He gives me a conspiratorial wink and my fists clench. "How do you know her?" I squint at him. "You called her Aria like you know her."

Shit. I did, didn't I? Would it be wrong if I told him I'm the guy who took her virginity? That he's going to remain her ex indefinitely because I have plans with her I won't fuck up this time?

"I grew up with her and Josh." I want to elaborate, but I have no idea how to describe her. Everything we went through feels too personal to reveal to him.

"Huh," Drew drawls, eyeing me for a beat before he plasters on a fake smile. Clearly, he can read through my bullshit. Good. "Anyway, thanks for that. Josh is a good guy, and Aria would be devastated if he didn't pull through."

He walks into the room with a cocky smile and an arrogant swagger and I decide I no longer like him. In fact, I want to kick his ass. He greets Rina and Margot and the unknown redhead, and when he reaches Aria, he bends down to give her a hug and a kiss on the cheek before he sits on the arm of her chair.

And now I want to kill him.

I enter the room before I can stop myself and when Aria's eyes meet mine, they're not smiling. Actually, she looks like she's ready to kill *me*.

"I heard he had a good day," I say to her and she nods. That's it. Something isn't right.

"Hi, Doctor Kincaid," Margot, one of the nurses says.

"Hi," I say to both her and Rina who are sharing the chair that Tyler typically occupies.

"I'm Halle," the redhead introduces. "I've heard all about you." I have no idea what that means, but it most definitely means something based on her if-looks-could-kill thing she has going on.

"You all here to keep Josh or Aria company?" I ask.

"Both," the three say in unison, then laugh like it's all just so funny.

"They met Aria through me," Drew oh so kindly offers. He's mocking me now. I can see it in his gray eyes. And really, who has gray eyes? They make him appear sinister and cold. Aria has to see that. Gray is barely a color.

Aria rolls her eyes. "You just love to take credit for my friendships with them," she replies dryly.

"I'm still waiting for my thank you present." She slaps his arm and he laughs, leaning his body into hers.

"You're not getting anything from me. In fact, you're too close Drew."

"There is no close enough."

I can't stand this. I can't stand him flirting with her.

"The way I hear it, you knew Aria long before any of us did," Halle says with a smile I can't interpret.

"Yes," Aria interjects before I can respond. "But I wouldn't exactly call us friends back then." *Ouch.* "Other than my brother, his taste in friends was always suspect."

What?

I stare her down, my eyebrows furrowed as a heavy, awkward silence ensues. "Well, I'm going to head out," Margot offers, standing up and trying to ease the tension. "I have to be back in twelve hours."

"Ditto," Rina agrees, standing up as well. "And Halle is going to come with us because Jonah is no doubt missing her." All of them walk over to give Aria a hug in turn.

"Later, asswipe," Margot bites playfully at Drew, who reaches out to swat at her. She dodges easily and says her goodbyes to Josh.

Rina and Halle do the same, minus the disparaging comment to Drew.

"Good night, Doctor." Margot waves to me with a smile. Margot has flirted with me before. She didn't now and I have to image that's as a result of whatever Aria told them. I'd be lying if I said I hadn't notice it or her for that matter. No denying she's very pretty with her dark hair and dark eyes. But I don't sleep with the people I work with. At least not the people I interact with daily. People in other departments, sure. But I've seen too many bad things happen when people go the first route.

"Have a good night," I respond to her and then turn back to Drew who still hasn't moved from Aria's side. They're having some sort of standoff with their eyes. Aria looks pissed. "Are you on tonight?" I ask him.

His head snaps up in my direction like he forgot I was still here.

Asshole. "Oh, no. I should be going too. Just hard to leave, you know." He smirks at me and then turns back to Aria with a gleam and a wink, and I hate him. "Walk me out? I want to tell you something."

She shakes her head. "I don't want to leave Josh."

He looks disappointed but gets over it quickly. "Okay," he replies, leaning in to kiss the corner of her lips. She stiffens up and pulls away before he can touch her.

I find a small amount of relief in that. Except her biting comments are still at the forefront of my mind. I move over to Josh and start examining him because he's my patient and who I should be focused on.

I do my best to ignore them as they say their goodbyes, but I don't miss him telling her that he'll come by tomorrow. That he'll call her later. She tells him not to bother and I try to hold in my smile.

Josh's surgical site looks good and his abdomen is soft and non-distended. His temperature and vitals are perfect. "How is he?" she asks, but I don't glance in her direction as I continue to check him out. I need another minute to get myself in check.

"Great actually. At least from a surgical standpoint. I'll peek through his chart later to see what neurology has to say."

"Are you still friends with Brady Hawthorn and Connor Shaw?" Her voice is quiet, her tone anything but. She doesn't look at me when she asks, but my stunned silence draws her attention in my direction and her eyes lock on mine.

It feels like a loaded question. Especially after seeing Connor not even twenty minutes ago.

"Sort of. Not really."

She doesn't like this. "What does that mean, Wes?"

I lower my head for a beat because I know why she's asking me this. I know that she deserves an honest answer, but…the truth is complicated. "It means I see them around from time to time. They live in Cambridge, which is where I live. I don't seek them out, but occasionally we run into each other and will grab a beer or something. In the year I've lived here, I think it's only been two times or so."

Aria stands up. "They tried to kill Josh!" she screams, not even caring that we're in the ICU of a hospital and that there are dozens of people just outside the door.

"You know that for sure?" I question softly.

She scoffs out incredulously. "You knew about this? That they were suspects?"

"I just found out tonight actually."

"They called him a faggot, Wes. That very night at dinner. Tyler told me all about it."

I nod once. "Yes. I know that too."

"How?" she challenges. "How do you know this? Did they call you? Did they seek you out?"

But because Connor was technically my patient, I feel no need to disclose how I know.

"I've spoken with one of them. They admitted to sitting at their table and talking shit. He told me they didn't do it. He said they have witnesses who can corroborate that."

"Oh," she snorts, her cheeks growing rosier as her anger rises to a crescendo, "like their *friends*? Please, Wes. I am not stupid. There is no one else who would have done it."

I shake my head, taking a few steps over to her. "You don't know that. The police interviewed them."

"And you believe them? Just like that? No way they could be lying?"

"Of course, there is a chance they could be lying. I'm not a fool, Aria. I have no idea if he told me the truth or not."

"But that's what you want to believe."

I nod my head. "Yes. That's what I want to believe. Because if they did do this to him, then guys I've known my whole life tried to kill someone. But that doesn't mean I'm taking him at his word either."

"I need to go." She rises quickly and starts toward the door, but I manage to intercept her, wrapping my arms around her and pulling her struggling body into my chest. "Let me go, Wes." She's fighting me, but I'm much larger than her so I hold on to her easily. If anyone were to walk in here right now, I'd be in big shit trouble. I spin us around, so my back is to the door in case anyone gets curious about the noise and then I bring my mouth down to her ear.

"No," I clip out in a harsh whisper. "No, Aria. Not until you listen to me."

"Listen to what? How your friends are homophobic assholes who beat a man to within an inch of his life? Are you happy about what they did to him?"

I flip her around in my arms so we're face-to-face. Bending down, my eyes lock with hers. "No. I'm not happy about what happened to Josh. I like him. A lot, actually. You know that. I know you do. You need someone to blame it on and they're an easy target. They are homophobic assholes. They were there that night. It's not a leap. But…" I tighten my grip on her arms as she tries to pull away again. "I don't know. I just don't fucking know what to think or believe. If they did it, I will do everything in my power to lock up their hillbilly asses. I will testify against them if need be. But until we know for sure who did it, you need to stop blaming me. You need to stop. Running. From. Me." I punctuate each word in a harsh staccato.

Her face crumples and her head falls. I tuck her into to my chest, much the way I did this morning in the rain. I wrap my arms around her and plant my lips into the top of her head. She smells like vanilla and jasmine and feels like everything my arms have been missing for the last ten years.

"I'm so sorry, baby. I feel like that's all I say to you. But it's true. I'm so sorry. For everything. I wish I could fix all of this, and not just Josh."

She draws back, her watery eyes meet mine. "It's never that easy, though. Is it? And you cannot fix this. This might be the unfixable. *We* might be the unfixable."

Fuck…that's just. A slap to the face? A punch to the gut?

But…

She's right. We might be. But that doesn't mean I won't fight like hell to prove her wrong.

Chapter Twelve

ARIA

My head is pounding. My eyes unfocused. My neck is stiff and my back aches. It's after two in the morning and I haven't slept. I tried. But I can't manage it. I tried sketching for a bit, but I can't concentrate on what I'm doing. Josh is lying here unchanged, Tyler never came back after he left, and Wes's words about Connor and Brady are tormenting me.

I understand him not wanting to believe it's his friends, but there is no one else who would do that. Standing up, I twist my body, trying to get rid of the perpetual crick that now seems to be in every muscle in my upper body.

"You need a break?" Wes asks. *Speak of the devil.* The guy is like a freaking ghost in this place. I never hear him enter. I never see him coming. And yet suddenly, he's there. His presence just as impactful as it was the first time.

"No," I reply. "If Josh can't complain, neither can I."

Wes laughs lightly as he approaches me. He moves behind me, then suddenly his hands are on my neck and my shoulders, massaging my irritable muscles. "Josh can't complain. He's got propofol keeping him asleep. You've been here for more than two days straight. You're allowed to complain and take a break."

"Propofol?" I ask, closing my eyes and doing my best not to moan at the exquisite torture that is his hands on my body. "Isn't that what killed Michael Jackson?"

"Yes," he says, breathing close to my ear, but I don't care because his hands are pure magic. "But we're much better at this sort of thing than his doctor was."

"Good to know. Oh, God," I groan as he gets a particularly tight spot in my neck. "That's so good."

His hands freeze for a moment before they continue. "Are you doing that on purpose to turn me on or is it really that good?"

I smirk, my eyes still closed. "Are you that easy of a target, Doctor Kincaid?"

"With you?" he questions, his breath brushing my ear and giving me goose bumps. Goose bumps he's now running his fingers across, eliciting chills and shivers and shudders. Damn him. "I'm the easiest target in the world."

"Would I be pushing it too far if I ask you not to stop?" I giggle, unable to help myself.

I shouldn't be flirting with him. But I'm too fucked to care right now. How many times has he said he was sorry? Why do I even care if he is?

"No. Keep going. It's driving me wild," he laughs with me. "Shit, you're so warm and tight."

My breath hitches.

"Too far?"

"Yes." Most definitely. Especially since my nipples are now harder than pebbles.

"Come take a walk with me. I want to show you something." I twist to look at him, missing his hands on my aching muscles instantly. "You can take a break, Aria. I have about ten minutes before I have to get back. Then you'll be free of me until the next time I come to bother you."

I shouldn't do it. That seems to be my motto with him. I shouldn't. But the way he's staring at me now… Like he's missed me for every second of those ten years. Like he wishes he could go back in time and fix all the mistakes he made.

Do you mean it, Wes or will I have to learn how to get over you again?

"Please, Aria. Please come with me."

"Okay," I say, looking up into his beautiful green eyes. Oh, how I've missed these eyes on me. The way they used to make me feel? God, I can't even. It would be so much easier not to feel so much for him.

"You'll need your coat."

My eyebrows hit my hairline. "It's two in the morning."

"Is it?" he muses. "I hadn't noticed. Time does not exist in the hospital. Well..." He tilts his head to the side like he's thinking about this as he slips my coat onto my shoulders, helping me put my arms into the sleeves like you would a small child. "Let me amend that. Time is everything in a hospital. Down to the second. The actual hour is irrelevant."

"Except when it's time to go home."

"Except then. Come on." He reaches out for my hand and I stare at it for a minute. "Are you nervous about people seeing you holding my hand or about actually holding my hand?"

I raise my eyes to his. "The latter."

He smiles big at that, like that was the answer he was hoping for, though I don't understand why. "Good. Now you can take it." He doesn't give me the option. He grasps my hand in his and guides me out of Josh's room. I turn back to get a quick glance at my sleeping friend. My heart hurts every time I look at him.

"Where are we going?" I ask as we walk past the nurses' station. No one really pays us any attention, even though I assume we look odd wearing winter gear and holding hands.

"It's a surprise."

"I don't like surprises."

He gives me a sideways glance. "Of course, you do. You just tell yourself you don't. Besides, when was the last time you had a truly good surprise?"

I think on that for a moment. I go back through all my moments. Things like birthdays and special occasions. Things like anniversaries in relationships. Nothing really jumps out at me. Probably because I always tell people I don't like surprises, so they never give me any. "I don't know."

"Then your ex, Andrew Albright, was a shitty boyfriend." My eyes bulge out of my head as I stare into the side of his face. "I wouldn't date him again if I were you." He peeks in my direction, an unstoppable smirk bouncing up the corner of his lips.

"You are in no position to talk."

"I was never your boyfriend, baby. If I were, your answer about your last truly good surprise would have been very different. Something I plan to remedy."

We reach an elevator that feels like a million miles from where we just were. He hits the up arrow and now my curiosity is really peaked. The doors open, and we step on. Wes stands absurdly close to me. His incredible scent infiltrating my senses and making me dizzy. Or maybe it's the anticipation doing that because my chest is tight with flutters.

We ride up in silence, but I still feel him. Everywhere. His proximity is consuming.

Then the doors open, and he leads me outside onto the roof of Massachusetts General Hospital.

"Holy shit," I whisper, walking across the large helipad. I wrap my arms around my chest, trying to stave off the blustery cold because even though I'm wearing a coat, it's freaking freezing up here.

It's just started to snow. I didn't even notice as I haven't looked out Josh's window in hours. From up here, we have a view of the entire city and the bay beyond. It's sublimely stunning and with the new snowfall, perfect.

"What if a helicopter comes in?" I turn away from him, my hair whipping around in the icy winds.

He's standing behind me, his body pressed against mine as his arms snake around my waist, his chin dropping to my shoulder as our cheeks press against each other. It's a very intimate position. One that should make me feel uncomfortable.

Instead, it makes my heart beat faster like it's finally coming back to life.

"I'd get paged." His voice rumbles into me. "I'm a trauma surgeon, remember?" *Like I could forget.* "It's beautiful up here, isn't it? Especially as the first flakes of snow fall."

"It is," I say softly as my eyes search around the city before me. I know what this is. What he's doing. A girl never forgets her first real kiss and I certainly am no exception.

"I come up here a lot, actually," Wes whispers softly, his warm breath brushing my face. "Down there…" He pauses. Takes a breath. "It can get to be a lot. Life and death and always having to be at my best. I come up here to just…I don't know, gain perspective. Get my bearings. Recharge." He squeezes me tighter. "I wanted to share this place with you. I think you need some of that right now."

I suck in a deep breath. He's right. I do need some of that right now. I need to gain perspective and get my bearings; recharge. I needed this moment. This place. I just didn't realize how much until he said that. I lean back into him, and I let myself go to places I shouldn't dare to venture again.

"No stars tonight, but a guy can only work so many miracles. Good surprise?"

"The best."

"Then why do you sound sad?" He holds me tighter against him and my eyes shut. Even though it is beautiful, even though it's a very good surprise, I am sad. A line from Jane Austen's, *Persuasion* flitters through my head. "You pierce my soul. I am half agony, half hope. Tell me not that I am too late, that such precious feelings are gone forever. I offer myself to you again with a heart even more your own than when you almost broke it."

That quote burned a hole in my soul the night he came back when I was eighteen. It wasn't even Anne Elliot, the female heroine, who said that. It was Captain Wentworth. That was always ironic in my mind because I never allowed myself to pretend Wes would ever feel half of that passion and emotion for me.

But now, after all these years, I'm afraid to offer myself to him again. Because there was no almost about my heartbreak. It was full-on, and if I do give in to this flirtation, into the things he's been saying and the promises in his eyes, what will he do to me this time when it ends?

So instead of admitting to my fears. Instead of giving voice to my sadness, I say, "I'm not sad. I love what the world feels like just as snow begins to fall." At least the second part is true.

"I know you do. It's one of my favorite memories of us. Did you ever paint the way it feels when the first flakes of snow fall?"

My throat constricts. How can he remember I said that? I hardly do, and I feel like every second of that moment is burned into my brain.

"Yes."

"Do you still have it? That moment when I kissed you for the first time?"

I shake my head against him.

He blows out a breath. "That's too bad. That's one I'd love to see."

Me too. But I sold it. It was another one I couldn't stand to look at.

Wes presses his lips against my temple, trailing down my face, hitting the corner of my lips and down my neck. He takes a deep inhale and I find myself closing my eyes once more, getting lost in the feel of his lips on me. His warm breath.

I could fall for you again, Weston Kincaid. God, would it be easy. And painful when I hit the ground once more.

The feel of his lips trickling back up has my heart racing in my chest. I want him to kiss me so badly I can hardly breathe with the want of it. "You should get back down." You should let me go now.

"I know. But I want to stay up here with you. Kissing you. Holding you."

"It's why you need to go."

"Probably. I wish we could stay up here longer, but I need to get back and I can't leave you up here."

I nod against him again.

"Are you ready?"

"Yes," I say, opening my eyes and facing the skyline one last time.

I step out of his embrace and turn to face him. He cups my face in his large warm hands, his eyes flittering back and forth between mine. He opens his lips, like he wants to tell me everything. And I can't do it. I'm not ready. I may never be again.

I step out of his grasp, forcing his hands away. Forcing my heart to close off once again. I realign my features into a stoic mask. "Thank you for bringing me up here. This was exactly what I needed."

Wes smiles like a boy on Christmas, undeterred by my brush off, and then takes my hand once again. He leads me back into Josh's room, helps me out of my coat, and then stares at me for a very long moment. So long in fact that my heart begins to beat faster with anticipation of his next move.

His fingers brush along my hair, tucking a few strands behind my ears. "You look tired. Beautiful, but tired."

"I am tired." And I mean that in so many ways.

"Get some sleep," he says, leaning down and kissing the corner of my mouth.

He's gone the next second, but instead of climbing into the recliner and closing my eyes, I walk over to the window and watch the snow fall. "Joshua Brown," I say, not even bothering to look over at him. "I realize that the last forty-eight hours have sucked way worse for you than they have for me, but I'm officially mad at you. Or maybe my heart is, because I think it might be about to go on strike. A girl can only take so much and I've just officially hit my limit."

I settle myself in the recliner, making sure all the lights are off, then I close my eyes. When I open them again, the room is filled with doctors. Doctors I've seen but haven't spoken to. They're discussing Josh's neurological state.

Sitting up, I rub my bleary eyes while trying to make myself appear put together. The guy who looks like the chief of things turns to me. He's got on glasses that are hanging precariously from his long, crooked nose, a rumpled white lab coat, a blazing yellow button-down shirt on top of brown slacks and his hair is a fucking disaster. He's the epitome of an eyesore. But I do not care in the slightest as long as he tells me good news. "Miss Davenport?"

"Aria," I supply.

"Okay, Aria. Today is going to be a very big day for Mr. Brown, here. Our plan is to take him for a series of tests that include MRIs and EEGs, amongst others. We're going to be putting him through the wringer, because our hope is that we can reduce his sedation tomorrow and get your friend to wake up."

"Really?" I'm smiling and I suddenly find myself standing. I want to hug this guy, I'm so excited, but that seems very out of place.

"Yes. We've gotten the green light from surgery who informs us he's stable and his ICP has been steadily improving with medication. Our goal for today is to remove that medication entirely and see how he functions without it."

"And that's safe?"

"I wouldn't do it if it wasn't."

I guess I can't argue with that. "That all sounds wonderful. I'd very much like him to wake up."

"I figured as much. The nurses have your contact information, so when he's back here, we'll be in touch. But until then, feel free to do whatever you need to do."

"What's your name?"

He grins at me, and Jesus, that's as off-kilter as the rest of him. "Samuel Clemens, but if you make a crack about my name I won't fix your friend."

I can't help the bubble of laughter that bursts out of me. "I wouldn't dare. Thank you so very much, Dr. Clemens."

"It's what we do."

In the next beat of my heart the transport people come in to move Josh. So, I guess this guy meant that those things were going to happen now. I kiss my friend goodbye and leave the hospital with a smile. I avoid the ER like the plague and take an Uber home.

And when I check my phone, I have texts from the whole world.

Rina and Margot and Halle. Wes and Drew. Even Brecken and my mom. I should really call her.

Instead of returning any of the texts, I go upstairs and shower. I practically scald myself in the hot water, then I towel off and change into my pajamas. My feet anxiously run upstairs to the third floor. My fingers itch with excited flurry as I pick up a paintbrush, ready my acrylics and a blank canvas. Then I paint what it feels like just as the snow begins to fall.

I've painted that moment before. But this is twelve years later and I'm much better at my craft than I was then. I paint my soul into this piece, and seven hours later, I know I will never sell what I've created. I'm going to hang this in my family room downstairs.

I abandon my life's blood in favor of another shower. I have plans with my girls soon and I can't be late. Or smell like paint.

Chapter Thirteen

ARIA

I take the T down to the hospital and hop off. I make my way down the stairs, across the street, and just as I reach the entrance, Rina walks out of the revolving glass doors, still in her scrubs. She scowls at me when she sees what I'm wearing, even though my coat covers most of it. "Why do you look like the fucking Sugar Plum Fairy?"

"You're such a bitch," I grouse. "Because I'm freaking exhausted after not sleeping for years, then painting too many feelings, and wanting to look pretty for the first time in days, hoping a doctor I shouldn't give a shit about notices me. And if you judge me for putting in the extra effort to look nice, I might smack you."

"Which doctor?"

"Ugh."

She gives me a hug along with an exaggerated pat on the shoulder. "I bet he would be sporting a chub with you dressed like this."

"Who?"

She grins. "Both of your smitten doctors. You're a vision of purity and loveliness."

I laugh. "Thanks," I say, stepping back. "That helps. Not so sure about the chub, but hey, I'll take whatever positive reinforcement I can get."

She nods. "No doubt. So what's our plan because you're dressed for fancy, and I'm dressed for greasy bar food and beer."

"I don't know…," I trail off as my phone rings in my purse. I slide it out and grin down at the screen, flipping it around so Rina can see it. I swipe my finger across to answer. "Well, hello there, M," I say to Margot. "How goes the night for you?"

"First of all, don't call me *M*. It makes me sound like a nineties rapper or a party favor. Second, I'm across the street at The Hill with Halle and we can see you and Rina standing there. Come join us."

I sigh. I do love The Hill, but that means really going out instead of just slightly going out. That might not make a whole lot of sense to the world, but it does to me.

"Isn't there anywhere else we can go?"

"No," she says. "We're already here with a table and Halle promised not to run home to her man-lover until later. Come have a drink. You sound like the beast got your voice." I have no idea what that means, but I don't question it either. Margot has strange expressions, and this appears to be another one.

"Do you even know what party favors are?" I ask, changing the subject.

"I work in the emergency department, Aria. Of course, I do. I'm not as clueless as you think."

"Okay then. I guess you have a point. Hold on, let me ask Rina if she's up for—"

"God, yes," Rina moans out before I can even finish my sentence.

"I take it you heard that?" I laugh the words. "We'll be there in five."

I hang up with Margot and sigh again. "I kinda wanted a Netflix and wine night. Not alone, though."

"Well, I took care of a girl who was stabbed in the chest six times by her ex-boyfriend. I'm not doing anything alone for the rest of my life."

"Jesus," I breathe out, utterly horrified. "Really? I think I might buy a gun and start sleeping with it."

Rina snorts. "You're not a gun girl."

"I was born in Texas." She gives me a look, but it's true. I may have only lived there for a year before we moved up to Mass, but still.

"That totally doesn't count."

"So that's a no to the Netflix and wine? Yes, to The Hill?"

"Yes, to The Hill. Because I know you, Aria Davenport," she threatens with a stern finger pointed in my direction. "If I agreed to Netflix and wine, you were going to force me to watch that documentary on the Nazis again."

"Hey," I bristle, feigning indignation. "That shit can happen again if we're not careful. Besides, it's fascinating. History is cool."

"So says the artist. Ironically, you have not one, but two doctors from your past after you, honey pie. I still can't get over the ridiculousness of that."

"You are way off the mark, doll. Neither are after my honey pie. They just like to tease the baker."

We both let out a real laugh for the first time today and it feels like a weight is lifting from us. "You are so very wrong. I saw Drew earlier today," Rina says, throwing me an eye as we walk further out into the cold January night, our breath coming out in bursts of white smoke as we hustle toward the crosswalk on Cambridge Street.

"Goodie on you," I snark, rolling my eyes. "And before you continue on with whatever bullshit you were about to spew, I don't want to hear it. Drew and I are finished. *Fini. Fertig. Terminado.*"

"Okay," she laughs, holding her hands up to stop my rant. "I get the picture. You don't have to tell me it in a million different languages."

"Glad to hear it." Drew isn't a bad guy. In fact, he's a great guy. I wouldn't have lasted for a year and a half with him if he wasn't. But the last three months of our relationship were not good, until eventually, he ended things. Believe it or not, I've had a harder time getting Wes out of my head than I had Drew.

We reach The Hill and I plaster on a smile as I open the door. We spot Margot and Halle at a table. Halle's eyes are widened in alarm, her fingers frantically pointing at something in front of her and that's when I see it. Margot's already got a shot in her hand.

"Shit," I sputter, practically sprinting over to her, about to knock the damn thing out of her hand, but she spots me coming and downs the sweet concoction in one smooth motion. "Ah, Margot. Tell me you didn't," I moan as I drop into the seat across from her and next to Halle, my back to the bar.

"I did. But once I tell you what happened, you'll understand."

"I was in the bathroom," Halle says, guilt etched in her fine features. "The little sneak snagged it at the bar while I was peeing. I swear, it's only her first, though. We got here together."

"I'm telling you—"

"Don't," Rina interrupts whatever Margot was about to say, taking the seat next to her swiveling until she's practically in her face. "I had the shittiest shift in the history of shittiest shifts."

"Yeah," Margot half-whispers, her expression laced with pain. "I heard about that girl." She shakes her head. "I don't even know how to process that. Are you okay?" she asks Rina, because Rina's ex stalked her back when she was in college.

Then we look over to Halle who is blushing furiously, her face downcast. Halle was attacked last summer by her crazy ex. He tried to kidnap her then very nearly killed her now boyfriend, Jonah. Christ. Both of my friends had it rough with an ex.

We all fall silent for a beat before Rina says, "I know this may sound super insensitive and I don't mean to be, because I ache for that girl. I know firsthand how nightmarish that is, and I'm so grateful she's alive and will eventually be okay. At least physically. But can we not talk about it anymore?"

We all agree. Then Margot jumps in with, "That's perfect actually because I need to talk about the one-night stand I had last night after I left you all at the hospital."

My eyes widen. So do Rina's. Halle purses her lips, leaning back in her seat and crossing her arms. All three of us exchange looks. "You said you weren't going to do those anymore," Rina reminds her.

"Clearly, I have impulse control issues. Blame my mother for my strict upbringing or something. Whatever." She blows out a breath, her long dark bangs flying up in the breeze. "I'm not going to anymore. I promise. But I really thought it was like a slot machine."

"Um. Yeah. You're going to have to clarify what you mean by that because as far as I can tell, the only slot machine is in your pants."

Margot rolls her eyes at me. "No. I just meant that if I pulled the lever enough times, eventually I'd hit the jackpot and the guy would know what he was doing with me. That's how it worked with Halle. She met Jonah like that and look at them now." Halle shrugs sheepishly. "The boy last night couldn't find my clitoris with a map and a flashlight."

"Shut up." Rina looks appalled.

"It's true." Margot nods dejectedly. "He was not giving in the orgasm department and whenever I tried to give him proper instruction, he got all pissy about it. Like my wanting an orgasm made me a bitch. Why is it so goddamn difficult? Am I orgasmically challenged?"

"Oh, honey." I reach across the table and pat her hand. "No. No way. You've just had some crappy partners. Better that you got that out of your system. An orgasm is everyone's given right and if this guy wasn't giving you them, then he sucks. Not you."

"It's true," Halle agrees. "And if you recall, I was with the worst men on the planet before I met Jonah. And meeting him like that was just…I don't know. Not the norm, I'm going to say."

"It's so deflating, you know? I mean, why can't I just find a decent guy?"

"You will. But most guys looking for a one-night hookup are only interested in themselves. Not in giving pleasure. And definitely not in a relationship."

As I say the words, of course, I think of Wes. We were only one night. Well, times two. But both instances were one night. But we're different, right? I mean, I've known him practically my entire life. I grew up with him. He knows my brother and my parents. Yes, I decide. Very different. We made out for months before we ever had sex. And he was very much invested in my pleasure. Crap. Now I'm blushing.

"But that's what happens in all of my romance books."

"You're fucking with me, right?" Rina asks, shaking her head slightly. "Margot, those are *romance* books. The fantasy. In real life, bad boys are just that. Bad. They're typically not misunderstood wells of love and feelings just waiting on the right woman to bring them out of their tragic whatever. They like to get in, get out, and be done. And if that's what you're into, cool. But if every time you have a fling, you end up miserable, face down in shots, then I'd say you need to change your tactics. So how about you remove the flashing vacant sign from your vagina, close up the hotel, and vet the boys a little better before you accept their credit card to stay the night?"

Her shoulders sag as she sighs dramatically then signals the waitress for another shot.

"Can we switch to beer?" Rina asks. "Or wine even? Last time I had to hold your hair twice, and you splattered vomit on my shoes."

"Fine," Margots relents, crumbling further. "But you order for me. I don't know what to get." We order our drinks and a plate of nachos to share. When our waitress leaves, Margot asks, "Speaking of one-nighters, how's Weston Kincaid? And for the record, I sort of hate you for him. He's godly."

I look down at the wood grain of the table for a beat, suddenly not wanting to talk about it. "That was years ago, Margot."

"But he still wants her." That's Halle. I can only shrug at her. I have no idea what he's doing with me. And I shouldn't care. I shouldn't think about it as much as I do. I'll blink and then he'll be gone, and I'll be a mess. Again.

"And while we're talking boys here," Margot chimes in, "Drew told me he wants to give it another try with you."

My face shoots up. "*He told you that*?" She nods, grinning at me like she knew it all along. "Jesus." I shake my head. "How am I supposed to tell you anything when you're friends with him like this? The two of you gossip together like old women."

"We totally do." Margot laughs so hard she snorts, slapping the table twice. "He reminds me so much of my brother it isn't even funny. They sort of look alike too, which is disconcerting if I'm being honest because I think Drew is hot."

"I have no words for you, Margot. Like none. Just keep your mouth shut when it comes to reciprocating gossip or I'm cutting you off."

"That's like the bitchiest threat ever. You know I don't do that. Chicks before dicks and all that bullshit."

"That's such a cliché," Rina says. "But in any event, you really need to figure this out, because Drew wouldn't say that unless he meant business, and Wes looks at you like you're the long-lost piece of something missing from his soul."

I scoff. "That's so freaking dramatic."

"But no less true." I glare at Halle who just smiles big at me. Damn these girls.

"Love is a twisted game with no winners."

"Did you ever tell your brother about Wes?" Halle asks and I have to laugh at that.

"What do you think? No way. I would never, and I talked Wes out of it way back when. Besides, that was forever ago. All of this male drama is too much. I just want to focus on Josh getting better and my work. I'm taking time off of relationships. It's just going to be me and Hermando for a while."

Margot snorts, choking on her newly delivered beer.

"Who's *Hermando*?" she asks all sweet and oblivious, wiping away the excess beer from her lips and chin. She's smiling so big practically all of her teeth are showing. Same with Rina.

"Her silicone boyfriend," a voice says from behind us.

I flip around at light speed and when my eyes land on the slate gray ones I am intimately familiar with, I groan. I'm not even embarrassed. Drew is well-versed in Hermando.

"Well, shit. How much of that conversation did you hear, Drew?" When I say his name, my friends crack under the pressure of trying to contain their laughter and let it all out. I flip them off while I wait on his answer.

"Only the part where you said it's just you and Hermando from now on." Well, that's a relief. I would not have been happy if he heard about Wes. Now the bastard is smiling down on me.

"Fantastic." I turn back to my friends. "Did you see him standing there?" I point behind me.

"Yeah," Margot replies, still grinning big as she looks over to Rina for backup. "But only for the very last part. We didn't know he was there before that."

"I'm totally innocent," Halle promises. "My back was to him so I missed out on all the fun."

"You could have warned me," I admonish Margot and Rina, folding my arms across my chest.

I'm pissed off.

I don't want Drew to be here. I don't want him eavesdropping on my conversations with my friends. I don't want to deal with him at all. I'm sort of getting sick of all the men in this town. Well, maybe just two, but I really am done for a while with the opposite sex.

I just want to eat some food because I'm hungry, finish my drink, and then go see Josh.

But when Drew pulls over a chair, placing it directly beside me and drops into it, scooting closer just because he can, I blow out a breath. There'll be no getting rid of him now.

Chapter Fourteen

ARIA

Here's the problem with Drew as an ex-boyfriend. I can never fully get away from him because two of my best friends work with him. Typically, when a relationship ends, you both go your separate ways and that's that. And that's the way it should be.

But with Drew, I'm not afforded that luxury.

No. The cocky bastard works with Margot in the emergency department and has known Rina for a while as that's where she started working as a nurse when she moved to Boston before she transferred up to the ICU. He knows Halle for the same reason, though she no longer works in the hospital.

He's an attending in the ER, but for some reason, he gets off on working crazy resident hours so he's always there. He's always. Freaking. There.

And when we were together, I found his work ethic admirable. Granted, he was still a resident for the first year of our relationship, but still.

But now, when I want to, need to, distance myself from him, I can't. At least not easily because he knows where I go and who I hang out with. I think he likes this. No, I know he does. Because he's grinning like the cat who ate the goddamn canary whole while he sips his beer and invades my personal space at our table.

"I don't remember inviting you to sit," I grouse, nudging him with my elbow so he'll move the hell over. He doesn't. Instead, he gives an unconcerned shrug as he stares intently into my eyes, manipulating me with his gaze.

And once upon a time, his whole arrogant, alpha dog thing was hot to me. It still sort of is if I'm being honest. I won't even lie and say that isn't what drew me to him in the first place.

But it also meant he had trouble showing and expressing his feelings toward me. Difficulty having a real conversation about our future. He was incapable of change in any way. Expected everyone, especially me, to bend to his will.

Maybe that's fine if you're just casually dating. But Drew and I were together for a year and a half. We were living together. When he began making demands that I give up my life and career to be at his beck and call while he worked all hours, I knew we were headed for trouble.

I foolishly stuck it out until he decided he was done.

After he ended it with me, I often wondered if he made those demands as a way to begin the process of getting rid of me. To make it easier for him to rationalize it after such a lengthy relationship.

Regardless, I really don't want him joining us tonight. I've got enough on my brain.

"So you've sworn off men in favor of plastic?" he asks, but he's not really asking. He's teasing me.

"Silicone," I correct.

He raises an expectant eyebrow at my evasive answer.

"Hermando is pretty much the embodiment of the perfect man," I say, winking at Margot who's turning a lovely shade of red to match Halle's hair. "He's always willing and able to give pleasure whenever I want it. He doesn't make ludicrous demands over my life. And he *never* shows up and sits down when he's uninvited."

Rina and Halle snicker, but Margot isn't laughing, and suddenly,

I think I know why she was blushing and it has nothing to do with my vibrator.

"You invited him, didn't you?" I point at her. Now she's full-on red.

"He texted me right after I got off the phone with you, so I told him you and Rina were meeting Halle and me here," she answers, her tone defensive and maybe a bit contrite. "I didn't *exactly* invite him."

"It's true," Drew admits, his attention focused on me. "I figured you'd be with your newest—courtesy of me—besties, so I texted Margot. And when she said you were drinking here, I came."

I shake my head at him. "Why, Drew? What do you want?"

"You," he says simply, and that dormant twinge of longing begins to reawaken in my gut.

"Drew—"

"Just hear me out, Aria," he pleads, his hand reaching under the table to clasp mine. "Just come up to the bar with me, have a drink, and let me talk. You can leave after that. I'll even walk you across to go see Josh."

"Josh hates you."

"He does not. He hates that we broke up the way we did."

I roll my eyes again. "That was not it." I can feel my friends' gazes boring into me, but I can't focus on them right now. I need to deal with Drew. "I don't think that's a good idea."

"It is," he says emphatically. "It's a great idea. Just one drink. Five minutes. Ten tops."

"Five minutes. That's it. And I want the drink to be expensive."

He grins like he just won, and I hate that I just capitulated with so little resistance. "Whatever you want, babe."

"Don't," I snap as I stand up because I'm a fool. I tug my hand back from his and look to my friends. "Five minutes." Margot nods, but she's laughing, I think. She won't be much help. She and Drew are good friends.

I can practically feel Drew's cocky satisfied smirk as he leads me down to the opposite end of the bar where there are two seats, just waiting for us. "Thank you," he says once I sit down. But the truth is, we need to have this talk if for no other reason than for him to know it's over for good.

Drew orders us drinks, a beer for himself and a fucking Grey Goose dirty martini for me. He's insane if he thinks I'm going to drink that. I need to stay clearheaded. When I said expensive, I assumed he'd order me a brandy or a nice glass of wine. Not four shots of alcohol in one drink.

Drew stays quiet until our drinks are placed in front of us. After he takes a sip of his liquid courage and I just stare at mine, he pivots to face me full-on.

He chuckles lightly, running a hand across his lightly stubbled jaw. It's his tell. He's nervous, and that's something he rarely is. I don't like that he's nervous. It makes me uneasy. It makes my heart begin to race.

He clears his throat—another tell—then leans into me, his hand resting on the bar next to mine. "I've thought about what I would say to you for weeks now. Maybe months. I came up with a million different things, but sitting here, looking at you, I realize I don't know what to say. Once again, you leave me at a loss for words."

I suck in a silent deep breath and hold it.

"All I know is that the last six months have sucked. Not being with you has sucked. More than sucked. I know I fucked-up. I know I hurt you and ruined everything."

He reaches out, cups my cheek in his large warm hand, and positions me so I'm staring up into his gray eyes.

"I'm sorry, Aria. I'm *so* sorry. I love you, and I miss you, and I think we should try again."

He blows out a breath like that was difficult for him to say. I bet it was. He was never big on this sort of thing. I think in all the time we were together he told me he loved me only a few dozen times. On the rare occasions he would say it, it had a tremendous impact. I asked him once why he never said it more and he explained that saying, *I love you,* is overused. That couples who say it all the time do so more out of habit than feeling. That every time he told me he loved me, it was because he meant it.

I hate that he just told me he loves me. Because it means he means it. And I don't want him to mean it. I want him to come across as insincere, because it would be so much easier to walk away if he did. I also wish this didn't happen today. At a time when I'm already so emotionally vulnerable. When I'm mentally hungover.

I blow out that breath I was holding and remove his hand from my face. "Nothing's changed, Drew. I paint like a madwoman. Seven hours today alone. I'm going to work and have a career. This is what I want for my life."

"I know," he says, his features growing severe as he takes a sip of his beer. "Do you know why I wanted you to slow down on that?"

"Because you wanted me home while you worked."

He shakes his head. "That's part of it, but not all of it."

I reach out and take a sip of my delicious dirty martini that I was not going to drink. I have a feeling I'm going to need it for this.

"I'll admit, I'm a bit of a caveman. I want to be the one to take care of and support my girl. But really, I was thinking of asking you to marry me, Aria." I choke on the sip I was swallowing, coughing and sputtering as alcohol drips down my chin. Awesome. Very classy. I wipe my face with a bar napkin and once I've regained the ability to breathe, I turn to him with a glare.

"So you *broke up* with me?"

"I know." He looks ashamed. "It doesn't make any sense. Even now as I think about it, I'm not sure why I did that. We had problems and they didn't feel like they were getting better. It felt like a stalemate and I was just so frustrated with everything that I got to the point where I didn't know what else to do. It was a mistake. I knew it instantly and I'm sorry for hurting you the way I did."

"What does that have to do with me giving up my art?"

The bastard is grinning at me as he reaches out and wipes some residual liquid from my chin. "You wanted to work as many hours as you could while traveling the world from one gallery opening to another. I never saw you. And that seemed to only be increasing. We both already worked insane hours, so the idea of seeing you less than I was, bothered me. I wanted to be with you. Whenever I could be, and that wasn't happening. It also didn't feel like you were willing to make any sacrifices to be with me more." I raise an eyebrow at that because I don't exactly remember him cutting back his hours. He holds up his hand, stopping me. "I know it's selfish, okay? I know I wasn't any better. That's what I'm here to talk to you about."

I shake my head. "I'm twenty-eight. My career is at a point where it's growing."

"I know," he agrees. "But I'm thirty-two and I'm ready for the next step. With you."

I shake my head again, totally and completely overwhelmed. My eyes begin to well up. I can't even stop them. Yes, I want marriage. Eventually. I just no longer want it with me.

"Listen, Drew. It doesn't—"

"I'm willing to cut back some of my hours if you'll agree to cut back on your travel. You don't need the money. Especially if we're together. You don't need to stop painting. I'm not asking that. I know what it means to you."

"Jesus," I whisper. "This is too much. Drew, I hear what you're saying. And if this had been six months ago, then maybe things would be different. Maybe we could have…"

I trail off, my eyes catching on something. On someone. And that's when I spot him.

At least I think it's him.

It's hard to tell from back here. It happened so fast, but I'm nearly positive Weston Kincaid was just staring at me before he turned around and walked out the door. I don't think about it. I grab my bag and run toward the door, brushing past people as I go.

But the moment I step out into the dark, cold January night, he's nowhere to be found. I don't see anyone matching him walking in any direction. I spin in a circle, searching every which way.

I wonder if I imagined him.

That thought frustrates me to no end.

I feel Drew come up behind me, his hands on my shoulders as he turns me to face him. "You ran out on me." He looks hurt as he places my discarded coat on my shoulders. Part of me feels bad about that. I don't want to hurt him. I'm not a vengeful woman.

He's talking marriage and commitment, and I'm running out in search of another man.

But he also broke up with me six months ago. He never said any of this to me before. It was all, *I don't want you working so much. You should stop painting and traveling and stay at home more.* It was never, I'll cut back my hours and I want to marry you and I want you here with me while we start a life together.

"I uh...," I shake my head. "I'm sorry. I need to go. I can't...I can't do this again with you. We're done. I want to get back to Josh."

"All right," he says softly. "I'll give you time if that's what you need."

"I didn't say I need time. I said—"

"Please think about it," he cuts me off. "Don't brush me off like this. Don't brush off our future like this. I meant everything I said, Aria. I want you back."

His hands move from my shoulders to cup my face the way Wes did when I was on the helipad in the snow with him, and I push Drew off, unable to handle his touch.

He growls, but quickly gets his frustration under control. "Can I walk you back to the hospital? Sit with you for a while?" he asks sweetly as he pulls back, searching my eyes.

"No." I shake my head fiercely. "I'm sorry. I really am. But I can't do this anymore with you. Tell the girls I'll call them."

And then I run off. As fast as my feet will carry me. I head to the hospital. To Josh. I need to get away from that bar. I need to get away from Drew. I just need to get away.

Chapter Fifteen

WES

My feet carry me down Cambridge Street, heading away from the bar back toward the garage I'm parked in. Today was one of the longest days I've had here. I was supposed to be off this morning, but instead, there was a massive car accident with multiple traumas and it was all-hands-on-deck.

I stayed.

There was no way I could leave.

And even though I was desperate to go home and crash after, I agreed to go out and decompress with a buddy of mine who had saved the life of a girl who was attacked by her ex. It was supposed to be one drink then home.

But the moment I stepped into the bar, I saw Aria there. With Drew. It wasn't just that she was there with him or that she was talking to him.

It was the *way* she was talking to him.

His body was leaning into hers, their faces close, and whatever they were discussing was intense. I think she was even in tears over it. It was at that moment I realized I was outmatched. Because he's her present and I've been nothing but her past.

Not even the best of pasts to her.

He knows who she is now and I'm grasping at straws. It was also the moment I came to grips with just how much I still want her. How deep this woman goes with me. How I don't think I can go back to nothing when she's always been my something.

For a moment, I very nearly went over to her. Was set to barge in and demand she allow me to plead my case before I begged her to pick me over him.

But I couldn't do that to her. I have zero right.

I told my friend Calvin I was done, and left.

My gut sinks further with each step I take. I don't know what I was expecting, but it wasn't that.

The frigid wind whips an icy path across my face and I duck to avoid it, but just as my eyes hit the sidewalk, my head flies back up at the sound of my name being called. I pause, listening to see if I was imagining things when I hear it again. "Wes," she cries out, the sound of her voice carrying in the opposite direction as it floats in the current of the wind. "Wait."

I do wait. I even turn around to face her.

Aria is running down the sidewalk to catch up to me, so I help her along and swallow up the distance between us. Aria comes to a halt when she's a few feet away, then she just stands there, staring at me like she doesn't know what to do now that she's caught me.

She's wearing a cream-colored sweater dress and tan leather booties. Her long dark hair is swept off her face, parted down the middle with the two front ends braided and tied together behind her head. Her eyelids are painted in something shimmery and her lips are pink. She looks like an angel or a fairy or something magical and mythical.

She's so pretty my chest hurts.

"You were there? You were in the bar?"

I nod and take a step closer, my eyes feasting on her. My heart picking up a pace I wish it wouldn't.

"I saw you leave, but when I ran after you, you were already gone."

"You ran out after me?"

Now it's her turn to nod, the color rising in her cheeks. "Why did you leave?"

I force out an aggravated breath, running a hand through my hair. What am I supposed to say to that? Or more importantly, how much do I want to reveal? Especially if she's with Drew.

Jealousy prickles my skin and I realize I'm angry. At myself. At her. At myself. I sigh.

She's going to pulverize the remnants of my battered heart and leave me for dead.

"Because things looked very intense between you and Drew and I didn't want to be there for it."

"And?"

"And?" I laugh out mirthlessly. "And this is just getting very complicated. I'm a possessive bastard, Aria. I love that you ran out on that asshole to come look for me. You have no idea how hard it was for me to see you with him. Or maybe you do because you know why I left. I just don't know what to do." I blow out a breath, glancing out into the street. I take a moment, forcing myself to grow some balls, reluctant to ask the question I need the answer to. I turn back to her, our eyes locking. "Are you getting back together with him? It certainly looked like that's what he was trying to do."

"No," she admits. Those two letters are surprisingly wonderful to hear and far more than what I expected her to say. "But that doesn't mean I'm saying yes to you instead. It's too late for us."

How is it fucking possible that it's too late again? I just got her back. And then something occurs to me. I'm not too late. She ran after me. She just doesn't want me to hurt her again and doesn't understand yet that I'd rather die than let that happen.

I can still fight like hell for her.

"Have you had dinner yet?"

She blinks up at me, clearly surprised by the change in topic. "No. I um…I was going to with my friends, but then Drew came along and wanted to talk and then well…," her voice trails off.

"Have dinner with me."

"Now?"

"It's as good of a time as any."

"But Josh..."

"I'll drive you back after. They're not reducing his sedation until tomorrow and last I checked on him, Tyler was with him. He's not alone."

"You checked on him before you left?"

I nod.

"Okay." She smiles up at me and my chest inflates. God, this girl. This crazy, sexy, stunning girl. I'm so gone on her. I reach out and I take her hand. She lets me and yeah, definitely not too late.

Within minutes, we're driving across the Longfellow Bridge into Cambridge.

"Where are we going?"

"My place," I answer, my eyes trying to find hers in the dark before I have to return them to the road. She's not going to like this and that has me fighting my smirk before I get smacked for it.

"I can't go to your place. I thought we were going for dinner."

"We're doing both."

Aria shakes her head, her arms crossed over her chest. She thinks I tricked her. Maybe I did a little. She's not happy with me. Fine. I can work with not happy. The bastard in me still loves getting a rise out of her. Still loves firing her up.

I pull into my spot, park the Jeep, and shut it off. I get out, running around to open her door for her. Her blue eyes meet mine and I can see the hesitation all over her. "It's just dinner, Aria. We can talk easier here than we could in a restaurant."

"Are you cooking for me?"

"Yes."

She tilts her head, appraising me. "And you know how to do that? Without poisoning me, I mean."

"I do," I say with a small chuckle. "I'm trying to impress you. You think I'd have you over to my apartment for dinner if I wasn't an amazing cook?"

"An amazing cook?"

"The best. No poisoning or secretly hiding food in your napkin before you leave to go eat a cheeseburger."

"I really like cheeseburgers though."

I grin. "I know. We'll get those next time. Come on. You can trust me."

I've imagined this moment so many times it's almost pathetic, but that's all it's ever been. My imagination. I never once believed I'd get this chance. But here it is and since I'm not one to squander a gift, I'm taking it. I give her my most charming smile. The one I know she secretly loves but will never openly acknowledge.

She takes my proffered hand and climbs out of the Jeep. I curb my smile before opening the door to my place. I have to work at checking my reaction when I take her coat.

Holy Jesus shit, she looks so fucking hot.

My cock instantly springs to life and if she were to so much as glance down, she'd see it. That cream sweater dress hugs her body like a second skin, showing just enough of her perfect soft curves that I have to intentionally avert my eyes before she catches me staring. The torture device stops just below mid-thigh and her wild, dark curls are all over the place from the wind.

I can't help but picture her on my kitchen counter with those silky legs spread wide, her dress bunched up around her waist, my face buried in her sweet pussy as I make her come. I can't help but picture those dark curls sprawled across my pillow as I sink inside of her. As I kiss those full bow-shaped lips before I dip down and worship her perfect tits. Lick the sensitive underside of them that I know drives her insane with pleasure.

Aria moves deeper into my apartment, and I adjust my aching cock, grateful for her preoccupation with my apartment as I get my shit together. She glances around, though she's trying to hide her curiosity by limiting her head movements. Still the same girl. Defiantly stubborn. Her hands are perched on her hips as she goes, but when she spots the piano in the far corner, she freezes.

I was wondering how she'd react to it. Her hand raises, almost reflexively as she reaches toward it with tentative, outstretched fingers. It's like she's magnetized to it. She glides across the room, her fingers lovingly touching the black and white keys without drawing sound out.

"Do you play now, Wes?"

I go into my kitchen, which is open to the great room, and get busy, pulling out ingredients, pots and pans. I chuckle softly, shaking my head. Aria's not looking in my direction, though. She can't take her eyes off the piano. "No. I rented this place mostly furnished when I moved to town. I think the previous tenant left it here and management didn't want to pay to move it."

She snorts, shaking her head like she can't believe that. I fill a pot with water and set it on the stove to boil, then I season the chicken before I get it going in the sauté pan. "You should sell this."

"Why's that?" I call over my shoulder, but she doesn't answer me. I get going on the sauce for the pasta while she stands there, staring at the piano in silence for way too long. I hate it when she gets introspective like this. It doesn't happen all that often. At least it didn't used to. I much prefer the Aria who can't stop talking. At least I know what she's thinking when she's loquacious. I add the pasta to the water and stir it around a few times. Then I remove the lid of the sauce I made and stir that too. The chicken is almost done so I pop some garlic bread in the oven.

"This piano is worth at least fifteen thousand dollars."

"Seriously?" I take out two wine glasses. I'm exhausted. I've been awake for a very long time and really, I'm dying to sleep. Except she's here, and she's letting me cook her dinner.

Sleep can wait. I have tomorrow off anyway.

The sound of a few of the keys being pressed resonates throughout the apartment, bouncing off the fourteen-foot exposed-beam ceilings. "Yup. It's a Steinway. Could use a tuning I'm sure, but it seems to be in good condition."

"You want it?" I offer only half-kidding as I set the two glasses on the counter.

She doesn't look at me, her only response is to start playing. And suddenly I'm wishing I had the foresight to have the damn thing tuned because her playing is exquisite. Aria addresses the keys with a straight back and delicately arched hands, but the sounds she's coaxing out of the piano are angry. Aggressive. Her body undulating ever so subtly with the force of her movements. She's playing what I think is Debussy, but I've never heard this song played like this. Debussy is soft, sensual and comforting. This is hard, full of rage and heated bitterness. It's fucking unbelievable and I find myself standing frozen in the center of my kitchen riveted by the woman playing music in my living room. *Jesus*.

I note she didn't play anything she could sing along with, and if things were different between us, I'd ask her to sing for me. She had a voice she enjoyed using once upon a time, but it's been forever since I've heard it. She finishes her rendition, her fingers gently resting on the keys, a stark juxtaposition to what she just created. Her chest rises and falls heavily, her cheeks are the loveliest shade of rose. The effort and emotion she put forth evident.

I internally breathe out my relief that she didn't run out the door after that and make my way back to the pasta that I'm praying isn't overcooked. I give it a stir, drain it into the colander then add it to the sauce. She's still at the piano, sitting silently, but I can feel her eyes on my back. Once that's finished, I plate it up along with the chicken.

This meal is a stretch. I know that.

I'm sure her favorite food has changed in ten years, but it was all I could think to make for her that I had the ingredients for, so I hope she likes it. Setting the plate on the counter, I wave her in, and when she catches sight of the meal I prepared for her I see the half-smile bouncing on her lips. I pour us each a glass of white wine, grab the garlic bread out of the oven, and join her at the counter.

I wanted us to sit at the dining room table so I could face her, but that felt too formal for an impromptu dinner. "You made me fettuccine Alfredo with blackened chicken and garlic bread."

It's a statement, not a question, but I answer all the same. "Yes. That okay? You didn't become a vegetarian or something, did you?"

She laughs, softly shaking her head. "No." She takes a small bite and a hum leaves her mouth. I'd love to press my lips to hers and capture the sound. "I'm just surprised you remembered it was my favorite." I shrug but don't respond because there isn't much about this woman that I've forgotten and if I tell her that, I'll scare her off. "This is really good."

I laugh, taking a sip of my wine and peeking over at her. I can't stop looking at her. It's almost surreal. Aria Davenport. Here. In my home.

I've screwed up so badly with this woman. More than once I know.

It makes me desperate in a way, having her here. I want to grab ahold of her and not let go, because I'm terrified that when she leaves, she won't come back. She's only here now because I tricked her into it.

"Why do you sound so surprised? I told you I was an amazing cook."

She smiles softly, taking a bite of her food to hide it. *I can still make you smile, Aria.* "When did you learn how to cook?"

"I dated a chef for a bit when I was in medical school. She taught me a lot, actually. It's come in handy over the years."

"Really?" She quirks an eyebrow. "What else can you make?"

I smile, leaning into her a little. "What would you like?"

Her eyes narrow, pointing the tines of her fork at me. "No flirting with me, Weston."

I hold up my hands in surrender, but I can't stop my smirk. "I wasn't flirting." I was definitely flirting.

"You're a bad liar, Doctor."

She's doing that half-smile thing she does when she's amused. Her powder blue eyes are sparkling. Damn do I love her calling me Doctor. It's a title that I hardly notice anymore, but coming out of her mouth?

Yeah, I like it a lot.

"Where's your restroom?" I point toward the hall. She wipes her mouth with her napkin before setting it down and standing up. "Thanks." She winks before heading in that direction.

"Now who's flirting?" I call after her and I'm treated to her sweet laughter. Aria has a great laugh. When she lets it out that is. These small little laughs don't really count. It's not annoying like many laughs can be. It sounds musical, and when done properly, you can't help but laugh with her.

My head inadvertently spins in the direction she just went as I realize in a moment of panic what's there. But I don't rush over to remove it while she's in the bathroom. I can play this cool. I can go for indifferent or flirtatious even.

But why?

Why pretend I don't want her?

Especially with Drew right there in the wings. Why not lay it all out for her? Let her know that this time is different. That I learn from my mistakes.

That I'm not going anywhere unless she's coming with me.

I hear the bathroom door open and close, but she doesn't return. Just as I'm about to get up to go find her, she says, "Incredible." I don't have to ask to know what she's referring to.

"Yes, you are," I reply.

Chapter Sixteen

ARIA

I stare at the painting hanging on his wall, transfixed by it. The way he said that, *yes, you are*, so cavalier, fills me with an onslaught of emotions that have been dormant for a very long time.

Ten years in fact.

I made this for him.

Well, I made it with him in mind. It was right after he left that second time and I poured my heartbreak out onto the canvas.

It was one of the first pieces I ever sold because I couldn't stand the sight of it and I couldn't stand to throw it out or burn it. I sold it to a very interested art dealer who sold it to a gallery in New York and I never paid attention to what happened to it after that.

I didn't follow the sale of it.

I didn't want to know.

In my mind, it was as gone to me as Wes was.

And now here it is, staring me in the face, living in the home of the man who is in every agonized brushstroke.

"How did you get this, Wes?" My tone dripping with accusation.

I take it in, following each line of color. It's almost odd to me how I used to paint. My style now is...well, I wouldn't necessarily say different, but more mature certainly. Less aggressive. More controlled. I lift the twelve by twelve square up from the hook it's hanging by and flip it around. I didn't write on the front of this one the way I used to. I wrote on the back of it.

It felt too intimate to write the words on the front. My pain was secret and not for public consumption, so I hid it. I've been doing that more and more if I write anything on them at all. I discovered I enjoy having people extrapolate their own interpretation of my art. To draw their own personal meaning from something I created.

But I wrote on this one.

I prop the canvas against the wall and reverently run my fingers across the lines of my pen strokes.

It was my moment of letting go. Of giving in. Of forcing my brain to accept what my heart already knew. "You are in my soul with every piece of my existence."

I haven't cried over what happened that day in a very long time. That doesn't mean I don't think about it. It was the defining moment of my life for so many reasons. It turned me into a closed-off, slow-to-trust, and emotionally unavailable person for a very long time.

In fact, Drew was the first man I allowed myself to really give in to and he hurt me.

I hate irony.

It was not as bad as what happened after Wes. I didn't bleed the same way. Maybe it was maturation or maybe I was too desensitized by the time Drew came around, but Wes shattered me that second time. I knew he was leaving. He told me so. He didn't hide anything, and he certainly didn't try to fuck me and run.

That's not what that night was about. The first time or the second time. I knew everything that was going to happen before it did. I'm the one who pushed for it to happen, but I didn't expect to feel that way.

I don't understand why he has this. Why is he making my favorite meal and asking me to a dinner that I know he considers to be a date, and why did he take me up to the roof of the hospital to watch the snow fall on the city? And why is everything happening at the same time? I mean, Jesus Christ. Josh being attacked. Drew and his declaration. And now this.

It's like my life is suddenly suffering from a bout of ADHD and my emotions are right there with it.

I hear his footsteps against the hardwood as he approaches me. I don't turn to face him. I'm not sure I can look at him yet. I just flip the painting back over and replace it on the wall.

I don't want him to comment on those words.

Suddenly they feel very private and I wish he didn't have them. Does he know they're about him?

His fingers brush my hair back from my face and I shift to him, gazing up at the man I can't seem to figure out. "Why are you hiding back here?"

"Where did you get this?" I repeat, my tone no less abrasive.

His eyes search my face, every one of my features. The way he's looking at me makes my skin warm and heat pool low in my belly. "I bought it from a gallery in New York."

"How did you know it was there?"

"Brecken."

I blow out a breath.

"You were still at home. You hadn't moved to the city yet, and I was there visiting him. He told me you had a painting in a gallery in SoHo. We went to check it out, and the moment I saw it, I knew no one else could own it but me."

I turn to stare at my painting. *His* painting. It's all color with the suggestion of two lovers in the background. They're not the focal point. In fact, you'd have to really study it to see them.

It's all about the emotion.

"I had no idea if you painted it after that night. If you wrote those words for me. But I imagined that you did, so I bought it, not even giving a shit what Brecken had to say about it."

"Why?" The word is out of my mouth before I can stop it, but I refuse to take it back.

His eyes sear into mine, the intensity in them almost too much. "Because I loved you."

I shake my head, taking a step back until I bump into the opposite wall.

It's like he just reached inside my chest, found my heart, and set it on fire. It hurts so bad to hear that.

My chest is so tight I can barely breathe. My eyes and the tip of my nose burn with my tears. But if I start to cry now, I'll never stop. If I let go and accept his words as truth, I'll be exposed. I'll succumb to all this…emotion inside of me. I'll drown in it. I'll drown in ten years of just getting by without him that has been brilliantly overshadowed by a life of professional success and other men.

My resentment is the glue that has been holding all of my shattered pieces together.

Because I resented him for leaving me that last time and having that be that. Or maybe I resented him for never coming back for me. Even though I had zero right to that resentment. I know that. I know what I told him.

And he never promised me anything.

Not once.

But in my defense, I was eighteen and alone and insecure. The guy I was in love with returned and told me he was leaving again. I wanted that night with him. I didn't really understand the implications. At least not fully. But we had…something together. A something so strong that childishly made me believe it was two-sided. That made me imagine that when the timing was right, we'd be together.

So. Stupid.

And yeah, it's been a good ten years. I've done everything I ever set out to do for myself. I met all my goals. But I loved him too and with every success I had, I wanted him to share it with me. Josh is my best friend, and I love him endlessly, but Wes and I understood each other on a different level.

Our connection existed on a different plane.

And when I lost him, I lost a piece of myself that I've never fully gotten back. So him telling me that he loved me, wrecks me. Because it's always felt easier to believe he didn't. Because if he did love me and he didn't come back for me? God, I don't know what to do with that.

"You're a goddamn liar," I choke out, my voice lined with the tears I'm desperate to tamp down.

"I'm not. I was just too much of a mess to do anything with it. That and you wanted a different life than what I could offer you."

"What does that mean, Wes?"

He stalks toward me, his eyes on mine the entire time. My heart is exploding in my chest. I can't breathe. I need to breathe and he's making that so impossible right now with his proximity and heated looks that invade every nerve in my body.

He puts his forearms on the wall on either side of my head, bracketing me in. "Do you remember what you told me that last night? You told me you were going to travel the world creating art. You told me you were going to see all the great works of art the world has. You told me that had been your lifelong dream."

"So."

"So, I wasn't traveling the world, Aria. I had two years left at Princeton then my plan was medical school. We were in different places and wanted different things. I would never have asked you to give up on that for me. You needed to go off and become the artist you are now, and I needed to get my head on straight about my family and my life and finish school. I kept my mouth shut, I bought that painting, and I bided my time. But when I was ready, you were gone. It was a mistake. All of it. I should have told you. I should have told you everything and I didn't."

"My fucking heart was broken when you left."

He winces, his body shifting closer to mine. He's right here. On top of me practically. His warmth and scent invading all my senses. Wes loved me. Shit.

"Mine too. Watching you leave my bedroom that morning and not stopping you was one of the hardest things I've ever done. One of the dumbest too." His hands clasp my face. His eyes search mine for answers I do not have. "I should never have done that. I should have stayed or brought you with me or I don't even know. All I know is that I shouldn't have walked away expecting you to wait for me the way I was waiting for you."

"I don't know you anymore." It's a whispered plea. *Don't kiss me, Wes. I'll never recover.*

"Yes, you do."

"I ned to go," I say softly, my voice catching on the last word.

"You need to stay," he says back, equally as soft. "Stay, Aria," he urges when I don't respond.

I shake my head and brush past him. That painting tipped the pendulum and now I'm swinging erratically. I just need more time to think. To get my head on straight. "I'm sorry," I call out as I find my bag and put it on my shoulder, grabbing my jacket in my hand. "I just…" I shake my head. "Thank you for dinner."

"Aria," he stops me with the force of his voice as he moves quickly across the apartment and grabs me by the arms, holding me close to him, forcing me to see him. He's done this particular move before and it sends a new swell of turbulence over me. His mouth crashes over mine, his lips claiming me.

His hands dive into my hair, cupping the back of my head as he presses himself against me without trying to deepen it. This kiss is a plea. It's desperation. It's the kiss of a rattled man who doesn't know what else to do.

I whimper into him, trying my best to fight something that feels so right I can hardly breathe.

"I don't want you to leave like this," he says against my mouth. "Stay. Play piano. Watch TV. Ignore me if that's what you need. Whatever. Just don't go. We're not done talking about this."

"If I stay tonight, I'll regret it tomorrow when it all falls apart."

He steps back, his eyes wide with shock. Beyond wounded. He releases me like I just slapped him across the face. "Is that what happened? You *regretted* what we did?"

"No, Wes. Never once. I would have regretted it if we hadn't. But I can't take the disappointment anymore. You never promised anything. I know you didn't, but I still believed you'd come back for me. Maybe that's naïve, but I couldn't help it. I thought our connection was that strong. But when I needed you to come find me, you didn't. You never came, and I had no choice but to go."

His eyebrows knit together as he stares at me. I see the confusion on his face, but that doesn't mean I understand it. Because everything I just said to him was true. I can't imagine he could see it another way. I step back farther, and his hands fall heavily to his sides. He just stares at me like he's never seen me before.

Like nothing in his world adds up.

Well, that makes two of us.

I run past him and out his door that slams with a heavy bang. That wasn't intentional, but it's too late to take it back now. My feet carry me down the steps instead of going for the elevator. When I reach the freezing night, I suck in a breath of much-needed air. And with this fresh air, comes even more confusion. I should go back to the hospital. I should go sit with Josh.

But I can't make myself do that. At least not yet.

I need to move, not sit, so instead, I walk. I walk with no purpose or direction until I see a line of restaurants and bars and realize I'm in Central Square in Cambridge. There's a bar across the street from where I'm standing. It looks like an Irish pub and that has me smiling. This city is known for them and right now, it's perfect. I quickly cross the street against traffic and open the solid wood door.

I just need to get out of the cold and gain my bearings before I can go to Josh. Or back to Wes. I want to go back to Wes, I realize. I want him to kiss me again. I want him.

A burst of warm stale air hits me and I inadvertently sigh. I'm here, so I walk up to the bar, find an open seat, and slide into it. The bartender saunters over with a friendly smile. "What are we drinkin' tonight?" He has a thick Irish brogue and well-groomed red wavy hair, and I think I like it here.

"Dirty martini?"

"Are ye askin' or tellin'?" He smirks at me, propping his elbows against the bar as he leans forward.

"Both. Dirty martini with Ketel One or something comparable."

"All right then." He stands up, smacks the lip of the bar with his fingers then leaves me to make my drink. Leaning back in my seat, I feel my phone rumble in my purse. Do I dare? I slide it out and see a text from Wes. Along with two missed calls, also from him.

Wes: ***I don't know what just happened, but we need to talk***. Just as I'm done reading it, another comes in. ***Where did you go, Aria? Tell me so I can find you.***

I debate that for a moment, before I text him the name of the bar, assuming he knows it since he doesn't live far. I want him to come find me.

It's annoyingly poetic.

The bartender slides my drink across the smooth mahogany top and just as my fingers glide around the thin stem and I verbally thank him, I feel movement at my right. And left. My head whips in both directions as my eyes grow wide and my jaw drops. My surprise isn't long-lived as anger quickly takes over.

"Well, well," Brady drawls, his hand wrapped around the dark bottle of his beer as he takes me in. "Look at what the cat dragged back."

"You look good, Aria." That's Connor. "Have to say, I never expected to see you again."

"Same here. Though that was clearly wishful thinking on my part." Both of them laugh in a surprisingly good-natured way. It only enrages me further. I take a slow pull of my drink before I set it down, lean back in my seat and cross my arms over my chest. "So, tell me," I start, my eyes flittering back and forth between both men, "what is it that Josh said that would make you two pricks go after him in a dark alleyway?"

They blanch simultaneously, exchanging quick glances with one another. I take another sip of my drink as I patiently wait them out. I really should stop drinking. Nothing good is going to come of that. My heart is pounding away in my chest, betraying my calm facade. It's so persistent I'm positive I'll have trouble hearing them over the rush of blood through my ears.

"Aria," Brady starts, adjusting his position in his chair like he's uncomfortable. "That's not—"

"Save it, you homophobic asshole," I interrupt, seething the words. "I don't want to hear your bullshit excuse. You two pricks were relentless with him in high school. You went after him time and time again. And for what? Because he's bigger than you? Better looking? Liked boys instead of girls? What was it? I seriously want to know why you felt you were entitled to try to kill my friend."

"Clearly, it doesn't matter what you think," Connor says firmly, his eyes narrowing as his lips form a thin line. "The police believe us." His arms extend out to his sides, his head scans the room quickly before returning to my direction. "Obviously, because here we sit instead of in jail." He gives a smarmy grin. "So maybe you should watch your pretty mouth before I stick my dick in it to shut you up."

My hand flies out to slap him, but Connor is faster than my alcohol saturated reflexes, and he has my wrist in a bruising grip before I even get close. He stands up, twisting my arm behind me until I'm forced to arch my back and lean forward to accommodate. Brady grabs my other arm and now he's got both of my wrists pinned behind my back. "In your dreams, you pathetic waste of life."

Both of them laugh and it's the sort of laugh that fills me with dread. It's the sort of laugh that says they're just getting started with me. "Come on, honey. Don't be like that," Brady coos in a sardonic tone, standing up behind me, breathing those words into my ear with his hot beer-saturated breath. His nose glides up the column of my neck. My stomach rolls as bile climbs up the back of my throat. "I have to admit, I've always had a thing for you. Always wanted to know what your tight body would feel like when I fuck it."

My knee comes up, colliding with Connor's balls as I struggle to get my wrist free of Brady, but there isn't much force behind the blow so all it does is piss him off more. "I like it when they fight," Connor purrs, leaning into me until his eyes are directly in front of mine. "It only turns me on more, darlin'."

"Forcing yourself onto some poor unsuspecting female is probably the only way you two losers could ever get laid," I force out. We're in a crowded bar. Though no one is paying us any attention, but if they try to drag me out of here, I'll scream. Wes. Wes is coming.

And just as that thought passes through my panic-mottled mind, I hear, "You better get your hands off her this fucking second, or I swear to God, you will both be spending the night in the hospital." Wes's thick voice is eerily calm, yet so menacing with his intent a chill runs up my spine.

Brady's hands squeeze me tighter, his smile spreading. He's always enjoyed this. Getting a rise out of Wes where I'm concerned. "We're just having some fun," Connor tells him with a cocky grin that suggests he's not afraid of Wes in the least. But his eyes tell a different story. His eyes betray his level of unrest. "I see you're still out to protect your little girlfriend. Always had a hard-on for her, didn't you?"

"You have one second."

Wes's eyes focus in on Brady, and something must pass between them because the next thing I know, Brady releases my wrists, freeing me completely. My arms swing back around in front of my body, and before anyone can say anything else, I stand up, down the rest of my cocktail in one impressive gulp, grab Connor's shoulders and knee him in the balls for a second time. Only this time, there is a hell of a lot more force behind the strike. Then I turn around and do the same to Brady.

It's not enough. I want to punch them in the face. I want to leave them both bloodied and bludgeoned the way they did to my friend, but now we're drawing a crowd and that's the last thing I need. "My drink is on them," I call out to the bartender. He's grinning at me, so I don't think he's all that upset over my little dramatic display.

Spinning on my heels, I push past Wes and leave the bar as fast as my legs will carry me.

The moment I step outside, I nearly collapse as the impact of what just occurred floods my body, the adrenaline I was coasting on fades as the alcohol takes over. My steps falter, my hand scraping against the brick exterior for support. My vision goes in and out.

Don't faint, Aria. Get it together. I can't. I suck in several deep breaths, but it's not helping to clear the fogginess.

Strong arms encircle my waist. I scream out, my elbow flying back, striking the person holding me in the stomach. He lets out a satisfying *oomph* before I realize it's Wes. He spins me around, one hand supporting my lower back, the other on my face cupping my cheek. "It's me," he asserts, forcing my wobbly gaze to his. "You have to slow your breathing, baby. You're hyperventilating." I focus on his eyes. On the way the pale green is nearly eclipsed with his black pupils. "That's right," he encourages. "Slow. Even. Breaths."

"Where are they?" I manage after a moment, realizing we're still in front of the bar.

"Nursing sore balls and black eyes," Wes says with a smirk.

"You punched them?"

He nods.

"In front of all those people?"

He shrugs, seemingly indifferent about that part of what just occurred.

"Your hand. You're a surgeon."

"I know how to punch without breaking anything. They're lucky I didn't do more. I sure as hell wanted to." He wraps his arms around me tighter, pulling me into his strong warm chest. I breathe in his scent. It's as calming as it is invigorating. That's the only way to describe it. My eyes close and I allow myself to sink into him. I had no idea comfort could feel like this.

He pulls back long before I'm ready for him to, then he lets out a long, slow, relieved breath.

"Come on," he orders, taking my hand and intertwining our fingers. I look down at our joined hands and wonder if I should put a stop to this madness now. But I think that time has come and gone. I think it's too late to pretend I don't still want him as much if not more than I did when we were young.

"Where are we going?"

"Back to my apartment."

"I should go back to the hospital."

"It's late, Aria. Josh is in good hands, and I don't want you left alone with your thoughts. I'll sleep on the couch, but you're staying with me tonight."

"And if I sneak out?"

He glances down on me with a playful smirk. The dimple in his chin more pronounced. "Go for it. As I recall, we had a lot of fun whenever we did that."

Chapter Seventeen

WES

Past

"YOU GOT ACCEPTED INTO PRINCETON TODAY," my dad says as I enter the house after a night out with my friends; what can only be my acceptance letter is balled up in his fist. "You're a traitor," he yells, his voice hitting me square in the chest. He's sitting on the third step, feet spread apart, his fist with my letter raised in the air like a threat. "You piece of shit. How could you do this behind my back?" I don't respond. "We had a plan. Alabama was our plan. *Football* was our plan."

I take a step in, swallowing so hard it rings through my ears. Through the now silent foyer. He continues to stare at me expectantly. But even as he patiently waits, I know he's just building up to his argument. That whatever I say, however I spin it, won't matter. Because I don't matter to him. I am a ballplayer. I am his do-over. I am not his son and he does not love me.

Sucking in the deepest breath of my life, I let it out slowly and say, "I don't want to play football professionally. I don't want to go to Alabama. I want to go to Princeton. I want to be a doctor."

"You're eighteen, Wes," he replies dismissively. "*Eighteen.* You have no idea what you really want. You have so much potential. You could be one of the greats, and if you go to Princeton, you'll be throwing it away," he screams the last words at me, spit flying out of his mouth, and it takes everything inside of me not to cringe. Not to shudder or draw back. Not to acquiesce and say yes, I'll go to Alabama for you. Yes, I'll throw away what I want for your dreams.

Instead, I shake my head as he stands up slowly, his feet positioned on the bottom step which gives him an extra six inches on me in total. And for a moment, for the briefest flicker of a second, I think he's going to hit me. And I decide I will hit him back if he does.

That's a powerful thing. Thinking that your father might hit you. Knowing you will defend yourself against him if he does. I stand here, and I face him, my gaze unflinching, but it is not without fear. Not without my stomach twisting into knots.

His eyes narrow and his lips form into a sneer. "Wanting to become a doctor will never happen. It's a dream bigger than you are capable of."

I had no idea a parent could say something so cruel to their child.

I'm struck with the irony of his words. There are a hell of a lot more doctors in this world than there are professional athletes. I understand why he wants me to go to Alabama. That's where he went. Both of my parents actually. They met their freshman year. Mom was a cheerleader and Dad was a quarterback and it was everything the clichés would have you believe. Until their senior year.

My father was slated to go pro. Was set to be a high number in the draft and their lives were laid out before them in perfect artful glory. Then my mother got pregnant with me. My father found out about it the day of his last game. A bowl game for that matter.

With ten minutes left on the game clock and the Crimson Tide driving down the field, my father took a helmet to his shoulder, dislocating it and injuring his brachial plexus nerve. When he landed on the turf, he did so awkwardly, unable to break his fall on that side due to the nerve damage, he fractured three bones in his hand. Did I mention this was his throwing arm? And the ball? Yeah, he fumbled that thing and the opposing team recovered it and returned it for a touchdown to eventually win the game.

That lovely football tragedy is why I can't wrap my head around his logic. Wouldn't you want your son to be a doctor over a football player? I like football. But I don't love it. Not enough to give it my all. The one hundred percent of blood, sweat, and tears it would require. I want to be a surgeon.

"There's plenty of time after football to explore other dreams. In ten years you'll regret this."

I shake my head again. "If I pursue football as a career, in ten years, I'll regret it."

"I will not pay for Princeton, boy." I know this. He already told me he wouldn't pay for Princeton. I believed him then and I believe him now. I have plans to take out loans.

"I don't need you to pay."

"You son of a bitch!" my father bellows, taking that last step and standing before me.

My fists clench in anticipation when my mother's voice startles both of us. "I'll pay for Princeton. If you won't pay for your son to go to the school he wants, to live *his* dream, then I will."

My father spins around on her and they start yelling back and forth. He won't touch her. I know this. If he was ever going to hit anyone, it would have been me. He loves my mother. Even if he resents her.

"Go to your room, Wes," my mother says, not taking her eyes off my father. I do as I'm told. I've had enough. I don't want to hear them fight about me. But wow. My mother just stood her ground for the first time ever. And she's going to pay for Princeton.

My father blames me for his injury. My father blames my mother for it too. In his heart, he believes if he hadn't been distracted with thoughts of his pregnant girlfriend, he would have shifted one way or another and deflected the hit. He would have gone on to football stardom, and he wouldn't hate everything about his life, including me.

I shut the door to my room and lock it. My hands go to my hips, my breaths ragged. Everything feels like it's spinning out of control. I don't know what to do. How to fix this. Everything I say and do feels wrong when all I want to do is make my father proud of me. That's all I've ever wanted. Being the only son of Alexander Kincaid hasn't been easy. He has expectations I've never been able to meet. And now this crap with Princeton and football. Our perfect family is crumbling, and sooner or later, the world will discover our perfection is nothing more than an illusion.

I walk over to the window and stare out at the dark night.

I sigh. Loud and hard with as much force as I can muster behind it. It fogs the glass of the window I'm standing in front of, but it does nothing to ease my tension. I want to punch something. I want to hit something so hard. My fist pounds against the glass, rattling it. No relief. There is no relief from this. If I give in to my father's demands, I'll hate him. I'll hate him, and I'll hate myself. I want to make him proud, but at what personal cost? And a part of me knows that even if I did go to Alabama and I did play football, it still wouldn't be enough. It'll never be enough. *I'll* never be enough.

The moon in the sky is big and bright and illuminates absolutely everything. An early spring moon, but still stunning. I can't help but stare at it. It's beautiful, but I'm left cold. My eyes wander over to the fence that separates our yard from Brecken's. From Aria's. I wish this was last summer and I could climb up to her roof and sit with her. Listen to her. Have her listen to me.

I never thought my world would be so complicated at the age of eighteen, but it is. Aria is part of that complication. A large part actually because the more time I spend with her, the more time I *want* to spend with her.

It's a vicious cycle.

Every day after school, I meet up with her in the art room. Sometimes Josh is there. Sometimes he isn't. On the days he isn't there, I kiss her. On the days he is, we just hang out. The three of us, as friends. It's…different. Fun. Unexpected for sure. But it's like a secret world. A lie I'm living right in front of everyone because in the light of the school day, we're strangers. Brecken has no idea.

None. And that fills me with another surge of guilt because he is one of my best friends.

But Aria insists he'd never understand. That she likes the secret. That there is nothing to tell anyway because we're not together. It's true. We can't be together. But that doesn't mean I don't want to be. I want to take her out on dates. I want to hold her hand. I want to make her mine and hide it from no one. She's almost sixteen and this could go somewhere great.

Until I leave.

My father's booming voice carries through into my room as my mother urges him to keep his voice down so I can't hear them. Too late for that. My fingers press into small indentations on the bottom of my windows. Before I can think too deeply about anything I'm doing, I push up. The window slides, but it takes a bit of effort as I haven't opened it in months. The cool night air blasts against my face, sending a shiver down my spine and a rush of adrenaline through my blood.

And for a moment, I just stare out into the muted darkness, allowing the gentle breeze to dance along my skin.

It's not enough.

Turning around, I grab a hoodie and throw it over my old worn tee. I'm already wearing flannel pajama pants and socks so I'm good to go with that. Shoes? Not necessary. Hopping out my window, I land silently. I stand against the house, surrounding myself in the shadows and twinkling lights I was just watching dance across the cold, dejected lawn.

I take a large step forward and then motion lights in my backyard illuminate, which is not an uncommon occurrence. They tend to flash on and off with regularity depending on which type of wildlife walks past them, but right now they make me visible to anyone looking out the window. I take off into a sprint, running at full speed through my backyard toward the fence line. I cannot tell where the hell I'm headed other than away from my house.

I just…I need a break. A breather. To escape.

I'm at least fifty yards back from the house and mercifully, the light shut off once I was out of its reach. Finding one of the large oak trees at the back of our property, I lean against it, panting lightly before I sink down onto the hard earth. I'm not out of breath from the run, but for some reason, I can't seem to catch it.

A motion light flickering on next door at Aria's house diverts my attention just in time to catch a flash of long dark hair whip into the night. A second later the light goes off, bathing everything in shadows once more, and I can no longer find the girl. But I know it's her. I'd know her anywhere.

I don't call out, I'm more interested in seeing what she's up to. I'm hoping she saw me and snuck out to meet me. It's a thought that has me smiling. Then I hear the sound of feet scraping up the old wooden lattice of the treehouse that our fathers built here when we were younger, maybe around eleven. I remember thinking we were too old for treehouses by that point, but after it was finished, Breck and I spent a lot of time in that house with her.

I have no idea what she's doing, but I plan on finding out.

The fence is shorter than it was when I was a kid, which is the last time I scaled the damn thing. Now it doesn't take much effort and after stepping on one of the horizontal boards that act as support on this side, I swing my body effortlessly over and land on my feet with a gentle thud.

The grass crunches beneath my socked feet as I make my way over and detect the sound of her shifting inside, probably wondering who the hell is out here. She might even think I'm her father.

"Speak low, if you speak love," she whispers down, and I can just barely see her peeking out through one of the windows. Her calling card makes me smile wider and want to shake my head at the same time. Only fucking Aria would use Shakespeare. I have no idea what story that line is from, but it can't be anything else. "Are you friend or foe?" she asks when I don't respond, and I realize she doesn't know who I am since my body is bathed in darkness and I'm wearing my hoodie.

"Friend, if you'll have me," is my only response, but I bite my lip as I say it, feeling just a bit ridiculous for it.

"Hmmm… you're not who I was expecting."

"And who were you expecting? Romeo?" I tease up into the

darkness, but really, that response pisses me off. Who the hell was she sneaking out to meet at this time of the night? It's quiet tonight and cool. My breath is fogging in front of me. *Just love me, Aria. Me and no one else. It's all I need tonight.*

"Are you coming up?" she asks instead of answering me. Without a moment's hesitation, I'm climbing the crooked, but hopefully sturdy, lattice up to the small treehouse. It bows and sways against my weight, but it holds, and I manage to crawl inside through the opening that once fit me with ease.

But I was a boy then, a small boy, and I'm certainly not now. My large body takes up the majority of the space, crowding Aria back until I'm leaning against the wood siding of the house with my knees bent up in front of me and my head resting against the sloped ceiling.

"Was this treehouse always this small?" I laugh, glancing up quickly. It's a wonder I didn't smack my head. Aria's sweet vanilla and jasmine scent permeates the room, her body heat infusing its way into me. It's distracting. Sort of like her, because I can just make out that she's wearing form-fitting leggings and a tight, long sleeve thermal shirt. No jacket.

"Breck tells me you got into Princeton today." I nod, trying to catch her expression, but not fully able to. "Congrats. You must be so excited. It's where you wanted to go, right?"

"Yup."

"Why don't you sound happy then, Wes?" *Because I'm not, Aria.* She lets out a harsh sigh, beyond frustrated with me when I don't respond. "What are you doing out here?" That raises my hackles. I had almost forgotten my jealousy by the time I got up here and saw her, but now it's back. Ugly and unwelcome.

"Who were you expecting at this hour?" I ask instead, leaning forward so I can see her better. So she's forced to see me better, too. I want to grab her and cover her small body with mine. I want to feel every gorgeous inch of her. I'm so crazy for this girl. And I need to lose myself. Forget the world. Forget what's waiting for me back in my house. She's the only one who can do that for me. The only one to ever truly get me.

"Don Pedro, of course," she says with a smile in her voice, leaning into me the way I'm leaning into her, like she's revealing a secret.

"So where is this mysterious Don Pedro then?" I make a show of glancing around. "Right now, it looks like it's just you and me, baby."

"Which is why I should make you leave. You seemed pretty damn content with Piper tonight. And the other night when I saw you and your cronies out at the Pizza Shack."

I smile. So goddamn big. I can't even hide it. It's like the weight that has been mooring me down all night is lifting. God, this girl. She's the antidote to everything. "You saw me?" She nods, her eyes narrowed. "Nothing, and I do mean nothing, is going on with Piper. But I can't help but love that you're jealous."

"I am jealous. I'm stupidly, pathetically, infuriatingly jealous and it's the last thing I want to be. Nothing good can come of me being jealous. You're leaving soon." Her eyes bore into mine, crystalline pools shining as they reflect the bright moon crawling through the small treehouse window. We fall silent, the only sound is our breathing, which is coming out just a touch faster, a touch harder. I love that she just admitted that. I don't think I've ever known a girl to admit when she's jealous or even mad. They hide shit while not hiding anything at all.

But not Aria. She just tells it like it is. At least to me.

"Would it make you feel better if I told you I'm insanely jealous of your mystery date?"

"No," she whispers back to me. "And yes," she adds on at the end, so quiet I have to strain to hear her.

"Who are you expecting, Aria?"

"Josh, of course," she says on a heavy breath like she's upset she can't continue to make me jealous. "And, if he's not here in the next five minutes, my guess is he couldn't sneak out without getting caught." She shrugs. "Or he's asleep and never got my text."

We're still the same distance apart, but it feels different. More intimate. An odd anticipatory tension is building between us. My heart starts to pound in my chest because this feels like a moment. A moment that might be so much more than the simple kissing and over-the-clothes touching we've done up until now. This feels like a moment where I can make her mine and erase every shred of doubt and jealousy from her. My fingers glide across the smooth surface of her face and into her hair.

"Here's hoping he's still asleep," I whisper, inching in ever so slightly.

"Wes?" she pants…and that sound. My dick is like a rock. Closing the small gap between our faces, I capture her lips with mine. Every time I kiss Aria, it feels like that first time. Terrifying. Exhilarating. Fucking incredible. I'm nervous. Always nervous she's going to push me away. But she doesn't. She never does. She wants me just as much as I want her. And God, is that a high.

She sighs, relaxing into me. Humming out her pleasure as her consent, I take full advantage of her lips. Suddenly, I'm ravenous. My hormones and desire kicking up to a degree they never have before. Aria's fingers dive into my hair, tugging me closer, as I demand access to her mouth. She opens for me, trying to seize control as I glide my tongue against hers, manipulating her head and lips the way I want them. Her kiss is strong and confident and sexy as hell.

Aria moans into my mouth and before I can make sense of what's happening, she climbs into my lap, straddling my thighs and dragging her nails down my scalp to my neck. I groan as she ever so gently rocks against my throbbing cock. *Jesus*. I'm going out of my mind.

"You taste like cinnamon toothpaste and smell like an erotic version of heaven."

She giggles against my mouth, making me smile against hers. I can't believe I said that out loud. My fingers slide from her neck, slipping down the back of her shirt until I reach her spandex covered ass and then I squeeze. I want, need, her so goddamn bad I'm blind to everything else but her sounds and smell and touch and my lust. "Aria," I breathe against her neck as I glide my lips along the smooth expanse down to her collarbone. My fingers run up under the fabric of her shirt, caressing against her lower back and around to her stomach where I pause.

"More, Wes," she moans, tilting her head back to give me better access to her neck. "More. I don't care about the bullshit. I just want more."

"God, yes." Grabbing her ass again, I shift us, lowering Aria to the cold floor before covering her with my warm body. This tree-house is far too small for me to stretch out, so I'm forced at an awkward angle. My head slams against the wood-paneled wall twice, eliciting a giggle from her throat. "That's not funny," I gripe, smiling widely against her lips. "It hurt."

"Aw," she coos mockingly, as she rubs the spot on the top of my head. "Poor baby. What can I do to make you feel better?"

"I can think of something."

"I bet you can." She giggles again, as I squeeze her side, my lips kissing her cheeks, nose, and lips. My fingers slide under her shirt, up to her chest, cupping and squeezing her unbelievable tits. She has no bra on and she moans as I roll her nipple between my fingers. I watch her face as I touch her, completely mesmerized. She opens her eyes, watching me back as her hand glides down my chest, over my pounding heart, to the elastic of my flannel pajama pants.

My breath catches in my chest, making her smile as she gazes up at me.

"I want you," I tell her, staring intently into her eyes. "God-dammit, Aria, I've wanted you for so long." She starts to shake her head, but I just continue on. "I know this is a lot. Whatever this is between us, it's a lot. It's real, and it's strong, and I'm leaving in a few months. I can't help that, and I can't stop it. But it's not because you're not everything I want. You are and more. I want to be with you. It's just so fucking complicated. I don't want to hurt you, baby."

Tears glisten in her eyes and I don't know if it's because she doesn't believe me or because she does.

"You're leaving in a few months and I get that. I do. I won't ask for more than you can give me." I hate that. I want to give her everything. It's just not possible yet. "This is fun, right? *Real* and fun. I want you too, Wes. I want you to be my first. But not out here. Not like this," she says, finding the strength to end this moment of stolen passion. We shouldn't be doing this out here. It's not the way I want it to be with her. Not our first time together. Not her first time. Aria is still a virgin. And though I'm dying to be that guy, I won't do that to her in a tiny tree house in the middle of the night.

"Not like this," I echo, my fingers brushing hair out of her face and curling it around her ear.

"Then we should stop."

I nod my head, my too long hair brushing my forehead. "We should stop." My dick cries out in protest. I don't think I've ever been this turned on in my life and I have to stop one of the hottest make out sessions I've ever had.

"I don't want to stop."

I smile, her thoughts echoing mine exactly. Leaning down, I kiss her. "Neither do I," I whisper into her mouth.

And then we hear it, both of us freezing instantly, wide eyes staring into the other's. How did we miss the motion light turning on? "Aria, is that you in there?" her father clips out, annoyed that he's outside in the middle of the night in the cold.

"It's me," she yells back with a big broad grin I can't help but return despite the predicament we find ourselves in. "I'm sleepwalking," she giggles at me, covering her mouth to muffle it. I can only shake my head, trying to hide my own amusement. I'm crushing her now, but I'm too afraid to move. Terrified Mr. Davenport will see me. He'll chop off my balls for sure.

"Who's up there with you?"

Oh shit. "Pfft," Aria exclaims, like the insinuation she could be up here with someone is insulting. "It's just me up here, Dad."

"Get down here, young lady, and into the house. Now," he demands.

"Yes, sir," she raps out formally, winking up at me as I shift so she can move out from under me, dropping a kiss on the corner of her mouth as I go. My head drops to the cold wood, face down. I need a minute before I can think straight. This is blue balls of the worst kind. "See you tomorrow in school, tiger," she whispers so only I can hear and then she's gone. Climbing down the steps and disappearing into the night with her father scolding her as they go.

And even though I'm in agony at the moment, everything seems better. Aria makes everything better. And one day, we'll figure this all out and she'll be mine. For good.

Chapter Eighteen

ARIA

Present Day

SLEEPING at Wes's seemed like a good idea at first. But now that we're actually walking in here, I'm not so sure. Before I ran away, things got pretty heated between us and now it's...well, it's not necessarily awkward, but it's definitely something.

Maybe tense is a better way to describe it.

Because I feel his eyes on me every few seconds. Like he's either gauging my reaction or waiting to see if I'll run again. I'm sort of strung between freaking out and doing just that so he's right on with his overzealous examination of me.

"Are you tired?" he asks quietly, the only illumination in his converted warehouse of an apartment is coming from a light in the kitchen. It's casting a soft sensual glow.

The way Wes looks at me has my heart rate going up just a bit more. Enough for me to feel the difference and make my stomach flutter. I nod. I'm not sure what this moment is between us, but I'm not about to encourage it. I've done that in the past and it didn't end so well for me.

"Come with me."

"We should ice your hand first. Does it hurt?"

"No. It's fine. Brady was the last person I hit before tonight." He grins, big and wide. "It was surreal given the situation, but no less exhilarating."

Men. I swear. All of them are such freaking cavemen.

He takes my hand and I follow behind him to the back of the apartment where his bedroom is. *His bedroom.* Now my heart is really going. Because even though I just said I was not going to encourage him, my body seems to have other ideas of what it wants. Wes releases me and goes over to a large dark wood dresser, taking something out of the drawers. His room is big with tall windows that take up an entire wall. His bed is one of those low-profile fabric types in a dark gray. And it's big. Like it seems way bigger than mine and mine is a king.

Or maybe I'm just more hyperaware of it because it feels like it's staring at me, sticking its tongue out and taunting me. The rest of his room is very bare. The walls are white and free of any art. The windows are also free of curtains. "How long have you lived here?"

When my eyes make the journey over to him, he's smirking at me. "Six months." He shrugs. "But in my defense, I'm not here a whole lot."

"I wasn't judging."

"You were. But we're not all artists and I couldn't stand to have your painting in my bedroom."

I stare at him for a moment. I have no idea what that means, but it feels like it means a lot.

"Here," he says. "Some clothes to sleep in. There is a spare toothbrush in one of the drawers of my bathroom. Help yourself to whatever you need."

"Where are you sleeping?"

"On the couch." I scrunch my nose and he laughs. "It's surprisingly comfortable. I've spent plenty of nights on it when I was too tired to make it to my bed. But if you're offering for me to sleep in here with you, my answer is yes."

"Just sleeping?"

"Just sleeping." He takes a step forward until my neck has to crane to meet his eyes. "But I don't have to. Like I said, the couch is fine if that makes you more comfortable."

"I don't want you to sleep on the couch."

"Are you okay? Do you want to talk about it?"

I shake my head. I really don't.

"If you change your mind, I'm here."

I nod this time and then he leans down to kiss my cheek. But not just my cheek. His lips glide along until they reach the corner of my mouth. He lingers there, his nose pressing into me and then he steps back, his expression swimming with so many different emotions it's hard to keep track as they flitter from one to the next. Regret. Longing. Lust. Disappointment. Relief. Contentment. The list goes on the longer I stare at him.

"I'll use the bathroom after you." Right. Bathroom. Sleep. Bed. "Good night, Aria."

"Good night, Wes."

I realize in this moment how quickly he's gotten to me again. It was the snow on the rooftop, I think. That started all of this. Or maybe he never fully went away. Maybe once someone gets under your skin they're impossible to free yourself of.

I walk into his bathroom, which is big and boasts a separate bathtub and large walk-in shower. I wonder if he's ever taken a bath. Then I laugh at that thought because Weston Kincaid is not the type of man who takes baths. At least not alone. I find that toothbrush he told me about and once I'm done with my teeth, I wash my face and change into his clothes that are a bazillion sizes too big for me.

But fuck all they smell incredible, and I definitely spend a few extra shame-filled minutes with my nose pressed into the fabric. When I exit the bathroom, he walks in, hardly glancing in my direction. I crawl into his bed and let out a mournful sigh. My eyes close and then immediately reopen as I stare blankly at the exposed ductwork along the ceiling.

That's when I hear the sound.

He exits the bathroom, flipping off the light and before I can process being alone in the dark with him, he crawls into bed next to me.

Under the fucking covers.

My head whips in his direction and my breath hitches when I see the intensity in his eyes. He's on his side, facing me and I roll to do the same. "After you crawled out of my bedroom window that last time, I lay in my bed for hours. I couldn't make myself leave. I kept hoping you'd come back. Or call. Or text. Something. But you never did. I didn't either because I couldn't make myself do it. I wanted so many things with you. So many things I didn't think could give at that point. So I went back to Princeton. I told myself it was for the best. That I, *we*, weren't ready. For months I couldn't figure out what that tightness in my chest was. I attributed it to stress. To trying to juggle too many things. To having gone home to the place my father used to live. But it wasn't any of that. It was not having you that was making me feel like I couldn't catch my breath."

I tuck my hands up by my chest. My heart so heavy it hurts.

"I made it through that year like that, because on the few occasions I had spoken to Breck, he told me you were painting and selling your work. That you were doing everything you set out to do and I didn't want to impede on that. You were happy and that made me happy. But by the following year, I became restless. I had just applied to medical schools and in my mind, I had a sort of countdown going. A mental timer that said, Twelve more months, eight more. Then six. I had just been accepted to Stanford, Harvard, and Dartmouth and was waiting on Columbia and NYU when I got to the point where I could no longer take it. I had to know.

"You see, I wanted Stanford. But I still wanted you more, which in my mind meant New York. I called Breck, and I told him I was coming for a visit. I figured at this point, I had nothing to lose. I could tell you what my plans were and see what you had to say about them. I was going to put myself out there, because in the year and a half since I had seen you, my feelings for you had not waned. If anything, they were keeping me grounded. Focused."

Wes reaches out and runs his fingers along my cheek, his eyes searching mine as he allows for his words to sink in. His words are everything. So blissfully perfect and so devastatingly painful.

"You came?" He nods. "I never saw you, Wes. And I waited for you." My voice catches on the last word as my emotions catch up to me. "For two freaking years I waited for you to come and you never did."

"It was pouring rain when I got to the city. Breck had classes all day, which was my intention, and I asked him where you were. He told me you were in one of two places. The studio where you worked from or this coffee shop near your apartment. He said you practically lived there. I didn't want to call you. I was too chicken-shit for that and I was looking to make a big entrance. I went to that coffee shop, and I sat there all day, waiting for you to come."

Tears start to leak from my eyes and onto his pillowcase. I can't stop them. Holy God, does this hurt. Part of me knows what's coming next. I don't know how I know, because I don't know exactly when he came to New York, but I can assume and that makes me close my eyes and release a shaky breath. I can't stand this.

"You did finally come in," he continues, like he's not about to rip me apart. "It was close to five in the evening and it was dark and gray and still raining. Your hair was wet because you didn't have an umbrella, but you were smiling. Laughing with the guy you were with." My eyes open to his and I see how difficult this confession is for him. "I watched for a few minutes. I couldn't look away. It had been so long, and you were so beautiful, and just as I stood up to come to you, that guy you were with leaned in and kissed you. He wrapped you up in his arms, lifted you off the ground, and kissed you again."

"So you *left*?" I'm incredulous. I dated that guy for a few months. That's it. I knew that's what he was going to say to me. But it doesn't lessen the blow.

"I told myself had nothing to offer you, Aria. You looked happy. Truth is, I was fucking jealous and hurt. It felt like you had moved on when I couldn't. You looked really fucking happy, and I wasn't, and I didn't know how to interrupt that. In all the years we had been apart, I was never like that with another woman. None of them were smart enough, or wild enough, or beautiful enough, or could recite obscure poetry from memory, or could make me feel alive.

"I was hurt and stupid and I fucked-up. I fucked-up so big with you. Again. So many mistakes I wish I could take back and undo. A month later, I saw that article in *The Times*, and then you were gone. And since then, I've had nothing but regret for the choices I made with you. Life got away from me somehow and then it was too late. You have every right to be mad at me. To accuse me of not coming for you or being open with you or fighting for you. I wish I could go back and do everything differently." He cups my face in his hand. "Please, you have to know, I want a second chance with you."

A sob breaks free and I bury my head in his neck, shaking with my silent tears. He holds me. He holds me so tight, and finally, when I manage to get control, he pulls back and wipes away my residual tears.

"What are you thinking?" he asks softly, his eyes affectionately staring into mine.

"You want my ugly truth?"

"Of course."

"I've been mad at you for a very long time. Even though I never felt I had a right to my anger."

"Do you want mine?"

"Of course."

"I've loved you for a very long time. Even though I never felt I had a right to deserve you." His eyes search mine, endless pools of green that I lose myself in. "Fall in love with me again, Aria." My eyes close. I can't handle the expression on his face. "Open your eyes and look at me." I do, but it's nearly impossible to maintain. "I know you loved me once. You never told me. Not outright. But I know you felt it too. Fall in love with me again," he repeats. "I'm not going anywhere. This is real and it's happening and I'm not going anywhere."

His lips crash into mine. Long. Deep. Perfect. He came to New York for me. And all this time, he's been unhappy. He's been missing me. He's been planning and plotting for us while I've gone on, living my life and loving another man.

Drew. I push thoughts of him aside.

I want Weston Kincaid. I want him inside my body.

I want him to own me, body and soul. I want to look into his eyes as we come together. I want to feel him in every sore muscle when I get out of bed tomorrow and I want to run and tell my friends about our wild night together.

"Aria, you were attacked tonight," he whispers against me, trying to stop this before it continues to the place we both want it to go. I shake my head, rolling on top of him, his hands drop to my hips, before he sits up in a flash. We're eye to eye and nose to nose as he pins me with a look that instantly has my panties wet.

I can't stop myself from rocking into him.

God, he's so hard. So big. So perfect.

He groans, his eyes closing for a moment as pleasure surges through him before he opens them again, his grip on my hips stopping any further movement. "You were attacked tonight, baby," he repeats. "I'm not doing this with you. We still have too much to figure out and I'm not going to blow it this time. I want you, Aria. I'm crazy about you, but I need you to be sure before I take you the way I need to take you."

If I have sex with him again, there will be no going back. I will be all-in. Is that what I want? Is that what I'm ready for with him?

"You're right," I tell him, looping my arms around his neck.

He smirks, rubbing his lips against mine. "What are you doing?"

I grind down on him. "What does it feel like?"

"It feels like heaven. But I don't want to take advantage."

"You can stop being a Boy Scout."

He laughs incredulously only to groan as I grind against his cock again. "A Boy Scout? I'm dying to watch you come. You think being a good guy is fun for me?"

I laugh, shaking my head, dropping my forehead to his shoulder. "Then stop being the good guy." I pull back and meet his eyes.

Before I can think about what he's doing, I'm on my back and he's hovering over me. "I've fantasized about this so many times, you'd probably never speak to me again if I told you. So, I'm going to make you feel good, and you're going to shut that big, beautiful brain off. Tell me yes."

Chapter Nineteen

WES

She stares into my eyes. Stares into me with those blue orbs that are bursting with desire and love and everything I've been missing for the last ten years. "Yes." She whispers the word, but it goes straight through me like she screamed it from the top of her lungs.

My heart thunders in my chest as I dip down, capturing her mouth with mine, our tongues lashing desperately against each other. Hunger swirls through me, making me greedy. Ravenous. Unapologetically lustful.

With my hand in her hair, I tilt my head, plundering deeper into her mouth. The throaty sounds she makes drive me wild and I press down on her, needing to be so much closer. I could spend forever just kissing her. Forever losing myself in her taste and scent.

So many years I've wasted without her.

Her legs wrap around my back and our bodies hum together in a mutual grind as I devour her with greedy kisses.

Sliding my hand under the oversized tee she's wearing, I cup her bare breast, squeezing her hard enough to make her moan into my mouth. Senses scatter at the feel of her, soft and swollen against my palm. She arches into me, begging for more. My tongue traces the line of her lips before sweeping back in, flicking her tongue as I flick her nipple, rolling it between my fingers.

Her body quivers as my mouth leaves hers, my lips trailing down her neck, sucking and nibbling on her as my hand slides the fabric of the shirt up her chest. Lifting her breast, my lips capture her nipple, sucking the gorgeously hard peak into my mouth.

She grabs a fistful of my hair, rocking into me, seeking relief. "Don't stop," she whimpers as I draw back, blowing on her before diving back down.

"Never," I groan against her, unable to control myself. God, she's so perfect. "So beautiful," I whisper into her heated flesh. Every part of me aches for her.

I watch enraptured as her eyes close. As she succumbs. As she gives into my touch completely. To the way my warm, wet lips caress her overheated skin. To the pleasure of my fingers as they dip into the boxers she's wearing, straight into her panties, sliding up and down her slit.

A growl sears past my lips when I feel how soaked she is, the sound vibrating across her nipple where my mouth is still consuming her. Air trembles past her lips as my thumb finds her sensitive clit, pressing in, and moving around in circles.

Aria angles up, ripping her shirt from over head, and throwing it away. I do the same with mine before I get to work on the boxers and panties she's wearing. My gaze eats her up, taking in every inch it can.

A flame bursts forth inside me, igniting low in my belly. This woman…

Two fingers slip into her hot pussy, rocking against her as she rocks against my hand. My thumb continues to work her clit, as I dip in and out of her at a pace that quickly works her up into a frenzy. Moans and breathy sighs and heated whimpers escape her lips, one tumbling after the other.

"You're so tight, Aria. I can't wait to slip my cock inside you." I bite her nipples. The underside of her full, gorgeous tits. "You'll take it. All of it. Any way I want to give it to you."

"Yes," she pants. "That's exactly what I want. Your dirty words and your big cock and your fingers making me fly higher."

Jesus Christ.

My hand rubs her clit harder. Faster. My fingers finding that perfect spot inside her with a simple crook. The smell of her arousal fills the air, making my mouth pool with saliva. I lick my lips, desperate to taste her, but my need to watch her wins out. Her head is drawn back, her eyes closed, and I stare mindlessly as she looses control.

She's so close. Right there.

"Come for me, Aria. Come all over my fingers." I pump into her harder, faster, flicking her nub as she rips at the pillow, the back of my neck, the sheets. Whatever she can grasp. "So hot. So wet. All for me."

That's it. That's all it takes.

She shatters. The orgasm rising up and ripping through her like a tidal wave. My mouth finds hers, swallowing her cries, and when the last of the spasms and aftershocks subside, I kiss her deeper, sweeter.

"That was..." Words fail her. She opens her eyes slowly, catching on mine, taking in what is very likely a dopey smile on my face.

"Good? Amazing? Perfect? Out-of-this-world fantastic?" My fingers covered in her cum slip into my mouth, licking them clean with a satisfied gleam to my eyes.

She watches me taste her, her eyes dark and dirty. "Huh? What?"

I laugh, shifting back over her, staring down into her like I've never seen her before. Like it's for the first time. "Speechless? I'll take it." I bend down and press a kiss to her lips, but she pulls me back, studying my face. A finger glides along the purple bruises beneath my eyes.

"When was the last time you slept, Doctor?"

I half-smirk. "Sleep? Never heard of it."

She laughs, kissing my jaw. "We have more to talk about."

"We do. And as much as I'd like to talk and then fuck you into tomorrow, I think it's already tomorrow. Are you wanting to stop?"

"No. I don't want to stop?"

I chuckle. "Are you sure about that? You don't sound sure. I just want to hold you while we sleep. Anything else is gravy."

She shakes her head. "No stopping. I want you."

"If I take you, Aria, there will be no going back. You'll be mine. For real this time. No more hiding. No more pretending. No more leaving. Mine."

"You're the one still talking. I'm the one lying here naked waiting on you to put this—" She squeezes my cock through my pajama pants, eliciting a groan from the back of my throat. "—inside me."

"Aria."

"Wes," she mocks my tone. "I know what you're saying. Do you see me running?"

Not yet, I think. Knowing Aria she'll likely freak out later. She's an in the moment girl. But if she runs, I'll chase her.

With that thought in my mind, my lips capture hers once more. Eating from her mouth in long, hungry kisses that leave us both breathless. My cock strains against her, her fists grasping the waist of my pants and tugging them down.

My tongue whirls around her nipple, sucking it in and trailing down. "Wes," she demands breathily. "I need you inside me. Now."

The corner of my mouth curves into a smirk as I spread her legs and lick her dripping pussy. She cries out, fisting my hair, and tugging harshly against the strands.

"Too much. Too sensitive."

I blow on her.

"Fuck!"

I rise up onto my knees, grab her hips, lift them off the bed, and sink inside of her. Another fuck streams from her lips followed by a low, throaty moan.

My hips buck against her, warm, so fucking wet, hot, needy, clenching. At this rate, I won't last more than a few minutes. I blow out a breath. My cock throbs inside her as I still my body, my hands finding the bed on either side of her head.

I thrust. Once. Twice. Rocking into her, my eyes entangle with hers. She whimpers at the intrusion, gasps as I drive in further, deeper, holding her gaze to mine because she will come looking at me.

Shivers explode down my back, snaking along my skin. Our foreheads meet as I roll my body repeatedly into hers with deep, heavy, long thrusts.

"Is that what you wanted? To be full with my cock?"

"Yes." A gasp. A moan. A plea.

I've never been like this with any other woman. Aria makes me an animal. Possessive. Feral. Predatory. I have to claim her body. Own it. Tell her every filthy thought as it hits my mind. I want to consume her and own her. The latter fantastical since she already owns me.

"What are you doing to me?"

"Stealing your soul," she replies on a sharp intake of air. "Same as you're doing to me."

"Thank god."

Feet digging into the mattress, I unleash holy hell on her body. I take. I ransack. I pillage. My body claims hers, digging and diving in deeper than I've ever been inside anyone before her.

She is it.

My kingdom and my precipice.

Breathless gasps become cries of pleasure. Moans of bliss turn to dirty curses as I take her, take her, *take* her. There is nothing slow or sensual about this. That will come another time. Our greed. Our hunger. Our years apart dictate this pace. There is no denying it. No surviving it unscathed.

I need this woman more than I've ever needed anything or anyone. I want her air in my lungs. Her lips on my skin. Her face on my chest. Her hair in my hands.

"Aria. You. This."

"Yes. Yes. *Yes!*"

She comes on a shout. A bellow. Her body trembling and

clenching me so tightly my breath stalls in my lungs. Fireworks seize my eyes and I follow her over the edge, shouting out my own release before collapsing, falling into her.

Her arms encircle my neck, her body clinging to mine, holding me so close.

I never want her to let go.

Ever.

Slowly, steadily our breathing returns to normal. I get up, returning with a warm cloth and cleaning her up. Then I climb back in bed, hauling her small body against me, kissing her lips, her forehead, her nose, her breasts.

"So sleep then?"

"Sleep." We both stare at each other and smile. Leaning in, I kiss her lips. "See you in the morning, baby," I whisper as I wrap her up in his arms, my body pressed impossibly close against hers.

"Night." Her voice is distant like she's already half-asleep. A second later, she's out. I can't imagine the exhaustion that sits on her shoulders.

Adjusting her small frame, I tuck her in. Needing to feel her. Uneasiness creeps up my spine. My fight for her isn't done. I already know that despite what she says.

Chapter Twenty

ARIA

The moment I open my eyes, I realize three things simultaneously. One, I'm in Wes's bed, completely and utterly naked. Two, he's listening to country music and humming along to it. Three, he's cooking something that smells out of this world amazing.

I can't figure out which one of these things has me smiling the most. Then his words from last night come crashing down on me with the force of a truck hitting a bunny. I replay them in exact detail. They feel just as excruciating and just as marvelous as they did then.

Mine.

I shouldn't have slept here. I shouldn't have slept with him. But I don't regret a second of our night together. It's him. It's always been him. I don't even care if I'm giving in too quickly to him. Life is short. And it's tragic. And unexpected.

It steals people from you. It takes and it takes and it takes. I've loved Wes my whole life. Even when I hated him, I loved him. So I could fight this. I could fight him. But everything inside of me is telling me to do the opposite. It's telling me to run to him and never look back.

I slept in Weston Kincaid's arms last night after he fucked me senseless. Hell, after he fucked me into an unconscious state.

I giggle. Like out loud as I roll on my back and make snow angels under his blanket. Then I pause as I think back on Brady and Connor. I don't even know how things got that far with them. How I allowed myself to be in that position. Last night may, in fact, be one of the most fucked-up nights of my life.

Not including Wes.

And now that the fear has all but dissipated, I'm so goddamn angry. Me aside, I want them to pay for what they did to Josh. How could it not be them? They didn't even deny it. If anything, they proved they're very capable of violence. And against women? I don't know if that was bullshit talk or not. But it's easily one of the most unsettling things anyone has ever said and done to me. My plan today is to talk to Tyler about it and see what he recommends. He's a lawyer, which automatically makes him more knowledgeable about these matters than I am.

Climbing out of Wes's extremely comfortable bed, I quickly change back into what I was wearing last night. I call the hospital and they inform me that Josh is doing well and that they're thinking about reducing his sedation later today. That's the best news I've had in a few days.

Creeping out of Wes's room, I hesitantly pad toward the kitchen. It's only a little after eight in the morning. Typically, I'm not up this early. I'm a late-night worker and a sleep-in sort of girl. But I want to get out of this confusing place.

I want to get back to Josh.

My eyes catch on my painting hanging on his wall.

Wes was my first love. Do people ever truly get over those? Especially when things are left unfinished?

I don't know.

But if I had to guess, given the thoughts I'm having, and the way he makes me feel when I'm with him, and the way I reacted to the things he said to me, I'd say no they don't.

I cannot fall for Wes again.

I can't.

I laugh. Kinda crazy out loud. *Too late, bitch,* my inner psyche chides. No kidding. But for real…

He likes country music, and I like indie rock. He's a doctor, and I'm an artist. I need to tell him where my mind is. That's what grown-ups do. They communicate and shit.

I'm stalling. It's pathetic.

The moment I gaze at Wes's muscled back straining against the soft fabric of his shirt, I wonder if I'll ever be brave enough to start that talk. I like this Wes. There, I admit it. Because he made me feel good in bed last night. The way his eyes held mine. The way his body owned me. Love. It was dirty and raw and passionate, but it was filled with so much love.

He made me my favorite dinner last night, and this morning he's making me my favorite breakfast. He came to my rescue at the bar.

And he asked me to fall in love with him again.

I mean, Jesus. How can I not?

He's still humming along to some god-awful country song that he clearly knows and loves. I love that he loves country music, and I love indie rock. I love that he's singing along to it and I can't because I don't know the words. I love that he's a doctor, and I'm an artist. Dammit, Wes. Don't do this to me again. Don't make me fall for you and then leave me a pitiful, heartbroken mess. I barely survived.

"Smells good," I say, stepping into the kitchen. I don't startle him. I wonder if he knew I was there watching him. He's smiling at me in a way that suggests he did.

"Morning, beautiful," he says, leaning in to kiss my lips like we've been doing this forever. Him making me breakfast and calling me beautiful and kissing me. When did we transition to this point? To this level of intimacy and familiarity. *After you let him fuck you in his bed.* Touché. "You still like blueberry pancakes, right?"

I nod. That's all I'm capable of because there is a very large lump in my throat obstructing my airway at the moment. "I need to get over to the hospital," I mention after I clear my throat, changing the subject and going back to business mode.

He frowns, and I can't help but feel just a bit bad about that. Okay. Fine. A lot bad.

"I take it I can't persuade you to spend the day with me then." I shake my head no and he gives a good-natured shrug. "I figured, but thought I'd try, anyway. How are you feeling after last night?" He gives me an impish grin. "I mean about Connor and Brady."

"Angry."

His eyes bore into mine. "I shouldn't have let you leave like that. I should have also done more than let them get away with a punch and a threat."

"It's not your fault. But you can't tell me you still don't think they hurt Josh."

His hand comes up to the back of his neck and he squeezes. Wow, it's amazing how some things never change. "I guess not," he says slowly like he still doesn't want to believe that people he's known his entire life are capable of such a thing. "Here," he says, plating two pancakes for me, "sit down and eat." I do as instructed. The considerate bastard even has butter and real maple syrup waiting on me. And coffee.

I cut into the pancakes and take a bite, the flavors exploding in my mouth. "Wow," I say through a mouthful of food and not even caring. "These are amazing. I might have to hire you to be my personal chef."

"I'll cook for you anytime." The way he says that has me looking down at my plate to hide my warming cheeks. "Since you won't spend the day with me, how about dinner tonight?"

"Wes—"

"I have a place in mind I'd like to take you. Seven-thirty. I'll pick you up."

"Did you get enough sleep?"

He grins, continuing on like I didn't interrupt him. "I want to know what happened to you. Where you went. What you did in those years we were apart. Your brother never said and I never asked. Incidentally I want to tell Brecken we're together."

"Seriously," I grumble, ignoring his comment about wanting to know about my life. The life he missed. "That's a no on telling

Brecken anything yet." I shake my head, studying him. "You're like a manic Easter bunny. What's the longest you've ever gone without sleep?"

Wes tilts his head to the side as if he's giving my question some genuine thought. "Hmmm… I don't know. Maybe somewhere around thirty hours. I've done shifts that have been longer than that, but I can usually manage a few hours here and there."

"And they let you cut people open like that?"

He throws me a cheeky grin. "Should I tell you how many sleepless hours I was on when Josh was wheeled into my OR?"

I shake my head adamantly. "Absolutely not. I might throat punch you." He laughs, leaning over and kissing the side of my head. "Why are you standing?"

"So I can look at you while I eat," he explains without any hint of sarcasm or artifice.

I have no response for that, which is a growing theme as this morning with him progresses. Yet oddly enough, it's not awkward. It's surprisingly comfortable. "What do you do on your days off, Doctor?"

A crooked smile twitches up the corner of his lips, making that dimple in his chin sink in deeper. "If I told you it would blow your mind. It's that crazy."

"Oh, yeah?" I laugh.

He nods, his eyes sparkling. "First, I'm going to start some laundry. After that, I'm going to Whole Foods to get some groceries and a few other things I need. I'll probably pay some bills, and then if I'm lucky, I might get over to the rock climbing gym for an hour or two."

"You rock climb?"

His smile becomes so big, his whole face lights up. "Yeah. You wanna come? I can teach you."

"No. I just didn't know that was something you did."

"Well," he begins, popping a bite of pancake into his mouth. I can't help but watch his mouth as he chews. The damn sexy thing is like a magnet for my eyes. He catches me doing it and winks. I forgot how playful Wes can be. How he likes to flirt. "I didn't start until I was in medical school and needed a way to reduce the stress."

"And now you're a trauma surgeon."

"Now I'm a trauma surgeon. So you can imagine I climb a lot." I scrunch my eyebrows in confusion. "It's a stress reliever for me, Aria. I think we already covered that. Keep up."

"Tool."

He laughs, his head rolling back and everything. "*Tool*? What are we, back in high school? Who says tool anymore?"

"I do," I tell him with mock indignation. I don't think my grin is selling it, though. I take another bite to try to hide it. I have a bad feeling I'm going to finish all of these pancakes and I most definitely finished all of my pasta last night. If I continue to let this man cook for me, I'll easily put on five pounds in a week. "Tool might, in fact, be one of the most underused disses around."

"*Disses*." He laughs harder if that's even possible. "Holy shit, I've missed you so fucking much."

He says that in a light way. In a way that goes along with his laughter. But it hits me in the gut and now I'm no longer smiling. I'm just staring at him, once again replaying everything that happened between us last night. And when he realizes what he just said, his laughter dies and his expression sobers. He rounds the counter in the blink of an eye until he's standing directly in front of me. Wes cups my jaw with both hands, his thumbs brushing up and down my cheeks as he gazes down into me.

"So fucking much," he whispers. His face descends the rest of the minuscule distance, and then his lips are on mine, full and soft. They move slowly against me like he's getting reacquainted and has all the time in the world to do so. But that lazy, languid kiss quickly morphs into more as one hand snakes into my hair and the other around my waist. Wes tugs me against him, his lips parting mine as his tongue seeks entrance into my mouth.

He tastes sweet and his kisses feel like sin.

It's so good that I can't help the moan that scurries its way out of the back of my throat. Wes growls something unintelligible as his other hand that is still cupping the back of my head pulls my hair. Not a lot. Just enough to let me know I'm driving him wild.

It's quite possibly the sexiest thing ever. His kiss is commanding and passionate. It has my toes curling in my shoes, my eyes in the back of my head. It has me moaning into his mouth again within seconds.

This is pure heat.

Unadulterated lust.

Painfully erotic.

His mouth dominates everything as his tongue invades, moving against mine until I'm so dizzy with need, I'm scratching at his shirt.

He's always had this effect on me. Even when we were young. It was like the moment his lips touched mine, every argument I could ever conjure against him instantly evaporated. And his kisses have only gotten better with time and age.

Wes pulls back, his teeth grazing my lower lip as he does. His forehead drops to mine and our eyes lock as we try to regain control, our breaths ragged. "Dinner, Aria. You need to say yes because I don't have a lot of time to convince you."

"Convince me of what?"

"To finally be mine."

Chapter Twenty-One

ARIA

I didn't respond. He wants me to be his and I am. I know I am. Body, soul, they're his. But my mind…she's having some trouble getting there. She's anxious and cautious. She's conflicted, teetering back and forth on a perpetual seesaw.

I want to stay here with him. I want to spend the day with Wes. But I also know myself enough to know I need space from him to take everything in that's happened. It's all come on so quickly and I need to regain my bearings.

Plus, Josh is waiting on me.

I told Wes I was going to shower and that's what I did. I locked the door and gave myself a few minutes of alone time. But I'm not alone. I'm in his place. Everything is Wes, all around me.

Stepping out of the shower, I wrap a towel around my body and another around my hair. Unfortunately I have nothing clean to put on and I can't exactly waltz into the hospital wearing Wes's clothes. Brushing my hair out quickly, I stare down at the soaking wet strands, wondering if Wes has a blow dryer. It's freezing outside and I hate leaving with wet hair.

I should go home. I should have gone home straight away. I

should have showered in my shower and put on clean clothes and ugh. What am I doing here?

Picking up the dress I wore last night, I take it in for a moment. It's wrinkled and way too dressy for a day in the ICU.

It seems I don't have a choice since this is all I've got, but just as I go to undo my towel and put the dress on, an unexpected sound stops me in my tracks. It's a light tap on the door.

"Aria?"

"Yeah?" I nearly giggle. I feel like a teenager all over again.

"I ran out and grabbed you some things."

I blink a few times, staring down at the dress in my hand. How long was I in the shower for? "Some things?" I parrot.

"Yes. Um. I hope that's okay. There's a store around the corner from here and I grabbed you a change of clothes and then I ran into the pharmacy and got you some things like deodorant and a face cream the woman who worked there helped me pick out. I also got you a blow dryer since it's so cold out and I didn't have one."

Was he reading my mind?

I run over to the door and fling it open, finding the man on the other side holding shoppings bags. For me.

And for the longest minute, I just stare down at him, unable to wrap my head around Weston Kincaid running out to the store to get me a change of clothing. To get me basic toiletries. He did all that. For me.

Because I think he loves me.

I think he's always loved me and he never stopped. Same as me.

I was devastated when he left. Because even though I tried like hell to hold myself at bay, it was an act of futility. I was in love with him long before he ever pressed his lips to mine. And to me, it never felt like adolescent love. It felt like the love the Brontë sisters and Jane Austen wrote about. It felt like the love I see between my parents. It felt real, and his loss was crushing even if I was prepared for it.

I cried a lot after he left.

A lot.

I didn't date anyone else for a very long time. Not until after I graduated high school and moved to New York. Not until I knew he wasn't coming back, wasn't going to call or email or even text more than that once. Not until I knew he was lost to me. I knew that's how it would be. Especially after his father died so suddenly.

I knew it would be too painful for him to return home.

Staying in contact wouldn't have been good for either of us. Especially me. I was an open wound where he was concerned, and I needed to sever the ties that held me to him. I knew the pain I would feel at him leaving would be rendered a million times worse if I held on to him.

Yet, I couldn't help but hope.

Wes was sad about it. He didn't try to hide it even if he knew it was the right thing. His kisses as he said goodbye to me that final time still fill my memories. But even though I never expected to stay in touch, I still expected him to come home occasionally.

And when he didn't, I couldn't decide if I was relieved or not.

I know his family fell apart. I know what his father did. She told my mom the truth, and I overheard them as she cried about it late one night.

Brecken told me he was a mess. That it had devastated him. There wasn't much I could offer him. I was young and living at home, and he was there, and we agreed we wouldn't make unrealistic expectations or demands on the other when we were so far away. In two totally different worlds. I still let him know he had my heart. Owned it is a more accurate description.

And now here he is, staring at me right back, those green eyes piercing right back into my soul without any resistance. I wasn't prepared. I hadn't built up my defenses. Dammit, how could he be so thoughtful?

"I can't tell if this silent staring thing is a good thing or a bad thing." He gives me a crooked smile, that dimple in his chin more pronounced.

"Good thing. I think."

That crooked grin I like so much turns into a full-blown smile and now I can't decide which one I like more. "I like you in my towel. I like you smelling like my shampoo and body wash."

"Caveman."

He chuckles, and I feel that damn chuckle in the pit of my stomach. I feel that damn chuckle on every surface of my skin that suddenly erupts in chills. Stupid traitorous body.

"What about you there, tiger?" His eyes sparkle at the use of my pet name for him. One I haven't used on him in a zillion years. "Are you going to shower?"

"Can I convince you to get back in with me?"

I bite into my lip, shaking my head. He's too good looking. It's that chin dimple. And the green eyes. And the thick head of blondish hair.

And the body.

Shit. That body.

I need to stop.

He brushes past me, into the room. "I got you a pair of jeans, a long sleeve shirt. In black, of course." He throws me a wink over his shoulder. "A pair of new panties and a bra. And before you start yelling at me for that, yes, I know your size. I've memorized everything about you. Every beautiful curve."

His eyes do a slow sweep of my body, taking it in inch by freaking inch and when he reaches my eyes, he just stares at me.

"Shit," he mutters, rubbing his chest absentmindedly with his fist. "God, Aria. If this is what ten years does to you, I don't think my heart will be able to handle another minute apart."

I'm dying to tell him that it doesn't have to. But I don't. I keep my mouth shut because our situation really isn't that simple.

"I've missed you," he says, turning to face me, the clothes on the bed forgotten.

"Me too."

"But you're still unsure."

He crosses the room, his hands grasping my bare shoulders, the towel tucked in tight, but that's all that separating us. This simple towel that could slip off so easily.

I pull back, our faces inches apart, and I shake my head. "I'm… I don't know what I am. I just know you're in my head. Back inside of me in ways I can't fight."

His lips crash into mine, his tongue sweeping in as he devours me. Wes's large hands cup and squeeze my ass over the towel, pressing me against his hardening cock. The sensation rattles me from the inside out and I can't stop how my body rocks against him.

"Tell me to stop, Aria. I'm crazed right now. I've thought about you for ten years, and now you're here and you look like this, and I'm crazed. I want you so fucking bad, but I don't want you to think that's all this is. It's not. I want *you*. I want us."

"Don't stop." Suddenly, I want this, him, more than my next breath. I don't care about the implications. I lived through losing him once, I can live through it again. I hope. Because I'm going for it. I will not squander this moment. If I do, I'll always regret it, and regret is for suckers.

"Aria," he breathes, losing his internal battle quickly, his mouth all over me.

I run my hands along the muscular columns of his corded arms and into his hair where I tug. He groans, his tongue taking over this kiss, and his resistance grows smaller by the second.

"Wes."

"God, Aria. I can't think when I'm around you. All I can do is feel. Something I've avoided my entire life, but with you, it's effortless."

It hits me then. The way he says that. The truth behind his words. It's true. Wes has avoided feeling his entire life. But with me, now, here, he's putting it all out there. Holding nothing of himself back.

I never stood a chance.

In a flash he has me against the wall, my legs wrapped around his waist. He groans into my mouth, his fingers frantically tugging at the towel, loosening it and throwing it away.

I help him out of his shirt, tossing it to the floor near where the towel ended up. Then his mouth is back on mine.

"Pants," I rasp against him.

"I don't want to rush this." He kisses a trail down my jaw. "I want to take my time with you. I want to worship your beautiful breasts. Admire the way they overflow out of my hands. I want to explore every dip and curve of your body. Taste every delicious inch. Reacquaint myself with the girl I've never been able to get over."

Dammit!

"Bed," I demand instead.

He sighs, almost like he's frustrated. I'm wound up and needy, and he's all patient. I point to my left like it's an order and he laughs at my persistence.

"You've grown very bossy," he quips.

"And that's a bad thing?"

"No. But I like to be in control."

Having control. Making decisions. Living with the consequences. It's what he's become. A precise machine.

"You take all my control from me. It slips through your fingers like fine grains of sand. You give my heart a beat. A pulse. A rhythm that's been absent since that fateful night ten years ago."

Jesus.

"I don't want to waste time." My eyes, so very serious, beseech his. "We only get moments, Wes. That's all life is. One moment that bleeds into another and this one is ours. We've lost so many already."

"Fuck. You're absolute magic."

He tosses his onto his bed and with a laugh I bounce only for it to quickly die as Wes's heated eyes take me in.

He stands here and just…looks at me. The color rise up my cheeks, visible, even in this very dim light, but I don't care.

"Spread your legs," he commands. That pink turns to rose, but without a word and on a nervous breath, I slide my thighs open as far as they can go.

"Pants," I direct because even if he likes control, I want my own say. His hands go for the hem of his track pants and mine skim down the skin of my taut stomach, hovering over my mound.

He sucks in a rush of air, his pupils blown out as he watches my fingers slowly start to rub myself.

I bite my lip, and that action, coupled with my fingers toying with my clit rips a primal growl from deep within his chest. The things he's going to do to me. I can already see it.

"Have you missed me, Aria? Thought about me inside your body? I have, baby. I've jerked off to you so many times. Last night was just a sample. Just the start. You're the one."

"The one?"

"The one you never get over."

My eyes close slowly, before they reopen to half-mast. I release a shaky breath. "I want to feel you kiss my entire body," I say, and that's it. That one naughty line from my lips is all it takes for him to be a goner.

All his patience shreds as he comes apart at the seams.

"Can I taste you? I need to taste you."

I don't get the chance to reply. In a second he's shoving me back, deeper into the middle of the bed and then he's climbing on. His pants gone, his body poised over mine, his gaze feasting on my wet pussy.

In a flash, he has me spread, my thighs wide, and he licks my pussy from my ass to my mound. My head falls back, as I moan loudly, my hands fisting the sheets before they find his hair and tug hard. It drives his insane.

"I can't get enough," he grunts into me, licking me harder. "Will never get enough."

He licks my clit, sucking it into his mouth as he slides a finger into my tight, dripping heat. His tongue flicks back and forth as his fingers pump in and out over and over, his pace relentless.

I gulp down one breath, followed by the other. It's too much. Too intense. I'm wild. Crying out as I yank harder on his hair, wrapping my thighs around his head. Grinding my hips up, fucking his face, no longer in control.

With reckless fucking abandon.

It doesn't take me long. His mouth and fingers are working me, his sounds of pleasure only spurring me on.

"So hot. So goddamn sweet. Absolute perfection," he purrs into me, licking every drop of me. And that does it. I lose my mind, I come impossibly hard. Without limits. Without restraint. Crying out his damn name.

My body writhes against his mouth until I'm spent. Falling back limply against the bed, I giggle, panting as my eyes close.

"Wow, that was…" And then I laugh again. "I think I am for once, speechless."

Climbing on top of me, he presses his weight onto his elbows and gazes down at me.

"I didn't get to do that with you before."

"No. You most definitely did not. I would have never let you leave for Princeton if you had."

He smiles, dipping in to kiss my lips, making me taste myself on him. "And I haven't even gotten started."

"Oh," I gasp as his mouth covers one of my nipples. "Okay. Um. Yeah, I'm gonna need you to fuck me now, because I'm like two seconds away from combusting. *Again*," I emphasize, needing to drill that point home.

He laughs, his breath causing chills to erupt across my skin and my nipples to pebble up.

"I love how responsive you are to me. To my touch."

I am. He's right. He may be familiar in so many ways, but everything we're experiencing right now is new.

He removes a condom from my nightstand drawer and covers his beautiful cock. I lick my lips. God, I want him.

"I want you on top of me," I whisper, suddenly very serious. "I know that's not the sexiest position in the world, but I want to feel your body cover mine. At least to start."

At a loss for words, he lowers his body to mine, kisses my mouth, and slide inside of me. We moan together, our eyes locked as we move like the last ten years apart never happened. Like that first time led to a million others. That's how perfect this is with us.

He pumps inside of me, in and out, my hips thrusting to meet his, our eyes never straying. I let him see all of me, and he does the same, and nothing has ever felt this good. Nothing.

My legs wrap around my waist, his hand gliding down to cup

my ass, lifting me enough that he's able to sink in deeper. I cry out, my head rolling back and to the side as he fucks me.

Loves me.

"You're so beautiful," he moans. "Everything about you was made for me and me alone."

"Harder," I pant and he gives it to me just the way I want. Our rhythm growing more frantic, less controlled. I come first, my nails clawing at his back and pushing him over the edge with me. He grunts out his release, my body detonating as I come harder than I ever have before.

And when we're done, he wraps me up in his arms, holding me against him as we continue to stare into each other's eyes, still lost in the happenstance of this moment.

"This is one of those moments," he whispers softly, kissing me. "Amazing doesn't even come close."

I nod as I sit up, getting dressed in to the clothes he bought me. "I have to go. Josh."

"This was too short. Can I take you to dinner? You never answered me on that."

"I know I didn't."

He tips my chin up until my eyes are on his. "What do you want, Aria? Tell me. Tell me what you're looking for from us. I am nothing. I am the empty man who ruins everything he touches. I broke your heart and I see that in your eyes. Please, we've always had the physical stuff down. Don't run from everything else."

Only the hope of forever feels like it's on the distant horizon.

I nod because there is nothing left to say. He kisses me. He kisses me, so I know that this was not just sex. That this was not just one night. That this is the beginning of us.

That he won't stop until he proves it to me.

Chapter Twenty-Two

ARIA

I told Wes yes. I told him yes, and he smiled and kissed me again. It was yes to dinner and yes to being his, but I'm not sure if he figured that out or not. He doesn't seem to. He seems anxious, like I'm going to slip through his fingers.

That kiss made my knees so weak when I stood up, I stumbled. He was a gentleman and didn't laugh at me, but I could see the inclination there.

Wes drove me to the hospital even though I told him he could drop me at the T. He refused, and when we pulled up at the hospital, he leaned in to kiss me again. For about ten minutes straight.

Believe it or not, I stumbled once again exiting the car.

I step into Josh's hospital room to find Tyler sitting there with his laptop in his lap and his feet propped up on the edge of Josh's bed. He's furiously typing away, his injured hand improved to the point where it's no longer swollen nor appears to be impacting his ability to type.

"Hey," he says with a warm smile when he sees me enter. "I was starting to wonder about you."

"How long have you been here?" I ask, ignoring the obvious question in his eyes.

"Shit." He laughs. "Hours maybe? I couldn't sleep so I came in to sit with him."

I smile at that. "I'm glad. I hate him being alone here."

"You just missed one of the doctors. His neurologist, I think. They're talking about reducing his sedation in a few hours."

I nod. "Yeah," I say, taking the seat on the opposite side of Josh's bed. "They told me that yesterday and again when I called this morning. Is it weird that I'm terrified?"

Tyler gives me a sad smile and shakes his head, his eyes gliding over to Josh's still form. "No. I know what you mean. What if he doesn't wake up? Or isn't Josh when he does?"

He spoke my fears aloud, and it makes my chest squeeze so tight I'm finding it difficult to breathe. I don't speak for a while, and neither does he. We're both lost in our own introspection about the fate of our loved one. I stretch my arms over my head causing Tyler's eyes to narrow on my wrists.

"What the hell is that?"

My hands drop into my lap and I glance down. I have bruises from where Brady squeezed me last night. How did I miss those? "I had a bit of a run-in last night," I explain, unable to pull my eyes off the bruises as I turn my hands this way and that to fully appreciate them.

"With Drew?"

I shake my head. That's almost laughable. Drew would never in a million years hurt me. Well, not physically at least. But there really is nothing funny about this.

"No. With Brady and Connor. I actually wanted to talk to you about it."

The color instantly drains from his face. He swallows. Hard. "What about it?"

"I can't think of anyone else who would hurt Josh. Who would *want* to hurt him?" He nods slowly, his eyes locked on mine. "They sort of got physical with me last night. I'm not entirely sure what would have happened if Wes hadn't shown up and saved me. So here's my question, what do we do about it?"

"Pardon?"

I would laugh at his bemused expression, but I'm still too worked up to display any other emotion but anger. "They're not in jail, Tyler. They're not even under suspicion from the sound of it. I want those fuckers to pay. I want them to pay dearly, and I don't know how to make that happen."

He points to his chest. "And you think I do?"

"You're a lawyer. What do you think would happen if I went and turned them in?"

He pauses, rubbing a hand across his smooth strong jaw. His black eyes going up to the ceiling in contemplation. "You say Wes saved you? What does that mean?"

Shit. Wes hit them. And threatened them. It was in defense of me, but then he punched them after they let me go and I walked out. I have no idea what he said to them after that.

"Nothing good for him."

"Then I think we need to tread carefully. Obviously, they're capable of violence. Josh is lying here in a coma, and your wrists look awful. Let's take some pictures of those bruises. And maybe we need to lure these assholes out. Get them to confess somehow."

The last thing in the world I want to do is lure them out. The last thing in the world I want is to ever see them again. But I get what he's saying. I understand what he's asking. And if I want justice for Josh, and myself, I think I need to do just that.

"Okay," I agree, formulating an idea in my head. "I can do that. Maybe I can get in touch with them somehow. Ask them to meet me somewhere."

"Your doctor won't like it. Either of them, actually." He laughs a little at that. Yeah. Ha. Ha. "And they might not admit to it. In fact, they probably won't. They'll most likely deny it because no one willingly incriminates themselves, and then where will we be? I don't know how wise this thing is that you're trying to cook up."

"I'm not doing anything this minute," I say slowly, my tone measured. I might have to stand Wes up. I don't want to. I want to have our talk. But I want this crap done. I want those assholes behind bars. I want to feel safe and I want the same for Josh.

"I don't think you should do this, Aria."

I see the concern in his eyes and feel his apprehension. But I don't think I can stop now. Stubborn and prideful are two middle names I could do without. But that doesn't make them less mine. "If you're afraid of the truth, Tyler, you'll never find it. It will always be lost to us, which means they go free."

"I know what you're saying. But what I'm saying is think of Josh. I know he'd rather have you safe and in one piece than see those boys in jail."

He has a point. One I can't exactly deny.

In truth, I really have no idea what Brady and Connor are capable of. At least not fully. I've seen it. Experienced it. But their limit might not have been reached, and do I want to put myself in a position where they could rape me? God, I can't even. Because that's exactly what I thought they were going to try to do to me last night.

"Okay," I say, rubbing my hands up and down my face and through my hair before I slap my palms against my thighs. "Okay. I'll wait until Josh wakes up. Maybe he remembers something anyway."

Tyler nods, his eyes flying over to Josh. "Maybe," he whispers.

We fall silent again, both of us focused on Josh. On his breathing. On the relentless beeping of machines. On the drip, drip, drip of his IVs. My phone vibrates in my purse, and as I pick it up, I see it's my personal assistant. Crap.

"Hey," I answer into the phone, throwing Tyler a wink as I exit Josh's room, past the nurses' station, and out into the hallway.

"Aria," she starts like she's out of breath. "Oh, thank God. I think I would have freaked my shit out if you hadn't picked up."

"What?" I ask as I lean my back against the wall. "Why do you sound like you're sprinting a marathon?"

"Because I am, bitch." Only Lydia can get away with this crap. Probably because I've known her a very long time and I absolutely love her. "You freaking bailed in the middle of The Broad Gallery exhibit. You missed both Friday and Saturday night and there was a huge turnout. I explained to the owner that you're out of town dealing with a family emergency, and he was cool shit about it, but still."

"Okay," I say rolling my eyes. Does everything always have to be so dramatic with this one? I was supposed to leave for New York the morning I got the call about Josh. And in truth, I've been anxious about the opening. I hate not being there. This is what I do. This is how I earn my living. But some things in life cannot be helped. "Is it not selling well?"

"No. It all sold. As in, every last motherfucking painting."

My eyes practically bug out of my head. This exhibit was supposed to go on for two months and it just opened on Thursday. It's also eighteen paintings. The biggest show I've ever done. Typically, I do small reviews or personalized sales. Rarely ever anything on this scope or magnitude. But when The Broad Gallery comes knocking on your door and asks for an exclusive, you say yes. "Jesus," I puff on an exhale.

"Yeah, Jesus. I also heard buzz that a few high-profile magazines and newspapers are reviewing it. The show will continue to run, but you've already got two other interested buyers as well as two other interested Galleries. One in London and another here in New York."

I think on this for a moment. Not about the other interested buyers. But about the other galleries. I'm not sure if I want to do that. I'd been contemplating purchasing a studio space for myself. Not a gallery per se, but a place where I can show my own work and meet with clients. A place where I can also have a studio set up somewhere other than my home. I'd like the option to work in more than one space if I can.

"I don't know," I reply. "I need to think on that. I only have about another ten or so finished paintings that I could use and I'm not exactly working much right now."

I don't mention the seven hours I spent yesterday. She doesn't need to know about that. I typically work every day. Even when I'm not feeling all that inspired. Sometimes it's just sketches. Sometimes it's just writing something that leads to art. Or sometimes I lose myself for hours or days. It all depends.

But with everything that's going on with Josh, and Wes and Drew for that matter, I haven't done as much as I would like. "Can you get some more done? I'm not pressuring you, but those clients said they'd come to you. They were both anxious to get the ball rolling."

"I don't know, Lyds. It's not like I have a ton of time right now. Josh is in the hospital in a freaking coma. I don't want to leave him. Can't you just show these people something I already have? You have digital pictures of everything I have finished."

She huffs out some air. "Yeah. I can do that. And shit, I'm so sorry about Josh. That was super insensitive of me."

"It's fine," I reassure her because this woman has the energy of a puppy on speed, and once she's on a roll, she doesn't stop.

"I'll show them what you have, and if they're not good with those, I'll tell them you'll be in touch as soon as you can. But hey," she continues and then she starts to laugh hysterically. Like loud and cackling. "You sold eighteen fucking paintings in under seventy-two hours." Yeah. I did. I smile big at that. "Do you have any idea how much money that is?"

"Not really," I laugh the words. "But I can guess."

"You can guess. So congrats. It's freaking awesome."

"Couldn't have done it without you."

"I know. And I'll be expecting my bonus once that check from The Broad clears." We both laugh, and then she says, "I gotta jet. But you should really think about buying that space now that you have all this money. I mean, why give these galleries a commission, right?"

"Yeah," I say softly. "Talk soon."

I hang up the call and lean my head back against the white walls. She's right. I should buy that space. But that means I'm staying here in Boston. That means I'm not going anywhere else. It's been nearly three years that I've been living in this city. I like it here. It feels like home in a way. And after this thing with Josh, I don't think I want to go anywhere.

But buying a studio space feels more permanent than owning a home.

"I sold eighteen paintings." I giggle like a little girl. Because holy crap balls, it feels so freaking unbelievable. This moment? It's the pinnacle of my career, thus far, and I'm dying to jump up and down and scream. I'm dying to run in and tell Josh. He's forever been my biggest supporter. I could text my brother or my father, but I know they're at work, so instead, I text my mother. But the moment I hit send, I realize my mistake. My mother hates texting. Which is why my phone rings in my hand the very next second. "Hi, Mom," I answer immediately.

"Are you calling to tell me you're coming home?"

I roll my eyes at that. "Nope. But Boston is lovely this time of year. You could drive the hour into the city."

She starts to laugh. My mother doesn't like to drive on the highway. I typically have to go to see her. "What's going on with you? You working today?"

"No," I reply. "I'm at the hospital. They're going to reduce Josh's sedation today."

"Oh," she exclaims, her voice raising an octave. "That's wonderful. I'm so glad to hear he's improving." I don't tell her what Tyler and I spoke about before. About the possibility of Josh not waking up at all or being impaired in some way if he does. "I miss that boy. He was always one of the good ones. I told your father that Weston Kincaid is his doctor. It made him feel better. You know your father has been so worried about Josh. Your brother had some real assholes he hung out with, but Wes was not one of them."

I let out a humorless laugh at her description of Brecken's high school friends. Especially after last night. She's not far off the mark.

"Drew wants to try again," I confess in a low tone. "He talked about marriage, Mom."

She's silent for a few agonizingly long seconds and then she clears her throat. "And what about your career?"

I puff out a breath. I really wish my mother drove on the highway because I'd really like her to be here right now. "He said he was fine with it as long as I cut back on my travel. He said his whole objection was that we never saw each other."

"Aria, don't bullshit me. Where's your head with him?"

"Done."

"Hmmm," she hums into the phone. "He went about this in a total fuck-wit way." Have I mentioned I adore my mother? "What did you tell him?"

"Just what I told you. That I'm done."

"Smart move."

"Wes kissed me. And I might have spent the night with him last night."

My mother does a cough, choking thing into the phone. "When it rains it pours. I knew sooner or later he'd be back for you. That boy used to stare at you like you hung the moon. How do you feel about him?"

"How do you think?"

"I think you're a mess."

"Thanks," I grumble. "Can't you give me any advice?"

"Okay. But you won't like it. My advice is to follow your gut."

"Yeah, that's not all that helpful," I laugh.

She laughs too. "I know. Love sucks, what can I tell you. But I have a feeling you already know what you want with him otherwise you wouldn't have spent the night. It's just a matter of making the tough choice."

"I sold all eighteen paintings at my showing at The Broad."

"Oh. My. God!" She screams into the phone so loud I have to hold it away from my ear. "I'm so proud of you. That's incredible, Aria. I can't wait to tell your father. Come for dinner on Friday if Josh is on the mend. Bring one of the boys who are messing with your head and we'll celebrate." She laughs like she just said the funniest thing in the world, but I do not care. I'm riding high.

I giggle some more, shaking my head. "I gotta go," I say. "I want to get back to Josh. But thank you for that. I needed your enthusiasm. And advice. I always need that."

She lets out a contented hum into the phone. "Okay, honey. Call me later, though. This Wes conversation is not done. Give Tyler a big hug from us and tell Josh we love him like he's our own. Love you."

"Love you too." I hang up with my mother and smile. The only thing that would make this day perfect is Josh waking up. I rest my head against the wall for a beat, thinking about what she said.

Love sucks, what can I tell you. But I have a feeling you already know what you want. It's just a matter of making the tough choice. But is Wes really a touch choice, or am I making him one?

Chapter Twenty-Three

WES

I hop into my Jeep, covered in sweat, my muscles aching from my climb when I hear my phone ring. I don't bring anything into the gym with me, so I flip open the glove compartment and take out my keys and my phone. It's Aria and I can't stop my smile. Probably because I'd be willing to bet she's going to try to bail on me.

"Don't even think about it," I answer into the phone instead of a greeting.

"He's not awake," she says, her voice thick with tears. "They reduced his sedation a few hours ago, and he hasn't opened his eyes, Wes." She lets out a sob. I pause, one hand on the key in the ignition, the other on the phone.

"Did they explain to you it could take more than just a few hours for him to wake up? It can take days or even weeks sometimes."

She sniffles a little and says, "Yes," so softly it's barely audible.

"Then why are you crying, baby? These things just take time."

"I don't know." And now she's really crying. Like full-on hiccupping sobs. "What if he doesn't wake up at all? That's a possibility, right?"

Shit. How can I tell her yes, when all I want to say is no? Sometimes being a doctor sucks.

"I can't…," she continues through her tears before I can even formulate a response. "I can't take it. He needs to wake up. I have the best news and I need to tell him and I don't know how to stop them anymore." I have no idea what any of that means. Aria has a way of babbling, sometimes nonsensically, when she's upset or nervous, and that's what she's doing now. I start my car up and head in the direction of the hospital. "They took that tube out, but he hasn't done anything other than lie there like he's sleeping." She breaks down again at that. "I can't stop crying. Like at all. And what if he wakes up and sees me crying and thinks he's dying or something?"

"Where are you? Are you still there with him?"

"I'm in the hall. I couldn't let him see me like this." I don't say anything to that. There have been cases where people coming out of comas can hear things. Can remember what they hear. So I'm not going to challenge her on that.

"I'm on my way, okay? I'll be there soon."

"Really?" She sounds so surprised, and I hate that she thinks of me as someone she can't count on.

"Yes. I should be there in like twenty or so depending on traffic."

"Okay," she sniffles, sounding slightly more in control. "Thank you." I snicker, and she huffs. "Yeah, that was as hard to say as it sounded. But, Wes?"

She pauses, waiting for me to respond, so I do. "Yes?"

"I'm really glad you're coming."

I grin, rubbing the back of my neck. "Me too," I tell her, even though there are so many other things I want to say to her. Things like, I'll always come when you need me. Things like, I might still love you. Things like, I might never have stopped. Things like, I don't want you to disappear when Josh wakes up, because this is our second chance.

I need this with her.

I don't think I realized how much until last night when fucking Brady and Connor had their hands on her.

I wanted to kill them. I wanted to break every single bone in their bodies. And I have to wonder if what Connor told me that night in the emergency department *was* bullshit.

They were both there.

They both talked shit to Josh.

Could they have done this to him? It's one thing to not like a guy, but it's another to nearly kill him. I wouldn't have thought it possible. In fact, I believed him outright.

But then I saw the way he was looking at Aria. I heard the words coming from his mouth, and now I'm not so sold. It makes me sick that I wasted so much of my life with friends who are able to do that to someone. Not only to Josh but Aria as well. Then I think about Aria with Drew. The way he was looking at her last night? Being jealous of a guy you work with is not a good thing. Especially in a non-professional way.

It takes me the better part of forty minutes to get there. Traffic in this city can suck sometimes, especially dealing with Storrow Drive.

I pull into the garage I always park in and I'm out of my car, walking across the main area and into the hospital in no time flat. I spot a nurse I had a one-night stand with months ago. She smiles softly at me, and even though I return that smile, I don't stop to talk. That's what my life has been. A series of one-night stands that do nothing more than assuage my needs. Scratch an itch.

Maybe it's wrong and maybe it's not, but it's not like they don't know the score before they let me climb into their bed.

I dated a woman in medical school for a while. That chef I mentioned to Aria. She was probably the closest thing to serious I've come. But when I was offered a residency at Mayo, she was not interested in Minnesota. I couldn't exactly blame her as she's a chef and wanted to stay in a city like San Francisco. And during residency, there was no time for dating. Not really. I worked hundred-hour weeks and never met anyone outside the hospital.

Now, the thought of a one-night stand leaves me cold. I don't find the same sort of satisfaction in it as I did before. I had convinced myself relationships were too much work. That I didn't want to add on to my responsibilities, and that's what a relationship with a woman felt like. A responsibility.

But the truth is, coming home to Massachusetts was the problem. Not my schedule.

Home always felt like it belonged to Aria.

Whenever I'd go to my mom's house, her house was right there, next door. Whenever I'd go into my old bedroom, I'd envision her sprawled out on my bed staring up at me. The treehouse. The school. Her roof. All of it was here waiting for me when I returned. It's one reason why I never came home to visit. Why I always had a million excuses for my mom to come see me instead.

Even after she remarried.

That and I never liked the reminder of my father.

Of how I spent my life trying to live up to his expectations only to have him destroy my mother and me completely. But when I returned, Aria seemed more in my mom's home than my dad did. Probably because my stepfather was already living there, and the place looked very different than it did when my father was there. My mother had completely redone the place. It was her way of moving on and moving up.

But my bedroom was unchanged.

I had thought about looking Aria up over the years. During some particularly dark moments or in the wee hours of the night when I was beyond exhausted and emotionally weak, she would unbiddenly creep into the forefront of my thoughts. I knew she was a successful artist before I even graduated college. I had literally been scrolling through *The Times* online one day over breakfast and there she was.

They'd called her work poetic art. Described her as immensely talented with a proclivity for encapsulating the essence of love, loss, and lust. I remember staring at that picture for more than an hour before I could move. It was a candid shot. A picture taken at some sort of gallery opening. She was wearing a long-sleeved black minidress with what appeared to be studs up the sides. Her wild hair was down, and her face was upturned with a brilliant smile that lit up everything around her.

She was smiling, and I was in agony.

Especially when I read she was planning on moving to London.

And yet, I was so unbelievably happy she had realized her dream. That she was successful. I mean, hell, a feature in *The New York Times*? They don't just give those away. But, God, did I ache for her. For the life I had envisioned with her. My life was all loss, and I don't think I ever fully moved past that.

At least not until now.

She called me crying. That is not something Aria does. That's not who she is. She needs me, and if I don't fight for her now, I'll regret it forever.

I reach the ICU and some of the nurses stare at me curiously. All I can do is shrug. I'm wearing gym pants and a threadbare tee. I have no idea what my hair looks like right now. I'm also sweaty. Probably covered in chalk. But fuck it. She called me.

I enter the room and find Tyler standing over by the window, staring out at the city beyond. Aria is on Josh's bed. Like actually on his bed, tucked in next to him. Even though she is absolutely not allowed to be since there are wires and tubes all around him. Since he just had two major abdominal surgeries a few days ago and has a head injury. I have no idea if the nurses have seen her like this, but I cannot imagine them not saying something.

Then again, this is Aria, and she most definitely doesn't give a shit if she's not allowed or even scolded. Her head is tucked into his arm, her hand placed over his heart. She's not crying anymore, but her cheeks are still that rosy color they get when she cries.

"Hey," I say softly. I'm not going to be the one to tell her she has to move. She's being gentle with her touch and mindful of her position next to him. Like I said, I'm in track pants, not scrubs. Tyler spins around at the sound of my voice. Aria doesn't move or even open her eyes. The heaviness in this room is suffocating. "You know," I say approaching the side of the bed to sit in the chair closest to her. My hand runs up the column of her spine and she lets out a shaky breath. "You're both depressing as hell." I hear Tyler let out a small snicker and Aria's lips twitch. "Seriously, if I were Josh, I wouldn't want to wake up to this either."

Her eyes finally open, and she tilts her head, so the corner of her eye catches mine. "What do you suggest then, Doctor?"

"Talk to him."

"Talk to him?" she parrots.

"Yup. He's asleep, so I don't think painting would do much. Plus, it would smell up the ICU." She laughs, and I blow out a breath. "Tell him something, Aria. Let him hear your voice."

"Josh loves it when you guys share stories of your misadventures," Tyler offers gently as he approaches the other side of the bed, and I'm unbelievably jealous that I don't really have those with her the way Josh does. "He has that video of you from that bar you sang karaoke in the last time he came to see you when you were living in Los Angeles. That time when he dared you to get up and sing, *Baby Got Back*." I can't help my smile, and neither can Aria. "He watches it every now and then. He swore me to secrecy and had me promise never to tell you, but maybe if he's pissed off enough that I broke my promise, he'll wake up."

"Such a goofball, Josh," Aria teases, and both Tyler and I laugh. "Did Josh ever tell you that he's got this thing for medieval times?" Tyler's lips bounce up into a full-blown smile. "I'm not talking the restaurant either. I mean real knights in armor and maidens in gowns and castles and swords and shit. It was a minor obsession of his."

"No," Tyler says, shaking his head. "He's definitely never told me that. I would have remembered."

"I'm not surprised," she laughs lightly, shifting her position ever so gently. "If he had, this story would have come up."

"So tell it," I push. "We're all waiting with bated breath here."

She throws me a look, and I raise an eyebrow in return. "When I was living in Paris, he dragged me all the way down, close to the Spanish border, to this castle place called Carcassonne. It's this huge real medieval castle that has a small city inside with shops and restaurants and an outdoor area where they play live music at night. There is also this amazing hotel in the center. It's actually one of the most incredible places I've ever been, but that aside, the restaurant in the hotel has phenomenal hot chocolate. Like liquid velvet chocolate in a cup. So Josh and I had this very French breakfast with this phenomenal hot chocolate, and at some point, he spilled some of it onto his chair. He was relieved, right, because he thought he missed his pants. We ended up exploring the city and the surrounding area for hours that day."

Aria snickers, angling her body so that she's facing Josh. A smile that cannot be helped brightening her otherwise sad face.

"All day long people had been laughing as we'd pass them, and we never quite got why. We just figured it was the fact that he was wearing bright pink pants and that the snooty tourists couldn't handle it. That night as we walked along looking for a place to eat dinner, an elderly woman who resembled my grandmother complete with a floral design dress and glasses perched on her nose, came up to us. She tapped Josh on the shoulder and said in French, 'Excuse me, I don't mean to be rude, but are you aware that you shit your pants?'"

Tyler and I burst out laughing. So does Aria, wiping away more tears from her face. "What did Josh do?" Tyler asks, through his laughter, his body leaning back in his seat as he continues to shake with amusement.

Aria shrugs. "He was a good sport about it. He thanked the old woman for her blunt observation and then she walked away, feeling like she had done the hot gay man a service. The best part? It really did look like that. The stain was in the perfect spot. My very style conscious best friend didn't change his pants, though. He said, 'fuck it, let them think I did shit my pants.' It was awesome. We spent the rest of the night trying to get other people to walk up to us and say something. No one else was brave enough, though."

"That's an incredible story," I tell her. "It sounds like the two of you traveled the world together."

She nods. "We did. We went everywhere. Any time I moved somewhere new, which was frequently, he came. The best friend a girl could ever want and then some." She sighs, and it's so wistful that my heart breaks for her. "I told an embarrassing story about you, Josh. Now open your goddamn eyes. I'm tired of this crap."

Of course, he doesn't open his eyes, and he doesn't speak, and he doesn't even move. A tear glides down her cheek. I don't mention the fact that we're supposed to have a date tonight. I know she's not going anywhere until he wakes up. *If* he wakes up.

I'm dying to pick her up and hold her against me. But I doubt she wants to be parted from Josh right now. "Aria?" I say quietly. She doesn't respond, but she does open her eyes again. "I'm going to go home, shower, and change my clothes. But I'll be back with some food for all of us."

"You don't have to, Wes. You're already here so much for work, and really, we're just sitting here watching him." She shifts so she's facing me. "I'm glad you came, I am, but I'm okay now."

"Stop being a stubborn pain in the ass. I'll be back in an hour. Call me if anything changes."

I lean in, and I kiss her. Even though she's tucked into Josh's body. Even though we're in the middle of the ICU and I work here. Even though Tyler is sitting right there, and I have no idea if she called Drew, asking him to come too. I kiss her because I don't want her to ever question my desire to be wherever she is again. To question that I wouldn't drop everything if she needed me.

"I'm sorry about our date," she whispers.

"Nothing to be sorry about. But don't think I'm letting you off the hook. I already told you, I'm not wasting time."

She lets out a small laugh, rolling her eyes. "Of course not. Were you always this domineering?"

"No. I was in college the last time you saw me. High school before that. High school boys are too chickenshit to be domineering. But I'm glad you know I am now." I lean into her until our faces are inches apart. "It will save us a lot of future fights if you just give in to me from the start." I wink at her. Kiss her smiling lips. "Keep talking to him. It's good for him to hear your voices. I'll be back soon." I kiss her again. Throw Tyler a shit-eating grin to which he laughs at and then I walk out of the ICU. I shouldn't be feeling like this with Josh in the state he's in. But I can't help it.

I'm high on Aria Davenport.

Chapter Twenty-Four

WES

Past

MY EYES FEEL like they're bleeding right out of my head. Three weeks at Princeton and it's exactly the way I imagined it to be. Fucking tough. But amazing. I've met some good friends, including my roommate Harrison, and the campus is beautiful, and football thus far is fun and not overwhelming. We won our first game, and from what I hear, Princeton football doesn't win shit ever so that's a step in the right direction.

I haven't heard from my father since I left.

Not. One. Word.

I said goodbye to him. Shook his reluctant hand. Took the Jeep he bought me and left. That was it. I have to wonder if that's all it will ever be. But right now, it's nearly eleven at night and I have the biggest textbook in the world in my lap. Art History. Which of course makes me instantly think of Aria. Right now, I wish I had her photographic memory. Or at least her knack for memorizing things because I cannot keep my head straight around these artists' names or the dates in which they created whatever work they're credited with creating.

Aria. I smile just thinking about that girl. I shouldn't. I left her. We both knew the score, but shit. Being inside of her was like nothing I've ever experienced, and even though I'm only a week shy of nineteen, I already know it will never be like that again with anyone else. The way her eyes looked into mine. The way her body felt as she moved. The way she looked as I slid in and out. I know it hurt. I did my best to make it not, but it did anyway. But after the pain was gone, I did everything I could think of to make sure that she only remembered the pleasure and not the pain. That when she thinks back on it, she'll only remember how incredible we were together.

I think I succeeded. I hope I did.

She's still all I think about. All I long for. The girls here? They're pretty and smart and so very…serious. I don't know. Princeton does have fun, but the girls think it's beneath them. Forgetting the parties, Aria had a light to her. The girls here do not, and I miss my light. I miss my girl. I can't wait until Thanksgiving. Or some random weekend I go home before that.

The knock on my door startles me out of my reverie. It opens a half-beat later and James from down the hall is there. "Hey, man," he says, standing awkwardly on the threshold of my door. "Sorry to bother you, but your mom is in the lobby."

"What?" I sit up straight, staring at my neighbor.

"Yeah. I don't know. That's what I overheard her telling the security guy." I grab my phone and see that I do have two missed calls. My phone is set to silent. Shit.

"Thanks for the heads-up." I stand and James gives me a head nod before he leaves. I call my mother back, and when her voice fills my phone, my gut sinks. "You're here?"

"Can you come down?"

I swallow. Hard. My heart suddenly resting in my throat. "Yes."

I hang up. I can't even stand to say anything more, because my mother is here, and I have no idea what's going on, but her voice was missing something crucial. Something vital. Something that makes her sound like my mother. I throw on my sneakers and a hoodie, grab my wallet, my keys, and my phone and leave the comfort of my dorm room.

I hit the lobby of my building and freeze. My mother hasn't spotted me yet. Her head is down, her hands are shaking, her posture is slack and something is so very wrong. My insides twist, my chest clenches. I feel like I'm going to be sick. My dad is not with her. "Mom?"

Her head snaps up and she doesn't even bother with an obligatory smile. "Wes," she says. "Hi, honey."

I walk toward her, reaching her as the first tear hits her cheek. "What's wrong? What happened?"

She glances quickly around the lobby, taking in the students, the security, and everyone else. I grasp her forearm and lead her outside. It's not cold out. It's barely the end of September and the air is mild. I walk and walk until I find a secluded area of green space, then I release her arm and spin around on her. It's dark here, but I can see her face well enough.

"Your father," she swallows so loud that I swallow in response. "He uh." More tears. More swallows. Her eyes hit the grass for a beat before they brave the journey up to mine. "I found your father in our bedroom this morning."

I pause. I wait her out. But she doesn't elaborate and I'm about ready to shake her. "What does that mean? You found him?"

"He hung himself. He's dead."

My world stops. There is no sound. My vision sways in and out, and I don't think I remember how to breathe. The next thing I know, my mother is hovering over me, I'm on the ground, my knees bent with my head between them as I pant helplessly. Her hands run through my hair, and I brush her away. I don't want anyone to touch me. My father is dead. I'm going to be sick, and I don't want anyone to touch me.

"Weston," my mother says with a tone that cannot be ignored. "Look at me." I do. But fuck is it difficult. "He was a very sad man. A very sick man. For many, many years."

"It's my fault."

She blanches, then shakes her head. "It's not. It's not my fault, and it's not your fault. He didn't know how to control his depression anymore."

"Did he leave a note?"

She nods. But it's a reluctant nod. "One to me and one to you."

"Did you read it?"

"Mine. But, Wes," she breathes, her tears out of control now as she wraps her small arms around my body and holds me tight, both of us trembling violently. "You don't have to read it. You don't. He didn't want a funeral, and I'm not giving him one. He's being cremated. I'm telling everyone he had a heart attack and that the service is private."

I can't wrap my head around this. Around what she's saying. No funeral? No service? Heart attack? I hear words, but it's taking me so much longer than it should for their meaning to penetrate. Blood is rushing through my ears, my stomach is in knots, my feet are like lead, and I can't handle this.

"Was his note to you bad?"

She pulls back and meets my eyes, heartbreak etched in every corner of her sweet face. Then she nods.

"Mine will be worse."

"I don't know, baby. But you did nothing wrong. You hear me? Whatever his illness made him think, you did nothing wrong. I'm proud of you. Do you understand? I'm so goddamn proud of you Weston Timothy Kincaid. You're such a good man. Smart and wonderful, and every day I thank God for you. Every. Day. Don't let this take over and ruin your life. Your father was never the same after his injury. I knew him for four years before that and the day he broke those bones and his football career ended, something inside of him changed. Died. I don't know. But he was not the man I fell in love with after that. He married me, but as the years progressed, he became even more angry and bitter. I'll give you his letter. He was your father and I don't want to withhold his last words from you. But if they're as awful as the words he left me with, then I hope you know that it was him and not you. Coming to Princeton was the best decision you ever made. Do *not* second-guess that. Ever."

After long minutes of tears, I pull myself up off the ground. "How can we not tell people the truth? Won't they find out?"

She shakes her head, her expression an odd combination of panic and resolve. "We can't tell them, Wes. I don't want anyone to know. Everyone has always seen us as this perfect happy family, and I don't want that to change. Even if he's gone. I don't want them to look at me any differently and they will if they know."

"Okay." What else can I say to that? The illusion of perfection is all we have left. There is no forever for us. No beauty in his death.

My mother leaves me with the letter my father wrote for me and checks herself into a hotel. She tells me she'll be back in the morning, but I hate night, and I hate morning.

I hate everything.

I should have gone to Alabama. I should have accepted the football scholarship. I should have pursued football instead of medicine.

I reach my room, and mercifully, my roommate is still gone. I climb onto my bed and I stare at the sealed envelope for so long my eyes burn with lack of use.

Do I open it?

Do I allow myself to read it?

My fingers rip the envelope and I slide out the folded white sheet. Opening it up, I stare at his not so neat script for a solid five minutes before I'm brave enough to read what I already know is going to be the most painful thing I've ever endured.

Wes —

I have no idea how you'll hear about this. How you'll interpret the news. Honestly, this is never how I imagined my life to end. I pictured a long life with your mother. With my son. I pictured endless hours of a life well spent and eventually grandchildren. I imagined a life in professional sports and the money and esteem that came with that. I imagined my son following in my prestigious footsteps. You didn't, and that decision took the last of anything I cared about away.

The day I was injured was the worst of my life. Your mother was newly pregnant, and my life felt like it was ending. Life continued on. The world continued on. I did not. Over the years, I've grown more resentful, angrier and increasingly depressed. I didn't want help. I didn't want life. My life ended that day on the field. I tried to live through you, only to be disappointed once more when you gave up on all your potential. I'm sorry, Wes. I am. I know this is not what you need from me. I'm just grateful I won't be around to watch you have the same regrets and disappointments that I've had in my life...

I stop reading after that. There isn't much left, anyway. Just his signing off and saying goodbye. Guilt and despair slam into me.

Consume me.

Like that sensation you have when a huge wave knocks you over in the ocean and just as you're about to stick your head above the surface and take a breath of air, another wave comes along and knocks you back down.

I can't reach the surface. I can't break through and take that much-needed breath of air.

I'm drowning, and at this moment, I hate my father. I hate him for doing this to me. For doing this to my mother. I hate him for placing all of his future happiness on one vision of his life.

Dreams change. Shit happens. Grow up and fucking deal with it.

How could he do this?

And how do I not blame myself when I know that if I had gone to Alabama and played football, he'd still be alive?

I lie on my bed, my eyes bleary and my mind restless. My days are bleeding into nights and nights into days. There is no stopping the endless vicious tormenting cycle. I can't sleep. Eating isn't happening much either. Class. Schoolwork. Stare at my ceiling.

That's the extent of my life.

My phone rings on my nightstand. Brecken. He's been incredible. We did not have a funeral for my father and my mother left after a few days here. Some of my high school friends have called. Once. Not Brecken.

He's called nearly every day. Even if he still thinks my father died of a heart attack. I don't have it in me to correct him.

I talk to him, but I don't have a lot to say.

Brecken makes me think of Aria and thinking of Aria makes me ache in a different way. I never pick up the phone when she calls. She's done so three times, and every time I watch her name flash across my screen, and I hate myself for ignoring her. But I have no words that I want to give her right now. And Aria has a way of reaching inside me, to the most hidden depths of my soul and pulling my words reluctantly from me. I can't do that. Not now.

I'm not brave enough to live through what I'll say if she does that to me.

"Hey," I say, answering the phone because it almost feels like it will be worse if I don't. Like I'll be fitting into some cliché of the depressed kid whose father is dead. That doesn't even make sense in my mind, but I still answer him. Every. Single. Time. Whether I want to or not. He's Brecken. Not Aria and I hate that every time I hear his voice. Hate the things I hid from him. He's a good friend and I'm a shitty friend for secretly loving his sister behind his back. I'm not a good man. A good man would have been honorable to both him and Aria.

"What's up, bro?" Brecken greets, his deep voice filling my ear as my eyes stare up at the ceiling.

"Just studying," I lie.

"Yeah. I do that shit a lot too. Maybe going Ivy League wasn't such a good idea." He laughs, but fuck, he has no idea what those words just did to me. How right he actually is. At least for me.

"Probably not," I reply and mean it.

"Aria told me she tried calling you." My fist comes up to rub that spot on my chest. The one directly over my sternum. "I told her not to sweat it, but I think she's worried about you." I close my eyes.

"Tell her I'm fine."

He clears his throat. "So there's this crazy party coming up," he goes on, ignoring my comment. "I want you to come up for it. Help take your mind off shit."

"I can't."

"It's not just Aria who's worried about you. I am too. You're like a brother to me." I nod, but I can't speak. Finally, when he realizes I'm useless, he blows out a heavy breath. "Just think about coming, okay? Even for one night. We don't have to go to the party. I live in New York City. We can go and do anything. Or we can just hang out. Drink some beers. Whatever you want."

"Thanks, man." My tone is genuine because even though I don't want to talk and I don't want to go to New York, and I don't want to do anything, knowing Breck is there for me means the world to me. "I'll think about it. I gotta run. I have this insane midterm coming up."

"Yeah. Cool. I'll talk to you tomorrow." I want to tell him he doesn't have to call me tomorrow, but then he disconnects the call. I really should be studying. I do have a midterm next week. That was no bullshit. My eyes close again instead.

My phone buzzes against my chest, startling me, my eyes flying open. It's been there since I got off the phone with Breck, and I have no idea how long ago that was.

It's a text. Not a call so I pick up my phone, glancing at the screen. ***My heart is with yours***. It's from Aria and it's her way of saying she understands I don't want to talk—I can't talk to Aria, I'll lose myself completely if I do. It's her way of saying she's not hurt that I don't pick up the phone or call her back, and she's here with me anyway.

I smile for the first time in…I have no idea how long.

Mine is with yours. Delete. ***I miss you.*** Delete. ***I think I love you, Aria.*** Delete. ***You have no idea how much that means to me.*** Send.

She doesn't reply and that makes me smile even more. If she did, I'd be done for. I'd give in and I can't give in. Not yet.

Yes, Aria, your heart is with mine. And I cherish it. I carry it with pride. I will not fuck with it, which is why I won't pick up when you call nor, will I call you back. And this is the last text I will send you until the time is right.

She's sixteen and now I'm nineteen. She's in high school and I'm in college. I'm a mess and she's perfect.

I have nothing to offer her.

At least not yet. But I'll hold on to her heart and maybe, if luck ever decides to come back my way, I'll find her and tell her she has my heart too.

Chapter Twenty-Five

ARIA

Present Day

"WHY DON'T you tell Josh all about your sexy doctor," Tyler suggests, leaning back in the chair and propping his feet up on the edge of Josh's bed. "I know he'd love to hear about nothing else."

"Cheeky bastard," I mumble, and he laughs. "Besides, there is nothing to tell."

"You're a crap liar. Like epically bad. He just kissed you. Twice."

"I know," I sigh. "But what's going on with the doctor is too new and fragile, so I really don't even know what to say. Wes and I have a very big history together. One that left me hurt on more than one occasion even if that was never his intention. It's not the sort of thing I can just brush under the rug with a few good kisses." Or one sweaty night of passion.

"So is he as good of a kisser as he looks?"

"Shut up," I laugh, making him smile big.

"You're blushing, Aria. It's a sight I never thought I'd see." I flip him off and he returns the crude gesture. "He loves you. It's obvious. You can play ignorant all you want, but I think things are going to get very interesting."

"Who loves you," Drew asks, walking into the room like he owns the place. "Are you talking about me? Because if you are, then yes, I love you."

Tyler's eyes widen and his mouth pops open in an *oh shit* expression. Me? I just sink farther into Josh who shall now be known to the world as my safe haven. My talisman. Protector from all straight men.

"I can't stay long," Drew continues like he didn't just interrupt that conversation. Or maybe he really doesn't know. "I just came to check on you."

"Thanks," I mumble, wondering why he's here after I told him last night we're done. "Um, Drew? We need to talk." I feel like I told him straight up last night, but now here he is. Maybe he still thinks I just need time?

"Do you remember that time the three of us went skiing?" Drew looks at me in a way that makes my chest tighten. It's the way he looked at me right before he told me he loved me for the first time.

"Yes," I reply softly. "I fell on my ass repeatedly while you and Josh flew down the mountain with ease."

Drew chuckles, as does Tyler, but my eyes are too busy staring at Drew to throw Tyler a death glare. "Did you know that was the moment I fell in love with you?" I can only blink at him. "It was." He nods like I needed the confirmation. "You were so goddamn cute in all your gear with your rosy cheeks and big blue eyes. And every time you fell, instead of getting embarrassed, you laughed. You were this angel in the snow and I remember thinking, shit, I really love this girl."

"Drew—"

He covers my mouth with his. The exact same place Wes's lips just were. I shove him away instantly, feeling sick.

"You can't do that anymore."

His eyes hold mine. "And yet, I'm not sorry. Text me when he wakes up. We can talk more later."

"Oh my God. What the motherfuck?" I half-shriek, burying my head in Josh's arm.

"That was some serious drama. I mean like daytime soap opera drama. Like the good shit. I wish I had popcorn."

"You're such an asshole," I grouse at Tyler. "Who says crap like that when there is real life insanity going on?"

"Oh, please, honey. You've got two hot doctors after you. Remind me to shed a tear for you. May we all have your problems." He rolls his eyes.

"I need to figure this all out. Drew is done. He knows that. I don't know what that kiss was all about. I told him last night we were done. But Wes. He'd be so hurt. I can't let Wes kiss me again until—"

"But you should," Josh mumbles, and I'm so startled by the sound of his gravelly, unused voice that I jump back and practically fall off the side of the bed.

"Was that the great and powerful Wizard of Oz or did you really speak?" I ask.

Josh opens his eyes slowly, blinking several times in succession like the light is painful. I immediately jump off his bed and shut it off and the moment I do, his eyes open wider. Tears spring to my eyes as I smile what is quite possibly the biggest smile in the history of smiles.

"I hurt," he whispers, his voice so quiet I have to strain to hear him, "everywhere."

"Do you remember anything?" Tyler asks urgently, his feet hitting the floor as he shifts his body to the edge of the chair, leaning over to Josh so he can see him. Josh frowns.

"No."

"I'm going to get the doctor," I rush out, but realize I can just hit the call-button and the nurse will answer. I don't think I can leave Josh. Maybe ever again. I know I've never been this relieved or happy before.

I hit the red cross on the large remote thing attached to his bed and the nurse asks if we need any help. I explain that Josh is awake, and she tells me that she'll page his doctor and inform his nurse.

My first instinct is to call Wes. It settles on me like a strange weight. I want him here to see this. To witness what his hard work did for my friend. To shower him with my overwhelming gratitude.

But I don't call him.

Wes called me stubborn and he's right. He said he was going to shower and come back within the hour anyway.

"Do you know why you're here?" Tyler presses and I sort of want to tell him to back off. The poor guy just woke up.

"No," Josh repeats, and it breaks my heart. Tyler takes Josh's hand, and Josh frowns again. I don't know why he's frowning. That's all he's done so far. Opened his eyes and frowned and said no. He's in pain and no doubt confused. I need to remember that. All that's important is that he's awake. A smile can come later.

Tyler looks like he's about to keep going with his inquisition, but a nurse walks in, followed directly by a doctor. They ask us both to leave while they examine him and though I want to stay, now is not the time to get crazy with things. The moment Tyler and I reach the waiting room, he begins to pace. Back and forth. Back and forth.

I have no idea why he's so agitated. I get that he's worried about Josh. I get that there is still so much uncertainty and that the road ahead is long, but I'm smiling while he's coming unhinged.

"He just woke up, Tyler," I say trying to calm him down with my tone. "You have to give him time. He'll get through this."

Tyler pauses mid-step like he forgot I was here.

"I know," he cuts out sharply before he blows out a breath, running his hands up and down his face. "Shit. I'm sorry. I'm just not good with this stuff. I'm scared for him, you know?"

I stand up and walk over to him, throwing my arms around his neck and hugging him tightly to me. "Me too."

Tyler steps back from me, practically pushing me off. "I'm going to go get some air. I'll be back in a few." And without another word, he storms out of the room. I'm left staring after him when the nurse walks in, informing me that I can go back in.

I practically sprint there and I wish Tyler hadn't left like that. I don't want him not being there when I return to Josh. But I guess everyone handles stress differently, and he needed a minute.

When I return, the head of Josh's bed is elevated a little and his eyes are still open, staring out toward the window. His head turns slowly when he hears me enter and now I see the smile I love so much.

"Hey," I breathe out, and immediately start to cry. Crap. That was not how I wanted this to go. "You bastard. I haven't cried this much in years."

Josh doesn't laugh, probably because it would hurt too much, but he's smiling even bigger now. "Come here," he whispers, moving the tips of his fingers across the white blanket he's tucked under. "I'm glad you're here."

"Wouldn't have missed it."

He rolls his eyes at me, wincing, as I sit in my favorite recliner and take his hand. It's warmer somehow. His hands have been nothing but cold since I got here.

"Tyler?"

"Went out to get some air. He'll be right back." Josh frowns again and I hate that Tyler did this right when Josh woke up. "Do you want me to go get him?"

"No," he answers softly. My eyebrows furrow.

Josh takes in a deep breath, his expression rigid as he closes his eyes slowly. I'm thinking they gave him something for the pain because he looks like he's about to go back to sleep. A few silent minutes pass before he speaks again.

"I remember." He tries to open his eyes, but it's a struggle against the pull of the drugs. I sit up straighter, clasping his hand tighter. I open my mouth to speak. To ask if it was Brady and Connor when he says, "I'm afraid."

Jesus. My heart just shattered into a million pieces. "Of what, Josh? You're safe here."

His eyes blink open and they lock on mine just as Tyler walks back in with a smile, a thing of balloons and a stuffed animal. "They don't let you have flowers in the ICU," he informs us.

But I can't acknowledge him because Josh's eyes continue to bore into mine. A feeling of dread crawls up my spine. My heart begins to hammer away as my stomach twists. Something is so very wrong. Tyler sits on the other side of Josh.

"This was the best I could do. But when you come home, I'm buying you whatever the hell you want. I'm just so relieved you're awake."

Tyler stands up just as quickly as he sat down and kisses Josh's forehead. Josh shuts his eyes.

But when Tyler sits back down, Josh opens them again, still staring at me, but that intensity is gone and I wonder if I imagined all that. He smiles warmly at me, setting me further at ease before he closes his eyes once more and this time, they stay closed.

"I think they gave him something," I whisper to Tyler.

"Probably," he agrees. "Did he say anything while I was gone?"

"He asked where you were," is my only reply. I hold the rest back. I don't even know why exactly, but I suddenly don't want Tyler to know that Josh remembers and that he's afraid. Tyler smiles, rubbing the line of his smooth jaw as he stares adoringly at Josh.

"I'm sorry I freaked out back there," he says. "I don't think I've gotten enough sleep, and it was like everything just hit me at once."

"I get it. Why do you think I've been crying so much."

Tyler laughs, leaning back in his chair and propping his feet back up on the edge of the bed.

That's when I see it.

The bottoms of Tyler's shoes are a light sandy color. But the toe of his left one is stained. Stained dark reddish-brown and smeared in a funny pattern.

Like he stepped in something.

Something I instinctively know can only be blood.

I can't pull my eyes away from it for the longest time as I try to come up with a different explanation for that stain. I tell myself it's not blood. That it could be a million different things.

But it's not.

I tell myself there are a million different ways that blood could have gotten there. But intuitively I know exactly how that blood got there.

Suddenly, it all comes together in my head, like the pieces of the puzzle. I understand why Josh said he was afraid. That look in his eyes. Why he didn't want me to call Tyler to have him return. Why he frowned when Tyler touched him, kissed him. Why Tyler was afraid to try and get Brady and Connor to confess. Why he was cold with the detectives.

Tyler is the person who did this to him.

All this time, I believed it was Connor and Brady. Never in a million years did I ever think it could be Tyler. Tyler who is always so loving with Josh. Tyler who punched a wall. Tyler who pressed Josh the moment he opened his eyes, desperate to see if he remembered.

Tyler who freaked out not even ten minutes ago.

Then I turn to Josh's sleeping form, and I'm forced to push it down. I have no idea what Tyler will do if I confront him in front of Josh and I will not risk my friend's safety. Ever so slowly, I rise out of my chair. I swallow hard, doing my best to get control of something that feels out of control.

"I'm going to call Wes."

I don't wait for a reply. I can't even look at him. I might kill him if I do.

I walk slowly out of the room even though my legs are begging me to run. I hit the edge of the nurses' station and the woman sitting behind the counter raises her eyes to me. Then she stands up with a look of concern when she notes my expression.

"I need you to call the police," I say quietly, but loud enough for her to hear me. Even if I'm wrong about Tyler, which I don't think I am, Josh said he remembers and he needs to speak to the police.

"I'm sorry?" she asks with an incredulous note. "Is there a problem?"

"The man in the room with Joshua Brown I believe is the person who put him here. I need you to call the police now."

She blinks at me and then her eyes glide past me over to the room. "I…uh…," she swallows and nods. "Okay. I'm going to call security to come and stand outside the door until the police arrive."

"Don't make it obvious."

"Right."

I spin on my heels and head back into Josh's room. I'm not leaving him alone with Tyler again. I take my seat, sitting forward and positioning my body until I'm practically leaning over Josh in what could probably be construed as a defensive position. Tyler doesn't even notice. He's lost in thought as he watches Josh sleep, his feet bouncing on the ground. His hands running through his hair so many times I've lost count.

He's nervous.

My trembling fingers grasp the arms of my chair. I'm shocked the wood hasn't splintered under the pressure of my grip. I'm hit with a sudden surge of adrenaline that's itching for me to fly across the room and hit Tyler with everything I have. To stand up and scream and ask him how he could do this.

All I see is red.

My vision is hazy with it. I taste it on my tongue. I feel it pulsing through my blood. My body humming with the force of my anger. It clouds everything.

What if you're wrong? that voice in my head questions.

And because I can't manage to stop myself, I blurt out, "Do you think he'll remember anything?"

Tyler's head snaps in my direction. "I don't know. He was hit over the head with a metal rod, right? Knocked unconscious instantly. Even if he does remember, I doubt he'd have seen anything."

I catch movement out of the corner of my eye outside of the room, but Tyler's back is to the door and the ICU behind it, so he doesn't notice that there is now a man standing there. But it's not the police. It's just security and I have to be careful.

"True," I agree, trying to keep my eyes on him and not make it obvious that I'm also watching the hallway behind him. But the moment I see two uniformed officers enter the ICU, I stand up because I have zero fucking cool left at this point. "How did you know he was knocked out instantly? And with a metal rod?"

Tyler blanches as he too rises, almost like it's a reflex. "I just assumed. That's what the police said."

Liar. Fucking motherfucking liar. The police said nothing of the sort. "How could you do it, Tyler?" I half-yell, my anger taking over my common sense.

"Aria," he sputters, his hands going out like he's trying to ward me off. "I don't know—"

"There's blood on the bottom of your shoe," I scream, interrupting him. "How could you do it?"

Tyler's expression grows murderous. So cold and detached. "He was having an affair," he yells back, his fists balling up so tight they turn white. One of the healing abrasions cracks open and begins to ooze. "Did he tell you that?" I shake my head. "I found the number in his phone. He was going to end things and I couldn't let him do that. He belongs to me and no one else."

"So you tried to kill him?!"

Tyler lunges for me across the bed, catching my cheek with his fist before his hands are yanked back by the police officers who flew into the room at the sound of our yelling. Tyler is shouting a million different things. He's bucking and fighting and the next thing I know, he's on the ground as one of the officers slaps handcuffs on his wrists while the other reads him his rights.

"His shoes," I call out, holding my smarting cheek with my hand. Hell did that hurt. When the one who just read him his rights looks up, I explain, "He has blood on the bottom of his left shoe."

"We'll take care of it. Someone will be in to speak with you shortly."

I glance over at Josh and his eyes are open, straining to remain that way as he watches everything unfold. Clearly, he heard the commotion, but the drugs and the extent of his injuries have a strong hold as he struggles to stay awake.

I walk over to him, take his hand, and press my mouth to his ear. "You're safe, Josh. He'll never be able to hurt you again."

Josh doesn't respond. He blinks at me a few times, his eyes glassy with the well of emotions threatening to run over.

He squeezes my hand back. Sighs. And closes his eyes.

Chapter Twenty-Six

WES

The moment I reach the hospital, I know something is very wrong. There are three police squad cars lined up, all with their lights flashing. Now, it's a hospital. A level one trauma center at that, so the police being here is not an uncommon phenomenon.

In fact, I see them almost on a daily basis. Trauma surgery and police often go together whether it's a hit and run or a gunshot wound or whatever.

But you don't always see their cars lined up with flashing lights. That's new to me and it instantly sets me on edge. It has me walking around toward the emergency department because I'm thinking maybe they need a hand. But when I enter the emergency department, it's quiet. Almost eerily silent as the doctors and nurses treat their patients.

There are no traumas. Those rooms are empty.

It's a relief, and yet it's not.

As I walk along the corridor, carrying a large bag of food and wearing street clothes, I'm noticing people staring at me. Not just staring but whispering about me in that obvious way people do when they're trying not to be obvious about something and fail. I check my phone but there is nothing from Aria.

"Hey," Margot says to me, her eyes wide like she's surprised to see me here tonight. Which really, she should be. It's technically my day off. "Were you able to get up there? Is everyone okay?"

"What?" My breath catches in my lungs and somehow her brown eyes widen farther. I have no idea what she's talking about, but somehow, someway, instinctively, I know she's talking about Aria.

"Yeah, um." She glances around quickly, noticing other people watching us the way I did before. "I heard there was an incident in Josh's room. No one will tell us what happened, they're not letting anyone up to that unit unless necessary, and Aria isn't picking up her damn phone. I'm going out of my mind. Drew threw a fit when they wouldn't let him up. He was ranting about being Aria's fiancé and how he needed to get to her."

"What?" I ask again, this time a little louder, and I feel like a broken record, but that one is fucking news to me considering I kissed her an hour ago. Considering I made love to her in my bed last night.

She shrugs. "I don't know. I think he was just saying it so they'd let him up there, but now he's pacing the back room, waiting for her to call him back. We heard she was attacked—"

I don't wait for Margot to finish. I take off at a sprint for the back stairs because the elevator will take too long. The door flies open and then I'm climbing the steps two at a time before I reach the fifth floor, panting and sweating and utterly fucking terrified. My heart is pounding out of my chest as I round the corner, swipe my badge against the pad and impatiently wait for the slow-ass doors to swing open.

There are two police officers standing outside of Josh's room. The nurses are all huddled over to the far side of their station, talking about whatever happened along with a few of the doctors and techs.

What the hell is going on? I've only been gone an hour. One hour.

How can so much change in such a short amount of time?

But I realize how ridiculous that thought is. Life-changing events aren't measured in minutes or hours they're measured in seconds. One second your life is great, and the next it's falling apart.

That hour I was gone is an eternity.

I sprint down the hall and over to Josh's room where an officer immediately holds his hand up. "I'm sorry," he says, his tone indicating that he's not sorry at all, "but you can't go in there."

"I'm Joshua Brown's doctor."

He shakes his head no and I try a different tactic. "I'm Weston Kincaid, Aria Davenport is expecting me. I was told she was attacked. You have to let me in." As I say the words I attempt to move around him, peering into the room, trying to catch a glimpse of them. I can't see anything. They have the glass door closed and the curtain drawn, and I'm going out of my goddamn mind.

"I'm sorry, you can't—"

"I need to know if she's okay," I snap at the cop who doesn't look the least bit bothered. "Just tell me if she's okay. If Josh is okay."

Vanessa, one of the nurses, comes over, standing at my side. "He's their friend and the surgeon who operated on Mr. Brown. He might be able to answer some questions about Mr. Ross. He was with them shortly before the incident."

Mr. Ross?

What the hell does Tyler have to do with this?

"Hold on a moment." The officer picks up his radio and speaks into it. "I have a Doctor Weston Kincaid." That's it. No other information is given to the officer on the other end and it's maddening. But then the curtain is drawn back, the glass door slides open, and instead of it being another officer, it's Aria.

A breath I didn't even realize I was holding rushes past my lungs as I step forward and wrap her up in my arms, burying my face in her neck. I don't even care if the whole ICU sees me do it. My relief overshadows everything else.

I kiss the spot between her shoulder and neck and then draw back to look her over.

She has a fresh bruise with a one-inch laceration on her right cheek. No stitches. My blood is boiling, but I grit my teeth, keeping it in check. If Tyler did this, his ass better be in jail where I cannot get to him. Christ. This is two times in as many days that this girl has been in trouble, only this time I wasn't here to protect her.

My hand cups her uninjured cheek and I stare into her. "You okay?" I ask, searching her eyes, and she nods. I take her hand and lead her into the room, but before the glass door is closed, I turn back to Vanessa and mouth, "Thank you."

She smiles and skips off, her job done for the moment. Josh is awake, the head of his bed raised to a forty-five-degree angle, and he looks uncomfortable. His body is tense like he's afraid to move, his features strained. Automatically, I check the patient-controlled analgesia device next to him. I can tell by the settings that it's been lowered significantly. There are two other officers in here, different from the detectives who had come around immediately after Josh was attacked.

"Doctor Kincaid?" one of them asks, and I turn my attention away from Josh over to him.

"Yes."

"Have a seat."

I shake my head. "He's in pain."

"We need to ask him some questions and we can't have him under the influence of opioids while we do that."

"He was attacked and had two major abdominal surgeries this week. His body's reaction to the pain is worse than him being on the medicine. Just let him hit the button for a bolus dose."

The two exchange meaningful glances, but then nod, one saying, "We're just about finished asking him questions anyway."

I walk in between them and the bed to reach for the button that will allow Josh to administer himself a dose of fentanyl. "Thanks," he says with a smile as he takes it and presses the red button. "I hear I owe you my life."

"Unfortunately, yes. And I plan on cashing in on that, so don't think it was a freebie."

Josh smirks at me as I walk back around the bed over to Aria's side. She's positioned herself on the edge of the bed, her hand holding Josh's, so I take her vacated chair and scoot it forward until my knees are brushing her leg. She smiles but doesn't look back at me or even comment.

The police continue to grill Aria and Josh, and within two minutes I've surmised that Tyler is the one who attacked Josh that night and the one responsible for Aria's cheek. When they finish with them, they ask me some questions about him. Things like how long have I known Tyler. About the interactions I've had with him. If I've ever witnessed him displaying any violent behavior.

I am zero help.

I've known Tyler for only a couple of days and in a very limited capacity. He's the significant other of a patient. A patient I know from childhood and he was very friendly with Aria, therefore, I was more casual with him than I typically would be.

But I do not know Tyler. Not really.

To say I'm floored Tyler not only tried to kill Josh that night but has been physically abusive with him for a couple of months, is an understatement.

Josh is a tall guy.

He's strong and bold and it's just not something I ever saw coming. It's not something you expect to hear. But in truth, no one really knows the inner workings of another. No one knows what can eventually lead someone to snap.

I know this firsthand, and it's taken me years to accept my father's suicide. To no longer blame myself for his actions. It wasn't an easy thing. And I know Josh is going to have a lot to sort through when this is all over. It's a sobering thought. Coming to grips with the knowledge that someone who says they love you, whom you love in return, is capable of hurting you.

I'm a man who dates women and it's not something I've had to deal with. I've never had an abusive lover and I've certainly never raised my hand to a woman. You don't frequently hear about relationship violence between men. That is not to say it doesn't happen, obviously, it does, but relationship violence against women feels more prevalent. At least to me. I've had several patients who have been on my operating table at the hands of their boyfriends or spouses.

But Josh? Never in a million years would I have ever expected this to be his life.

His relationship. My heart hurts for him.

But much like we don't know the real inner workings of another human, we also don't know what happens behind closed doors. It's easy to judge. Easy to place blame or make comments. Society punishes the victims enough. The world is faster to excuse the abuser and condemn the abused for not doing more to stop it.

At least that's been my experience. Nurses and doctors will say things like, "How did she let it go on for so long?" or "Why didn't she leave him sooner?"

I've always kept my mouth shut, because if I've learned anything from my experiences with my father, judgment is easy when you've never walked in someone else's shoes. When you've never lived in their world or their pain firsthand.

But really, I thought Josh and Tyler seemed like the perfect couple. I should have known better than to assume something like that. There is no such thing as a perfect anything.

The police eventually leave, satisfied with what they have. There was a lot of discussion about Tyler's shoes, and I'm not entirely sure what that means, but the police seemed please about them, so I'm hoping Tyler will be in jail and Josh will feel safe.

The moment they exit the room, Josh lets out a weighty sigh. His eyes close as he says, "I lied to you."

I assume he's speaking to Aria, but I'm not entirely sure at this point. She lies down next to him again, the way she did before he woke up. "Yes," she agrees. "You could have told me, Josh. I would have done everything I could to help."

"The first time he hit me, it was a slap." Josh shakes his head like it's the most ridiculous thing in the world. "It was like nothing, you know? We had a fight after a couple of glasses of wine each and things got out of control. We had both said things we shouldn't have, and that slap was the result. He was full of remorse. Said he couldn't believe he did that. I told him if he ever hit me again, I was done. He didn't hit me again for another couple of months. Then we had another fight and he really let me have it."

Aria's eyes slam shut as she burrows her head into his shoulder, gingerly wrapping an arm around his chest. "That was when you blew me off for two weeks? Wasn't it?"

"I couldn't let you see me like that, cowgirl. I was ashamed and embarrassed, and I didn't want to hear you go all preachy on me."

She raises her head, her eyes narrowed. "I would not have—"

"You would have," he interrupts her. "You absolutely would have because if the roles were reversed, I would have done it to you. You would have told me to leave him. You would have told me I deserved better, and I needed to go to the police and a hundred other things."

"Yeah," she says, her tone contrite. "I probably would have." I move to leave. I feel like an interloper who should not be here for such an intimate discussion between friends. "Don't go," she whispers without even looking over at me. I smile at that, but I peer over at Josh who nods his head.

"It's fine. Hang out a bit, doc." I sit back down silently, my hand reaching over and grasping Aria's calf, rubbing my thumb up and down against her silky skin. "I wasn't having an affair. I wasn't cheating or any other word there is for that. That name he saw in my phone was the therapist I started seeing to deal with this. That night at the restaurant, I told him I was done. That I didn't want to move in with him and that I needed a break. Then Brady and Connor showed up."

Jesus. Those assholes. I almost forgot about them. It wasn't them, and I'm relieved by that, but I will never see or speak to them again after what they did to Aria.

"I'm glad you remembered what happened," Aria says softly. "And I'm sorry about it. I love you, and you can always come to me. With anything. And if I get preachy, just tell me to shut the fuck up."

"I'm glad one of the men who loves you is a surgeon—"

Aria shoots up, her cheeks warming as her eyes burn holes into Josh. "Fucker."

"—Otherwise who knows what shape I'd be in."

"Like I said," I lean forward, squeezing Aria's calf, I don't even bother contradicting him, "you owe me. Tit for tat and all that shit, right? You think I work for free? I've got a million loans to pay off. These are some very expensive, well-educated hands we're talking about."

He gives me a tired half-smile and a small chuckle. "How about I let you win next time my team plays yours? And I won't tackle you." He hits his pain button again, and since the nurses lowered the dose, I'm sure he's feeling pretty rough.

"Considering it's *tag* football, you shouldn't have been tackling me in the first place."

Josh smiles, but I can see how difficult that is for him. He's still in a great deal of pain and no doubt beyond fatigued. But his vitals look really good, and his eyes and speech are clearer than I would have anticipated given his injuries and the medications they have him on.

Aria's brows scrunch at him before her head pivots to me. "What?"

"That rec football league I play in? Wes here also happens to play in it."

Her head whips back to Josh. "You play in a football league with *him*?" She juts her thumb in my direction and Josh looks like he wants to roll his eyes at her, but it requires too much effort.

"Yep."

Her eyes bug out of her head. "Dickface, you never mentioned that to me."

"Of course not," Josh says this like it should be obvious. "For the last decade we were not allowed to talk about he-who-shall-not-be-named. He was like freaking Voldemort."

"Did you talk to him about me?"

"No. I was dying to, though, and I could tell he wanted to ask about you, but never did. Believe it or not, Aria Davenport, the world does not revolve around you. I don't chat about you to the very straight guys I play football with. I have way more important things to focus on."

"Yeah, like how they look in their tight football clothes," she grouses, but she's smiling a little too.

"Exactly. That is far more important. And I can happily report Wes looks super-hot when he plays. Like way hotter than he did when we were teenagers. I *so* wanted to tell him you were back in town and single."

I can't help but laugh as I sink back into my seat. I'd mention that I can hear him, but what's the point. He knows I can, which is most definitely why he's saying all of this. "You do remember I had a broken heart, right?"

"Who could forget." Josh rolls his eyes. "But seriously, it's time you get over that. He's a surgeon, Aria. And I know you like him. It's *so* obvious. Plus, I like him better than I ever liked Drew."

Now her cheeks are on fire. "Girl code! He's right here. He can hear you."

"But I have a penis," he protests.

Aria beams at him, dropping her nose to his cheek. I love watching them together. Even if they are talking about me. "Good thing you're gay then, otherwise I wouldn't have lost my virginity to him." She points at me again and now it's my turn to look surprised.

"What?"

Aria laughs, her blue eyes so very bright at the moment. "Sorry, but Josh was *really* good-looking in high school. If he weren't gay, I'm just saying things might have gone differently."

"Not possible." I glide my hand from her calf up to her thigh. "There was no way I was letting anyone else have you."

"God, could you imagine? That would have been the worst sex of my life," Josh says on a sleepy smile, his eyes growing heavy.

She laughs, nodding her head, not the least bit bothered by his barb. "That's because I have a vagina."

That she does. And I'd really rather her not discuss it in front of Josh. I think this conversation is done for now. Plus, Josh looks like he's at his end. I stand up and walk around the bed, over to him. "I'm going to have one of the nurses come in and adjust your pain meds."

"Awesome."

"And I'm taking her with me."

"Even better."

“I’m staying here with you,” she complains adamantly.

“I’m tired and need my rest, cowgirl. Isn’t that right, doc?” A small one-sided smile pulls up the corner of his mouth before it’s just as quickly gone.

Running a hand through his hair, Aria says, “I don’t want to leave you after everything that happened.”

“No,” Josh argues in a firmer tone than I bet he typically uses with her, his eyes still closed, his voice growing fainter. “I want details tomorrow. I want good, *sexy* details. And no more fucking it up you two.” He’s out. That last word was barely audible.

I look at Aria.

She looks at me.

No more fucking it up.

Chapter Twenty-Seven

ARIA

Wes is leading me out of the ICU. I reluctantly follow. I really don't want to leave Josh, but I also think he might want to be alone. I mean, yeah, he's going to sleep for a while. But I'd bet he also needs time to process everything that happened with Tyler.

How do you make sense of your lover doing that to you? I have no idea. Honestly, I never would have pictured Tyler being capable of that.

I knew he had a temper. I saw his fist from the wall he punched, and I've heard him yell a time or two, but nothing like this. Nothing like trying to kill the man you claim to love.

"I don't want to leave him," I say again.

"I know," Wes responds with a warm smile and a squeeze of my hand. They're drugging Josh back up as we speak. Wes made sure that the nurses made him comfortable. I like that. I don't want Josh hurting. "But he needs to rest, and you'll come back in the morning. Tomorrow they'll try to get him up and moving. He'll need you then. Believe me. It's going to be a hard day for him."

I shake my head as we step into the elevator. My phone vibrates in my purse and when I pull it out, I gasp. "Holy shit." I have like a million missed calls and texts. From Rina, who isn't even working right now. About ten from Halle. More from Margot and Drew. "We need to stop down in the ER."

Wes peers down at me with an indecipherable expression. "To see Drew?"

"And Margot. They're worried about me."

Wes gives me a tight nod before he glances down at our joined hands. "Is this okay?" I look down at them too and then raise a questioning brow at him. "Because Drew said he was your fiancé. And if that's true then I need you to tell me now."

"He's not my fiancé. You already know this. You said if we sleep together, I'm yours. So I guess that's what I am."

Wes pivots his body so I'm pushed back into the wall of the elevator and he's standing before me. His hands cup my cheeks and he tilts my head so I'm forced to stare up into his eyes. "Is that what you want? To be mine? I want you to be happy. But if he's still making noise, then I'm going to fight for you. I've let you go too many times to make that mistake again."

I can't speak, nor can I stop the tears swimming in my eyes. His head dips until his nose runs along mine.

I blow out a weighty breath. How do you tell someone you love them when you're afraid?

"Have you ever been in love? Horrible isn't it? It makes you so vulnerable. It opens your chest and it opens up your heart and it means that someone can get inside you and mess you up."

He grins against me. "Who said that?"

"Neil Gaiman."

"I like it. Even if I hate its meaning." He pulls back just as the doors to the elevator open and we're greeted to the sounds of the emergency department.

He steps out ahead of me and does not retake my hand. I stare down at his for a moment before I hear Margot yelling my name. My eyes fly up to find her as she sprints across the bustling hall in my direction. I laugh and shake my head. Fucking Margot. Always so dramatic.

I feel Wes lean into me, his breath tickling my ear as he whispers, "I look at you and I see my forever. Give me a chance to win you back for good. To show you I'm your forever too. I swear, I won't mess you up this time."

My breath catches in my chest. Doesn't he already know? How can he still question it?

I twist to tell him the second Margot engulfs me in the biggest hug I think I've ever had. "Oh my God," she half-sobs, half-shrieks. "I was so scared. What the hell happened and why didn't you pick up your goddamn phone?" She pulls back and catches sight of my cheek, her eyes bugging out of her head. "Holy duck shit. What happened?"

"It's a long story. But I'm fine. I swear." I have no idea how bad my cheek looks. I haven't had the opportunity to see it.

"This is *so* not fine. Was it really Tyler? Was he really the one who did that to Josh?"

"News travels fast."

"Hospital employees gossip. Haven't you ever watched *Grey's Anatomy*?"

"Not since they killed McSteamy."

"Right?" She laughs so hard. "Is Josh okay? I have no words for what he must be going through."

"He's hanging in there."

Margot peeks up at Wes who is quietly standing with us—insanely close to my side, I might add—and then back to me. "Should I tell Drew you're fine or do you want to go find him so he can see for himself?"

"She doesn't have to," Drew says from behind me.

I spin around at the sound of his voice, and suddenly I feel like I'm doing something wrong. Like my parents just caught me kissing the boy I snuck into my room. Which would have been Wes if I was being literal since my mother did catch me kissing him once, but whatever. Semantics and all that.

Drew's eyes flitter over to Wes quickly, something very deliberate passing between them before Drew reaches forward and grabs me.

He tugs me into him, hugging me close. "I was so worried about you. I'm so relieved you're okay."

"I'm sorry to interrupt," a voice says from behind me, and I swear, it's like craziness in my head. We all pause, turning to catch the eye of a nurse. "Dr. Kincaid, I know you're not technically on right now, but I have a hernia patient you operated on last week back here today complaining of abdominal pain. Can you just take a quick look?" I step back, out of Drew's arms.

Wes blows out a heavy breath, his eyes closing, his face twisting into a frustrated grimace before he reopens them and focuses on mine. In them, I see the promise behind his words. "I'll just be a few minutes," he says to me. And then he turns to the nurse who continues to apologize profusely as they walk off together.

"Do you want me to get someone to cover the rest of my shift?" Drew asks, diverting my attention back to him. Literally, his fingers are on my chin and he's guiding my face away from Wes's retreating form back to his steely gray gaze. "I hate that you were attacked, and I wasn't there to protect you."

And that's like six months too late. I mean, that's the first thing that pops into my head. Obviously I do not need a man to take care of me.

I never did.

But most of all, Drew is not the man I want. Not the man I love. Wes is.

I shake my head. "Drew, can we go somewhere and talk?"

"Well, this is awkward," Margot interrupts and I completely forgot she was still here. I roll my eyes at her. "I'll let Rina and the Hallster know you and Josh are alive and well. I have patients I need to get back to, but you better freaking call me tomorrow, because wow." Her eyes go wide before she blows me a kiss and then jaunts off.

"About what?" Drew asks, picking back up where we were before Margot interrupted us. His expression tells me he knows exactly what I want to talk about.

"I'm sorry, Drew. I really am. You're an amazing guy—"

"Don't," he snaps quickly, cutting me off. His face drops to the floor and his breathing grows heavy. But he had to know this was coming. That we couldn't just start over like the last six months apart never happened. "You don't even want to try to work this out, Aria? That makes no sense to me. We had a good thing for a very long time. We were amazing together. Don't let one speed bump throw us off course."

When Drew ended things with me for his unexplained, bullshit reasons, I was hurt. I won't even lie and say I wasn't. I was hurt. But I wasn't *devastated*. My world didn't feel like it was ending. The darkness didn't feel like it would never clear. It took me months, not years to get over him. Here I am, six months after we broke up and I'm right back to where I was before I met him.

Or close enough at least.

Maybe I was too young and too immature when Wes and I were Wes and I. Maybe that's why his leaving felt like that. But his leaving *did* feel like that. And Drew's didn't. And Wes is telling me I'm his forever, and he wants to convince me he's mine.

I don't see that when I look at Drew. That forever thing.

When I look at Drew, I see a lot of personal sacrifices I would have to make. I see giving up a large piece of who I am.

When I look at Wes, I see infinite possibilities because he knows me. He. Knows. Me.

He knows what my art means to me. He would never expect me to give that up for him. Never. It's why he let me go all those years ago. Why he never told me he came to New York for me. I believe that. I know it in my heart.

"Aria?" Drew asks impatiently, grasping my hand and staring at me intently when I don't respond. "You cannot be serious about this? You barely know Wes. Me?" He points to his chest. "Me, you know. It's me you love."

I shake my head. He really has no idea, and I don't think this is the moment to explain everything. At least not fully.

"Drew," I start again. "You're so special to me. You always will be. That will never ever change. But I've loved Wes for a very long time. I've known him practically my whole life. We grew up together. He was my first everything. And while that may suck to hear, it doesn't mean I didn't love you. I did. You know I did. But if I did try again with you, we would end the same way we did last time. I don't want to give up my art. It's part of my soul. The way medicine is for you, and I would never let you sacrifice your dream for me. You like your long hours and I like mine." Truth be told, we never made the effort. Neither wanting to make the sacrifice for the other. If that's not telling, I don't know what is. "We're just not right together, Drew. I love you and I care about you, but it's not the way it should be."

He shakes his head, incredulous, I think. "No," he says. "I think I just waited too long to try to get you back." He lets out a harsh, bitter breath, his hands going to his hips. "And for the record, I think this is a mistake. What we had was good and should not be thrown away without giving it another try. I love you, Aria, and I was willing to go the distance. To finally make the sacrifices. To give it my all."

I'm tempted to mention that he's the one who threw us away the moment things got tough, and that it shouldn't take all this to finally make him want to give it his all, but I keep my mouth shut on that.

It's not relevant. It's not why I'm doing this.

"I'm sorry," I offer instead. "I hope in time you'll see this is what's best for both of us and we can be friendly if not friends."

Drew's eyes pierce into mine for the longest of moments and then he gives me a tight nod. "Yeah. I'd like that. I don't want to lose you completely."

I smile genuinely, even if this does hurt some. I reach up and give him a hug that he returns. His lips plant themselves onto my cheek and then he turns away, marching off to go back and do his job.

But before he gets too far, he spins back around and says, "Wes better take care of you. I'll kick his ass all over the place if he doesn't." He throws me a wink and a smirk and then turns the corner out of sight.

I laugh. I can't help it. Drew might be an asshole. He might be arrogant. But he's been through a lot and has a heart of gold at his center.

I feel better now. Lighter. I know Drew and I will remain close. Despite all of our drama, I really do care about him. He's a good man. A very good man.

But he's not my Wes.

Speaking of…

Chapter Twenty-Eight

ARIA

I text Wes asking how long he's going to be. I don't want to rush him, but I'm dying for a shower. And I'm starving. I haven't eaten anything in hours, and I bet it's the same for him.

The food he brought us was somehow discarded.

I don't want to go find him.

First, he's with a patient. Second, I don't exactly belong back here in the patient area. I don't work here and I'm not a patient and I've gotten yelled at before.

I step out into the waiting room and well, I wait. I wait ten minutes and I don't hear anything back. I'm not annoyed, I'm just...okay, I'm a bit annoyed. Because we talked about dinner and forevers, and I thought this was going to be our night. Our start. And I get it, his patients come first. Someone is sick and hurting and I don't want to diminish the severity of that.

But come the fuck on!

He could at least text me back. Or have one of the nurses do it.

I sigh and text him again, letting him know that I'm heading home for a shower and to call me when he's finished so we can meet somewhere for dinner. I walk outside, hop in a waiting cab and fifteen minutes later, I'm home. I feel like I haven't been here in years. But Josh is awake and will be okay, and Tyler, freaking *Tyler*, is going to jail.

All I can do is shake my head at that one because it is beyond reasoning.

I jog upstairs, strip out of the clothes Wes bought me, and jump in my shower. I swear, I've never been happier that Josh talked me into the multiple jets thing when I renovated the master bathroom. This might just be the best shower ever. After I get out, I wrap a towel around myself as I go digging through my closet.

I checked my phone like an obsessive teenager the moment I got out of the shower, and I'm already hating myself for feeling this sort of disappointment at seeing nothing from Wes. Because if this is the way things will be with him, then I'm not interested. It's why after staring at all of the cute clothes I own, almost an hour after I left Wes in the hospital, I vacate my closet in favor of my dresser that houses all of my comfy clothes.

Fucking men. Fucking Wes. I should know better by now.

Just as my hand reaches for the knob of my dresser, there's a knock at my door, followed by the bell and another round of persistent knocking. I fly down the stairs, practically tripping over my feet as I do. Drawing back the edge of the curtain I catch a glimpse of Wes's jacket. "Crap," I mutter and then I hear him cough.

"Open the door, Aria. I know you're in there."

"How can you possibly know that?"

"Other than the fact I heard you say crap, you just answered me."

"You didn't return my texts. Or call me."

"I know. Open up."

I sigh but unlock the door and swing it open. A blast of cold air rushes over me and I'm suddenly very aware I'm still wrapped in a towel. Only a towel. And judging by the way Wes's heated eyes travel down my body, I see he's realizing the same thing. "Are you trying to kill me?"

I glance down. "Hadn't thought about it. But if my being in a towel causes you to drop dead, that's fine."

Wes steps inside and I close and lock the door behind him. He squeezes the back of his neck and tries his best to keep his eyes on mine. He fails a few times and it makes me smile despite my ire and frustration with the whole male gender.

"I'm sorry. I know you're pissed and you have every right to be. I left my phone in my car in my haste to get back up to you and Josh earlier and I didn't see your messages until I looked for it to call you. I figured I might as well just come here instead of texting you a restaurant because I was already late. Now go get dressed." He points to the stairs behind me. "I can't fucking think with you only in that towel. I'm a second away from ripping it off your body and calling it an accident."

"What? This old thing?" I twist around in a circle.

"Aria," he groans. "Now it's a half-second."

I laugh, but scoot away from him, heading for my stairs. I feel his hand smack my ass and I yelp, laughing louder. "That hurt," I call to him as I ascend the stairs.

"Did not," he calls back.

"Can we order food in?" I yell out as I quickly dress with my door open. I throw on a pair of jeans and a black sweater before I run a brush through my drying curls. They're going to look crazy, but I don't want to waste time blow-drying my hair. "I'm starving. Like officially. I'm liable to become a cranky bitch if I'm not properly fed within the hour. I'm borderline there now. So, can we just order food in? I sort of have a hankering to eat something terribly greasy in front of the fire with a bottle of wine."

"That sounds perfect," Wes says from my doorway, and I let out a shrill screech, jumping a foot into the air at the surprise of him being up here.

"That was mean." I raise my eyebrows and point at him. Christ, I think I just died.

He smirks as he shrugs. Stepping into my room, his eyes sweep over everything including the discarded red lace bra that's been gracing my floor for the past two days. I wish I was wearing that one right now instead of the black one. Red feels naughtier. "We can definitely order in cranky girl."

"Thank God," I sigh dramatically, trying to ignore his presence in my room and the desire to jump him and tackle him to my bed. "Because if you had pitched a fit about it, I was going to tell you to scram while I raided my fridge."

Wes laughs. Reaching over, he takes my hand, tugging me into his body. His cheek glides across mine as his mouth reaches my ear, his breath tickling my sensitive skin and awaking every nerve ending in my body.

"Nervous, Aria?"

Shit. Was I babbling? Of course, I was babbling because I am ridiculously nervous.

"Yes. But I'm also hungry, so please don't discount that. I need you to order food while I open some wine because I'm thinking we're going to need wine." *Shut up, Aria!* I was not like this last night in his bed. It's all that talk of forever. It's having him in my space and committing to this. To being with Wes. Finally.

Shit. That really didn't help my nerves.

"I can order food." He steps back and pulls out his phone. He does something with it that I cannot see and not even two minutes later he looks up at me as he slides his phone back into his pocket and says, "Done. It will be here in about an hour. Can you manage until then?"

"I can manage," I say because suddenly I have an amazing idea. "Come with me." I take his hand and lead him out of my bedroom and up the third-floor stairs to my studio. I walk him over to the sofa I have positioned in front of one of the windows and I shove him down until he's lying on his back. I stand over him, doing my best to ignore the way his eyes are feasting on my body, and think about how I want him. "Place your right arm behind your head and cross your legs at the ankle." He does, and I smile. "Eyes on me. Hold that pose."

He doesn't say anything. He just watches as I walk over to a blank canvas I have set up. I'd love to paint him, but I don't have the time and I think charcoal will capture this better anyway. My hand raises to the stretched material and then I pause. Something isn't right.

"Take off your shirt," I command, and he grins impishly.

"You want to draw me without my shirt on?"

"That's exactly what I want to do."

"I will if you do too."

My cheeks heat and my heart rate quickens. I remove my sweater. A wicked grin pulls up the corner of his lips. He sits up, his eyes raking me in as he reaches behind his head and tugs his shirt off with one smooth motion. "Go back to your pose."

He stands up instead, stalking toward me, those delicious muscles in his abs and chest flexing with each step, and when he reaches me, he hooks two fingers through the belt loops of my jeans. He tugs until I step toward him, his warm muscular chest pressed against me. His lips descend, crushing into mine in a dominating kiss that has me grasping his upper arms for support. "You have a photographic memory, Aria," he breathes against my lips. "Don't pretend I don't know this amazing fact about you. Draw me from memory if you must, but pretty soon you won't be able to stand so you should start drawing now."

He spins me around to face the canvas, lifting the hand still holding the charcoal up to the white cotton. I do start to draw from memory because even if I didn't have a photographic memory, the image of him on my sofa staring at me like I'm his next meal is forever burned into my brain.

I start my sketch, the smooth edge of the charcoal gliding across, creating rough lines as I try to gain control of my shaky hand. My breathing is no better and shifts from soft pants to ragged when I feel Wes's fingers glide achingly slow down the contours of my back. They reach the waist of my jeans, running along the seam before dipping under the hem. I shudder violently. Embarrassingly so. "You've stopped drawing," he whispers in my ear and chills erupt across my skin. "Keep going, Aria. I want to see what you create while I make you come with my fingers."

I moan. It can't be helped. I also close my eyes because his words take over everything, and I need a moment to compose myself. But when I open them again, I realize that's an impossibility, because his hand is snaking around to the front of my jeans, tickling the tender flesh of my lower abdomen before he releases the button.

And then lowers the zipper. I moan again, this time with an added whimper, and he hasn't even touched me where I need him to yet.

My hand continues to advance on the canvas, but I can't focus on anything other than the tips of his fingers as they glide against the lace of my panties. "Mmm…so wet for me."

His fingers press against my clit, using the texture of the lace as added friction and driving me wild with the need to come. But before I can comprehend the sweet torture of his ministrations as he moves along the fabric, Wes slides them aside and dips his fingers inside of me. "Oh, God," I cry out so loud I'm positive my neighbors just heard me.

"What do you think my mouth licking your sweet pussy would do? Do you think it would alter your drawing more than my fingers?"

I can't speak. I can only focus on breathing and his fingers and the way this feels. Because every time he pushes in and out of me or rubs my aching clit, is better than the last. He snakes my jeans down my thighs, his fingertips pressing into my heated flesh and now I have no idea what I'm doing. My hand is moving, and his hand is moving, and I'm stepping out of my jeans, and my panties are following, and the second I'm aware he's on his knees in front of me, his mouth is on me, licking me, sucking on me until I'm dizzy.

"Draw, Aria. I stop the moment you do."

Shit. He wants me to keep drawing a stupid picture I no longer care about when his mouth is doing the most unbelievable things to me? Is he fucking insane? I'm trying too hard to remain upright. "Please," I beg. I have no idea if I'm still drawing, or standing, or moaning, or talking. All I know is that I never want this to end. And if this is what his tongue is capable of now, after ten years apart, I'm marrying him tomorrow. Because… Oh. My. *God!*

"Tell me, baby. Tell me what you want. I'll give you anything you want."

I have no idea what I want. Except… "Don't stop."

"Not until you come on my tongue. Then I'm going to bury my cock so deep inside of you. You're mine, Aria. Say it."

"Yes," I pant, so very close.

"No. Say you're mine or I stop. I can't share you. I can't be inside you unless this is real between us. I told you that last night and I meant it."

Goddamn sexy alpha domineering bastard. "I've already told you, Wes. I'm yours."

"That's all I needed to hear."

And then he licks me, flicking his tongue before sucking my clit between his lips. His fingers pump in and out of me until I come like I've never come before. I scream. I might never have screamed before, but I'm most definitely screaming now. And my hand is still sketching, an afterthought that I'm oddly aware of.

And when my spasms slow, he glides up my body and kisses me, breathing into me as he whispers, "You're so beautiful. So perfect." He leans back and stares intently into my eyes. A warm, glowing smile lighting up his handsome face. "I love you so much, Aria. I never stopped. It's always been you."

I can't respond. I'm just an endless pool of emotion, and lust, and possibility.

"Keep drawing. This is something we're keeping always."

Wes's hand presses down on my belly, his other hand guiding his cock up to my entrance. My eyes close and my breath shudders and my body shakes. Has it ever been like this before?

With one smooth motion, Wes is inside me. He gives me a moment to settle in, to adjust to his size as he stretches my walls.

"Are you ready?"

I nod, my breath stalled in my chest. With his hands on my hips, he controls the pace. He slides in and out, slowly at first, his cock hitting that magical spot inside me with each thrust as I continue to draw.

Then he lets go. Gives in.

His cock pumps into me, hard, his arms wrapping around me, squeezing my breasts, holding me upright. I'm a mass of sensation. A deluge of pleasure. His fingers find my clit, rubbing in a rhythm so perfectly attuned to the thrust of his hips.

This is the most erotic moment of my life and I'm capturing it on canvas in charcoal as the love of my life fucks me senseless. Loves and worships my body. Kisses me and talks to me, telling me how perfect I feel. How this is only the beginning for us. And when I come, my hand slashes across the canvas. I fall back against him, his arm holding me up as my legs are officially Jell-O and are no longer capable of supporting my weight.

I pull back and meet his eyes. "I love you, too," I tell him with so much conviction my chest tightens like a vice is squeezing me. "I never stopped loving you. You've always been the love of my life. The one I compared everyone else against."

His mouth meets mine in a bruising kiss. And when he pulls back, he's giving me the same smile he gave me on my roof the first time he kissed me under the new snow. He opens his mouth to say more, but the doorbell rings. "Food." Thank God, because now that our lovemaking is done, my stomach is about to implode. "Get dressed and meet me downstairs."

He pulls on his clothes as I turn to stare at what I just created. It's madness. Nonsensical. It's all lines and smoky brilliantly constructed chaos. It's fucking fantastic. The best thing I've ever done.

His hand grasps mine, pulling it until it covers his chest over his pounding heart. "As long as this is beating, it's yours. And we're going to make a million more like this. One day, we'll look back on our story and realize how painfully exquisitely perfect it all was." He kisses me again and then he's gone, running down the stairs to get our food.

Painfully exquisitely perfect. That's us. And it's just our start.

Epilogue 1

I should propose to her. Again. It's the perfect day for it and really, it's a long time coming. A year, in fact, since that first day she walked back into my life. Since I stood on the precipice of Josh's ICU room and saw her twisting her body, speaking to her comatose friend. I felt my heart start to beat. It hadn't done that in an observable way, in a palpable way, in years. Not since she walked out of my life and I let her go.

Aria is a mess. Covered in paint and too many layers to count. Yes, layers because the heat to our townhouse broke last night, and it's the middle of January, and she refused to leave in favor of Josh's, or Halle and Jonah's, or a hotel even because she was, and I'm quoting here, "in the zone." Naturally, I refused to leave, too, and we survived on the gas fireplace, lots of blankets, and those layers. But even dressed like the abominable snowman, she's the most breathtaking creature I've ever come across.

The heat is back on, has been for a few hours now, so she really could do without so many layers.

I fell in love with Aria staring up at the heavens, watching the snow fall. I fell in love with her over a decade and a million minutes ago. But I continue to find small things that make me fall in love with her again and again and again. Like right now. She's wearing her earbuds, as always, and from all the way across the room, I can hear the music blasting into her ears. It's fast with a steady beat, but more than that, I can't tell. But what really stops my breath is the way she moves to it. She's dancing. But not just dancing like you'd see women in a club do. No, Aria is letting it all out. She's jumping around and twisting her body and rocking her hips and bouncing her head from side to side along to the beat.

I'm enraptured. Totally and completely.

She shifts to the side and I catch a glimpse of the colorful art in front of her. This is no ordinary piece. Her painting is bold and sensual. Far too sexual for me not to hope it's us she's extrapolating from. But it's also very angry and violent. It's a storm of color and emotion.

Aria begins to sing, and I pause all over again, smiling like the stupid love-crazy bastard she makes me. And I am crazy about her. Like nothing and no one could ever be.

"I don't like hovering interlopers, Weston Kincaid," she says, not even bothering to slow her brushstrokes as she does.

An uncontrollable smile bursts forth and I find myself moving slowly as I approach her. "What about hovering interloping fiancés?"

She sighs. "I don't like them either. And you're not my fiancé."

"But I should be."

"I'll think about it." She's smiling. I can tell. She likes this conversation, though she refuses to give me a real answer. Even though I've already asked. Well, sorta. I didn't get down on bended knee. I didn't give her a diamond. I just asked if she'd marry me and she gave me the same answer she just gave me now, I'll think about it.

I wrap my arms around her waist and press my lips into the crook of her neck. "I'm thinking a summer wedding."

"Too hot. And my mother would like that way too much. So would yours. Besides, I don't want a real wedding. It's too…traditional. No white dress or wedding march or tuxedos or fluffy gowns. It's gross. And too expected."

"I'm thinking I get you pregnant before we get married."

"So people can ask if the only reason you're marrying me is because you knocked me up?"

"Precisely. But until I can convince you to marry me, I need you to come with me."

She turns her head over her shoulder and glares at me. "Absolutely not."

I don't give her the choice. She's been going for hours and she needs a break. I take her hand and intertwine my fingers with hers and I lead her down to our shower. She doesn't pull away and she doesn't object further so I know she's finished for the day whether she says so or not.

She's a mess. No way I can take her anywhere like this. I wash her hair and her body, resisting the urge to make love to her against the tile, or shove my tongue inside her, and I help her out, wrapping her up in a towel.

Then I hand her the cream-colored dress she wore last year that made her look like a winter fairy. It's my favorite thing she owns. She ran after me in the cold in this dress. It was the moment I realized the ten years apart were meaningless. That she was still my one.

"Where exactly are we going?" she asks as she sits and does her hair the way it was last year on that night. I don't even have to prompt her for that. She remembers and she's doing it. She's feigning annoyance, but I know she's not. She likes this. Even if she's too stubborn to ever admit it.

"Dinner," I tell her. "It's our anniversary."

"What?" she scoffs. "It absolutely is not."

"It is, Aria. One year ago today, I saw you again. The rest is just semantics."

"That's romantic," she snorts, rolling her eyes, her tone dripping with sarcasm. But she's putting on her makeup and ten minutes later, we walk out of our home to my Jeep that I have waiting directly in front. An amazing feat given parking in the South End of Boston. I help her in, and then I sprint around, starting the car up because holy fucking shit it's cold.

She doesn't ask where we're going again, and it's a relief

because the last thing I want to do is lie to her. I'm not very good at it, and she's like some rabid bullshit detector. Reaching across, I take her hand in mine and squeeze. Her eyes shoot over in my direction and she smiles warmly.

I want to play a game with her.

"When was the first moment you knew you loved me?" I ask.

"Hmm…I don't know." She tilts her head, contemplatively. "I was young. Not sure I have an exact moment. I liked you forever."

"I did too."

She crosses her legs and pinches the skin of my hand. It stings, but not enough for me to pull away. Instead, it makes me laugh and her groan. "I don't know why you keep telling me that. It's a total lie."

"Is not."

"Is so. You ignored me forever."

"Because I liked you."

She laughs, shaking her head, but that smile on her lips is unstoppable. "That's so juvenile, I almost believe you." This is an ongoing argument. One I always seem to win. Mostly because she likes it when I say this. Loves this particular game we play.

"The moment I realized I loved you was the first night I kissed you. I'm pretty positive I loved you before that. I know I did, actually. It happened one of those nights under the stars, but I didn't admit it to myself until that night when I was climbing up that tree to your roof."

She leans across the space between us and gives me a kiss on the corner of my lips, whispering in my ear, "I was a goner way before that. I hated that I was so young, and you were older and Breck's friend. I hated all of it."

"And now we're going to have a summer wedding with you…," I catch her eye, "three months pregnant?"

She laughs, sitting back in her seat and crossing her legs at the knee. "Shut up with that. Either propose the right way or don't."

"I can't do that. Not until you say yes."

"That makes no sense."

"It makes perfect sense, baby. You don't do traditional, remember? And what if I ask and you say no? I can't handle that sort of rejection. I think I need you to say yes before I ask you in the traditional sense."

"God, that's so dumb." She's smiling like crazy and my plan is working.

I love her smile. I love the way her pale blue eyes look at me. I love the way her dark curly hair falls around her face, framing it perfectly. She laughs, and I realize it's because I'm still looking at her even though I should be focusing on the road. It seriously makes me question how I made it through those ten years away from her. "Wanna marry me?"

"I'll think about it. But for now, how about you drive?"

"Sure. We can set a date later. I'm thinking The Four Seasons for the reception." She lets out a loud sigh as I take a turn on Newbury and park the car behind a building. A building with a For Sale sign in the back window that now has a SOLD sticker on it. "Wes," she barks out, her eyes wide. "What the hell are you doing?" I turn off the ignition and face her. "No, seriously. Just what the absolute fucking hell are you doing?"

So here's the deal. I was offered a position in Dallas, Texas. A position I told her I was taking. We talked about it. She said she was in, but I could tell her heart was not. She always said Boston wasn't the best place to sell art, but Aria has been selling art like a master. People come from all over the world to see her. So Boston isn't an issue. And Josh is here. And Halle, Rina, and Margot, and even fucking Drew is here. And our parents.

Besides, MGH is one of the best hospitals in the country. Boston is our home. Which means Dallas is out and Aria needs a proper studio. "There are two stories, Aria. The first floor is a gallery space where you can show whatever you want. The second floor is also open, baby. Like your studio in our house, but it's not in the house, and the lighting is incredible and the best part? The roof."

"The roof," she parrots, her eyes growing glassy.

"Yeah. The roof. Come on."

I jump out of the car and she does too. She's too excited to wait for me to open the door for her. Pulling out my key, I insert it into the lock, twist it until it disengages and then I lead her in, flipping on the lights as I go. This place cost my entire inheritance my father left me when he killed himself. I never spent it. Not on my loans. Not on a place to live. Not on anything. Because it always felt tainted. Like I would disappoint him more if I spent it on myself and the career he never wanted me to have. But Aria is different, and I can't think of a better person to spend it on.

"Wow," she breathes in an awed half-whisper. "This is gorgeous."

Her fingers skim along the white walls. That's all that's here. White walls and neutral hardwoods and openness. But the moment I stepped in, I knew it was for her. There are so many things she can do with this space. So many ways she can make it hers.

And then she stares up at the high ceilings. "I love it."

"You do?"

"Most definitely. But what about Texas?"

I take her into my arms and I hold her tight. "Texas isn't Boston. And Boston is where we live."

"Boston is home," she agrees, echoing my thoughts from seconds ago with a contented smile spread across her face. "Are you sure?"

"Positive."

A smile lights up her entire face. "Show me the rest, Doctor Kincaid."

"Yes, Mrs. Kincaid." She lets out a half-groan, half-laugh to that as I lead her to the back of the building where the stairs are.

"So stubborn," I muse as I lead her up.

"Right," she puffs. "*I'm* stubborn."

We go past the darkened second floor where she balks. "Roof first. We'll work our way down."

"But it's cold up there."

"Freezing," I add. "And snowing." I turn back and flash her with a smile before I open the door. "Come here." I pull her back against my chest and cover her eyes with my hands. Her hands fly up, grasping onto my wrists as we step forward, her movements more careful than mine. "Do you love me?" I ask in her ear.

I can feel her smile as my cheek presses against hers. "Always."

"Good. So you won't be mad at me then."

"*What?!*"

I remove my hands from her eyes and laugh as she sucks in a deep breath. But before she can fully appreciate everything I've done for her, I swivel her around and finally get down on one knee, staring up into her eyes. "Aria, I love you. You are the automatic beat of my heart. The pump of blood through my veins. The color to my black and white. I need you. You are in my soul with every piece of my existence." She smiles down at me, tears streaming down the sides of her face as I speak the words she wrote all those years ago on the back of my painting. I mean them just as much as she did when she wrote them. "Will you marry me?"

"You sneak attacked me."

I grin. "I did. But I still need an answer."

"Yes," she laughs, throwing her head back. "I'll marry you."

"Now?"

She nods. "Absolutely." I stand up and kiss her.

"You're supposed to do that after you say, I do," Brecken yells out and everyone, all of our family and friends, laughs. Brecken got over the initial shock faster than I expected. Good thing, because he's moving to Boston and if he didn't agree then Aria would be out a brother. Only kidding. But not.

"Then I guess I should let your father walk you down the aisle." I kiss her cheek.

"Please. It's very cold up here. Those heaters you ordered aren't nearly enough to keep your new mother-in-law warm. She's already complaining." That's my new father-in-law. And if I've learned anything, it's that my new mother-in-law does not like the cold, or driving, or snow, or anything medically related. But that's another story for another time.

"I am not," Aria's mother yells out and then Margot yells back, "She is, Aria. Please help us. I want to see you get married so I can get my drink on."

"Oh no." Aria laughs, and I lean in and kiss her again.

"Enough. Patience and all that." Aria's father takes her hand, throws me a wink and escorts her away from me. He leads her down the aisle. Well, it's not really much of an aisle. And it's true, those heaters I ordered really aren't doing much. And this wedding technically isn't legal because Aria didn't sign a marriage license and neither did I. But hey, it's what we're working with and I wanted this all to be a surprise. Because Aria would never have planned anything. She would have dragged me down to city hall, and I want this memory. I want to tell our children about the night I married her in the freezing cold as the snow fell on us.

I meet her at the front of the line and Josh and Brecken are standing next to me. The snow is starting to fall a little harder and I can't think of a better way to marry my girl. My life's love. The woman I was never able to get over. The woman who kept me alive when I felt so very dead.

I've had a lot of regrets in my life. Things I've done wrong and wished I could change. My father will always be the biggest. The most prominent, and tonight I wish he were here to watch me marry Aria. To finally see me for the man I became. Because I'm proud of this man. And I don't regret my choice to pursue medicine instead of football. But he's not here, and over the years, I've accepted that some people are unable to be helped. Maybe he was one of them, and maybe he wasn't, but I wasn't at a point where I could do more for him than I did. I accept that now. I do.

And Aria. I always regretted the way I treated her. Which is why I want her to have everything. Need to show her that there is nothing more special in my life than her. She's all I'll ever need. The rest is gravy.

This whole thing is very impromptu. There is no officiant. It's just our friends and family, and it's just us promising forever. We'll make it official another time, but this is the one that matters.

When I'm her husband, when it's finally officially unofficial, everyone claps and cheers. I dip her back and hold her close, and I kiss her like a husband should always kiss his wife. With lots of tongue and exchanges of breath and a passion that can never be rivaled. "I love you," I whisper against her, making her smile and her bright eyes sparkle. "Forever."

"And ever," she says. "You're stuck with me now, Doctor."

I grin against her. "Finally."

"Here's to finally not fucking it up." That's Margot.

"Here's to true love." That's Halle.

"Here's to shutting up so we can get somewhere warm." That's Josh. And her mother, actually.

"Here's to all of you shutting up. Let them finish and then we'll go. You only get this moment once." That's Rina.

I grin at our people. Our family. "Come dance with me?" I whisper against her. "I want to hold my wife while I dance with her in the middle of her new studio. Before I get her pregnant later. That's going to be a lot of fun."

Aria rolls her eyes at me. Only, I'm not kidding. That might be a conversation to start later. But for now…

"I thought you'd never ask," she says, and then I right her body, take her hand to lead her to the second floor where I have food, and yes, alcohol, and music waiting on us. She spends the rest of the night in my arms. And that's where she'll spend the rest of her life. Because distance and regrets are a thing of our past. And this is the start of our forever.

Epilogue 2

Margot

THE SALTY BRINE of the Atlantic sweeps across my face and through my hair, lifting it until it whips back behind me. I'm aiming for screen goddess right now and I think I'm nailing that one pretty hard with this hair whip going on and my white chiffon dress, à la Marilyn Monroe, dancing with it. I'm standing on the edge of the grass line, staring down at the beach and ocean below. Waiting. For him.

It's been four months since he left for London. Four months since he ended things with me so he could move back home. At the time, the move was perceived indefinite and we weren't together long enough for him to ask me to go with him. At least, that's what I told myself. Three months of a relationship is not enough time to make a trans-Atlantic move with someone.

Except, I would have.

That's how deep into him I was.

But he's back now, so the last four months hardly matter, right?

Behind me, the happy din of the party, complete with the

melody of glasses clinking and people laughing, makes me smile. I love parties on The Cape. I don't get out to Cape Cod as often as I'd like – lack of my own personal digs and tons of money are to blame. But this year, a friend of a friend invited me to tag along, and when I heard the party was to help celebrate a certain someone returning from London, well, I jumped. Literally. I practically gave Doctor Forrester a hernia when I leapt into his arms with squealing delight.

The wind changes direction and with it the mood of the party.

A tingle works its way up my spine as his name floats over to me on the breeze. Julien. A bubble of nervous anticipation swirls in my belly. Unfortunately, the glass and a half of champagne I've had seems to enhance my jitters instead of squelching them.

I give myself a quick once-over. Dress? Perfection. Hair? Well, I'm hoping the windswept look throughout my long brown locks is sexy and not a frizzy mess. Breath? Cupping my hand in front of my mouth, I breathe out and quickly catch the remnants of the mints I've been relentlessly sucking on. Makeup? Shit. Where is my phone when I need it?

Riffling through my purse that's strapped over my shoulder, I locate it all the way at the bottom. Just as I pull up my camera app and flip the image so it's facing me and not the ocean, I catch sight of the man himself strolling up behind me. An amused smile curls up the edges of his lips when he catches me staring at myself on the screen of my phone.

Oops. Well that sucks. Not exactly the entrance I was hoping to make with him.

A hand runs along his smooth, tanned jaw and I realize I'm still watching him through my phone. Quickly shutting it down, I tuck it back into my purse, blow out a silent heave of a breath and spin around. And God, I almost forgot how good-looking he is. Tall with unruly wavy blond hair, soft-hued brown eyes, strong angled jaw, and the lithe yet muscular body of a man who runs marathons. Our eyes meet, and I smile before I can stop myself, my heart beating to that familiar thrum–a rhythm only he's been able to produce.

I take a step toward him, almost magnetized, my body unable to wait for him to finish the journey across the spacious–especially for

The Cape–backyard. But then I catch a flash of honey out of the corner of my periphery, and my eyes automatically track it, scanning down and to the left of Julien. *My* Julien. My Julien who has a petite blonde woman stuck to his side, her hand resting comfortably in the crook of his elbow.

Time slows, deciding to take this particular moment to fuck with me and draw out the torture of what my heart has already seemed to process, but my brain is slow to capture. The petite blonde woman is stunning as she smiles brightly at me through a sheen of pearly white teeth surrounded by too plump, cherry-red lips. That beautiful rhythm my heart was just beating to shifts drastically into what I can only describe as a drumroll.

This must be what ventricular tachycardia feels like.

Now I understand what my patients go through in the seconds before their chests are zapped with 1700-volts from a defibrillator. I wonder if I pass out and die in this crowd of mostly doctors and medical professionals if they'll resuscitate me or just let me go and put me out of my misery.

But what the fuck?

He was all fucking heartbroken when he left me four months ago, and in that time he's met a woman? A woman he clearly has on his arm? A woman who likely came back with him from London since I know for a fact that he just returned the other night?

My smile slips a notch, and once I realize I'm no doubt exposing my incredible displeasure and probably snarling like a feral cat at the woman on his arm, I do my best to reform it. I have no doubt it looks as awkward as it feels.

"Margot," his voice floats over me like melting butter, all warm and soft and so deliciously perfect. The upward lift at the end of my name makes him almost sound pleasantly surprised to see me here. A fact I quickly discover is true when he follows my name up with, "What a lovely surprise finding you here."

"Julien," I manage, my voice far calmer than I would have thought given the rather large frog stuck in the back of my throat. "It's nice to see you. When did you return?" I ask, feigning ignorance. I don't fool him for a minute. That's what happens when you have sex with a man for three months and give him part of your heart.

He learns all of your tricks. Knows you inside and out.

"Just the other night," he replies in that annoyingly yummy English accent of his. The sun takes this particular moment to burst through the scattered clouds and shine directly on him, proving once more that he's a God and can command the heavens.

My heavens.

My heart.

My poor, sick, absolutely ruined heart. I had given up on Julien. He had left the country, after all, with no plans to return.

But then hope came rearing its ugly head back in when I heard he was returning, and suddenly it was as if he had never left. Like those last four months of us being apart never happened. All those feelings I felt that were so perfect and so right crashed back through me with the force of a tsunami.

"Wow." I smile a little too brightly as I swallow down my stupid feelings. "Amazing. How long are you in town for?"

He chuckles, glancing down at the woman on his arm and I hate everything.

"Brielynne and I are back in Boston indefinitely." Brielynne? That's her name? Whatever happened to the names Brie or Lynne? Brielynne is a dumb name and it seems I'm officially hating on her. Probably because I've heard the words indefinitely before, but when they were spoken to me, my name was definitely not included in the sentiment.

"Wow," I say again and then cringe at the repeat, but in fairness, my brain is rapidly swelling to twice its natural size while my heart shrivels up and dies. It's good at that. Has had tons of practice. "Well...," I swallow, staring over at the woman who is now eyeing me in an all-too-familiar, territorial way. "Welcome back. To both of you."

"Thanks," he answers smoothly, taking another step until the three of us are only a few feet apart.

Why can't he just go? Why does he have to engage me with her on his arm? Is he trying to hurt me? Prove that he's met *the one* while

I was just a placeholder? I get it. Thanks. I don't need him to blast it in front of my face in high definition picture and sound.

"I'm Margot," I say to the woman since Julien seems to have forgotten his typically very polished British manners. I reach out for her to shake my hand and she does. Her hand is like an ice cube. Cold and hard and slippery wet in mine. What he sees in her is beyond me. Hands should be warm, not cold. "It's nice to meet you."

"You too," she replies softly, and I catch her English accent, same as his. How perfect are they? I bet they'll have English children who will play with the royal family. They'll all have tea and pristine play dates together.

And this is the point where he needs to walk away. I can't. I was here first. But instead of leaving, his eyes search my face, trailing slowly down my body before he finds my face again.

"You look beautiful, Margot. Have you been well?"

NO! I want to shout. No, I have not been well. I've been okay. I've been getting by. Actually, I was doing fine until this. Until he decided to come back to Boston like the ghost of Christmas past and haunt my ass.

"Yeah," I laugh, shifting my weight and resisting the urge to drop my eyes to the grass. It's a habit of mine to look down when I'm feeling most insecure and I hate it. It makes me feel weak when I do it and I will not be weak in front of him. "I've been good. You know me." It's a throwaway line, but Brielynne doesn't like it one bit.

"Yes," he chuckles, agreeing almost a bit too enthusiastically and now her eyes are flaming. "You still working all hours at the hospital?" I nod, humming out something that's meant to sound like a yes. "Not much time to meet someone new when you work like that."

Is he fucking kidding me?

How dare he.

Is he seriously asking if I'm dating someone right now, right here, in front of his indefinitely? I open my mouth to respond, to say something, when someone beats me to the punch.

"She doesn't need to meet someone new when she has me." My head flies to the right, my hair catching in the wind once more and plastering across my face. Peeling it back so I can see, I do a double-take because there is no way the person whose voice I heard would say that.

Andrew Albright, aka Drew my best friend, saunters over to us, a devil-may-care grin etched on his too-perfect face. His gray eyes are alight with the same mischief, but if you didn't know him, it would come across as arrogant. Which he is. Make no mistake about that. But this look has purpose and it makes me uneasy.

"Drew," I say, somehow able to accurately label him with his proper name. But that's as far as I get.

"Hey, sweetheart." His smile widens as he approaches me. "I was looking for you."

My eyebrows furrow for about two seconds before I realize what he's doing.

He's saving me.

Julien and Drew never met, which is kind of weird if you think about it. I dated Julien for a few months, and in all that time, he never met my best friend. He never met my girlfriends either. It was like I was his dirty secret. We stayed in a lot and ordered food or cooked. Had a lot of sex, and most times, I'd leave without spending the night.

Which actually makes me think…

But before I fully formulate my question, Drew reaches me, wraps his arms around my back, tugs me to his chest and plants his lips on mine.

I'm so stunned that I freeze up, my eyes wide before I feel him nudge me in the thigh with his knee, urging me not to mess this up, I assume. So I do the last thing I ever thought I'd do. I close my eyes, snake my arms around his neck, and kiss my best friend back.

I kiss him back hard.

His lips are full and soft and commanding as he takes my mouth with determined ardor. Tilting his head to the side, he instantly deepens our angle and before I even know what the hell is happening, our mouths are moving together.

Touching. Testing. Tasting. Breathing.

It's like the beginning of a symphony. The slow build that you know–if allowed–will reach a soul-crushing crescendo. My fingers twirl up into his hair, the ends just long enough for me to twist my fingers in. His hands rake down my body, pausing above the crest of my ass where he presses me toward him ever so slightly.

Just enough to let me know he likes this.

That he wants more of it.

His tongue sweeps across the seam of my lips, begging for entrance, and I open willingly for him. A groan tears from the back of his throat, his grip on me tightening. The moment our tongues meet, someone clears their throat rather forcefully and Drew jerks back, his gaze dark and his lips wet from our kiss.

Holy hell, Andrew Albright can kiss.

Jesus, my knees are weak, and that kiss couldn't have lasted any longer than a few seconds. What the hell just happened? Drew keeps one hand glued to my lower back, turning to face Julien and Brielynne.

"Hi," Drew says. "Andrew Albright. I don't think we've met." He reaches out his other hand for Julien who appears like he just smelled rotting garbage.

"Julien Westover." Drew shakes hands with Julien, while Brielynne stands there like a quiet doll, not saying a word or reaching out to shake Drew's hand. "How long have you two been together?" Julien asks, his steely gaze concentrating on me before bouncing back to Drew like he's ready to kill him.

Drew angles his head down to me with a warm, adoring smile. "It's been what? A couple of months, right?" I nod numbly, still unable to speak after that kiss. *That kiss!* "Feels like longer though. In a good way." Drew throws me a playful wink.

"I'm sure. You must be a nurse, as well, then? I can't imagine there are many of you about," Julien asserts with an unmistakable air of superiority. Like somehow being a male nurse is a cardinal sin for the male gender. I roll my eyes at him before I can stop myself.

Drew laughs, tugging my body closer into his side and dropping a kiss on top of my head. "There aren't many male nurses, no.

Which is a shame considering all the important work nurses do." Drew peeks down at me with that smile still planted on his sexy, full, amazingly kissable lips. *Shit. Stop it!* "But no, I'm not a nurse. I'm an emergency room physician. I work with Margot. What do you do?"

"I work in pharmaceuticals."

Drew nods his head, but doesn't ask anything else about that. "I think I remember Margot mentioning something about you once. You moved to London, right?"

"Yes. But we're back now."

My eyes widen at Julien's slip, and I know Drew catches it too. Because I cried on Drew's shoulder for a few nights after Julien ended things with me.

"Very nice. How long have you two been dating?"

"Oh," Brielynne laughs sardonically, her grip on Julien tightening. "We're not dating. We're married. Have been for…," she trails off, glancing up at Julien, *her husband*. "How long, darling? Five years now?" My stomach drops into my feet. My vision sways, likely because I just sucked in a giant rush of air and I'm holding it in tight. She eyes me hard with a very fake smile. "How do you know my husband again?"

THE END

Continue reading Margot and Drew's funny, sexy and unexpected story in The Edge of Reason. You'll also get more of all of your favorite The Edge characters including more of Drew and Aria's HEA.

If you want a future glimpse (beyond these stories) into Aria and Wes's HEA keep reading bonus epilogue.

Also by J. Saman

Wild Minds Duet:

Reckless to Love You

Love to Hate Her

Hate to Love Him

Crazy to Love You

Love to Tempt You

Promise to Love You

The Edge Series:

The Edge of Temptation

The Edge of Forever

The Edge of Reason

The Edge of Chaos

Start Again Series:

Start Again

Start Over

Start With Me

Las Vegas Sin Series:

Touching Sin

Catching Sin

Darkest Sin

Standalones:

Just One Kiss

Love Rewritten

Beautiful Potential

Forward - FREE

End of Book Note

For those of you who have read my books before, you know this is the part where I sort of break it all down. First, thank you for reading this book. Your support means everything to me and I couldn't do any of it without you! I want to thank my husband and my girls who are absolutely everything that is everything in my world.

I wrote this book forever ago. I've updated and revised it since (obviously), but when I initially wrote it, it was before Touching Sin which had a huge domestic violence theme to it. Josh is a fictitious spin on a real person. He is a patient I once treated when I was working in the ICU as a nursing student many many years ago. His partner had bludgeoned him because he thought he was cheating. Unfortunately the patient was transferred to a different hospital and I never found out how he ended up. But his story always stuck with me. It went along the lines of do we ever really know someone. What they're capable of? It went along the lines of everyone has secrets. Hidden pieces of their soul.

My characters aren't all good and they aren't all bad. They are flawed and damaged and experience emotions we all do - insecurity, doubt, frustration, jealousy, depression… The list goes on and on.

This book was sort of about that for me. This was a life is motherfucking messy and raw and occasionally brutal. But it's also beautiful and full of hope and love and that's what I love most about writing romance.

These weren't the perfect CEO alpha men out for world domination (though I do love those heroes). These weren't the feisty girl that knows just the right buttons to press and how to get under the skin of that perfect CEO (though I love those heroines too). To me, these were real people. People you could see being in your lives. Being your friends. Your secret crushes.

I liked that Aria dressed up for Wes, hoping he'd see her like that. I liked how Wes was a total mess of a man - even though his world was outwardly perfect for a while. I liked how he felt undeserving of her and realized he fucked it all up by letting her get away. Even the side characters are messy. Margo? I mean, talk about issues. We obviously know about Josh's demons.

Okay, enough babbling. The Edge of Temptation is part of the Illicit Boxed Set - it's a limited edition series though so in May I'm going to release that book as a standalone. This summer/early fall (?) I'm going to be releasing the second book in the Las Vegas Sin series. It's Maddox's book and I'm getting really excited for it! This fall/ early winter, I'm hoping to release a rockstar romance I wrote and I've got a few more coming as well. It's going to be quite the year!

Check me out on Facebook, Instagram, BookBub, Pinterest, Goodreads or on my Website! Signup for my newsletter and get one of my books FREE!

Thank you so much! XO ~ J. Saman

Keep reading for the first chapters of Start Again

Reckless to Love You

Lyric

I can't stop staring at it. Reading the two short words over and over again ad nauseum. They're simple. Essentially unimpressive if you think about it. But those two words mean everything. Those two words dive deep into the darkest depths of my soul, the part I've methodically shut off over the years, and awaken the dormant volcano. How can two simple words make this well of emotions erupt so quickly?

Come home.

I don't recognize the number the text came from. It shows up as Unknown. But I don't have to recognize it. I know who it's from. Instinctively, I know. At least, my body does, because my heart rate is through the roof. My stomach is clenched tight with violent, poorly concealed, sickly butterflies. My forehead is clammy with a sheen of sweat and my hands tremble as they clutch my phone.

It's early here in California. Not even dawn, but I'm awake. I'm always awake, even when I'm not, and since my phone has, unfortunately, become another appendage, it's consistently with me.

It's a New York area code.

Goddammit! I suck in a deep, shuddering breath of air that does absolutely nothing to calm me, then I respond in the only way I can.

Me***: Who is this?***

The message bubble appears instantly, like he was waiting for me. Like there is no way this is a wrong number. Like his fingers couldn't respond fast enough.

Unknown: ***You know who this is. Come home.***

I don't respond. I can't. I'm frozen. It's been four years. Four fucking years. And this is how he reaches out? This is how he contacts me? I slink back down into my bed, pulling the heavy comforter over my head in a pathetic attempt to protect myself from the onslaught of emotions that consume me. I tuck my phone against my chest, over what's left of my fractured heart.

I'm hurting. I'm angry. I'm so screwed up and broken, and yet, I'm still breaking. How is that even possible? How can a person continue to break when they're already broken? How can a person I haven't seen in four years still affect me like this?

I want to throw the traitorous device into the wall and smash it. Toss it out my window as hard as I can and hope it reaches the Pacific at the other end of the beach, where it will be swept away, never to return. But I don't. Because curiosity is a nefarious bitch. Because I have to know why the man who was my everything and now my nothing is contacting me after all this time, asking me to come home.

Unknown***: I'm sitting here in my old room, on my bed, and I can't focus. I can't think about what I need to be thinking about. So, I need you to come home.***

I shake my head as tears line my eyes, stubbornly refusing to fall but obscuring my vision all the same. Nothing he's saying makes sense to me. Nothing. It's completely nonsensical, and yet, it's not. I still know him well enough to understand both what he's saying and what he's not.

Me: ***Why?***

Unknown***: Because I need you to.***

Me: ***I can't. Too busy with work.***

That's sort of a lie. I mean, I *am* headed to New York for the Rainbow Ball in a few days. But he doesn't need to know that. And I do not want to see him. I absolutely, positively, do not.

Unknown: ***My dad had a stroke***

My eyes cinch shut, and I cover them with one hand. I can't breathe. A gasped sob escapes the back of my throat, burning me with its raw taste. God. Now what the hell am I going to do? I love his father. Jesus Christ. How can I say no to him now? How can I avoid this the way I so desperately need to? *Shit.*

Me: ***I'm sorry. I didn't know. Is he okay?***

Unknown: ***He'll live, but he's not great. He's in the ICU. Worse than he was after the heart attack.***

I shake my head back and forth. I can't go. I can't go home. I was there two months ago to visit my parents and my sister's family. I have work—so much freaking work that I can barely keep up. I don't want to see him. I won't survive it. I'll see him, and I'll feel everything I haven't allowed myself to feel. I'll be sucked back in.

Things are different now.

They are. My situation has changed completely, but I never had the guts to call him and tell him that. Mostly because I was hurt. Mostly because I felt abandoned and brushed off. Mostly because I was terrified that it wouldn't matter after all this time apart. If I see him now, knowing how much has changed…Shit. I just…Fuck. I can't.

I don't know what to do.

I'm drenched in sweat. The blanket I sought refuge in is now smothering me. I'm relieved his father is alive. I still speak to him once a month. Wait, let me amend that—he still *calls* me once a month. And we talk. Not about Jameson. Never about him. Only about me and my life. I'm a wreck that Jameson is contacting me. I can't play this game. I never could. It was all or nothing with him.

Unknown: ***I miss you.***

I stare at the words, read them over again, then respond too quickly, ***Liar.***

Unknown: ***Never. I miss you so goddamn much.***

I think I just died. Everything inside me has stopped. My heart is not beating. My breath has stalled inside my chest, unable to be expelled. My mind is completely blank. And when everything comes back to life, I'm consumed with an angry, caustic fury I never knew I was capable of.

Unknown: ***Are you still there?***

Me: ***What do you want me to say?***

Unknown: ***I don't know. I'm torn on that. Please come home.***

Me: ***Why?***

Unknown: ***Because I need you. Because he needs you. Because I was always too busy obsessing over you to fall for someone else. Because I need to know if I'm making a mistake by hoping.***

I shake my head vigorously, letting out the loudest, shrillest shriek I can muster. It's not fucking helping, and I need something to help. Clamoring out of bed, I hurry over to the balcony doors, unlocking them and tossing them open wide.

Fresh air. I need fresh air. Even Southern California fresh air. A burst of salty, ocean mist hits me square in the face, clinging to the sweat I'm covered in. It's still dark out. Dawn is not yet playing with the midnight-blue sky.

I stare out into the black expanse of the ocean, listen to the crashing of the waves and sigh. I knew about him. I would be lying if I said I hadn't Facebook-stalked him a time or twenty over the years. Forced myself to hate him with the sort of passion reserved for political figures and pop stars. But this? Saying he misses me?

Me: ***Seeing me won't change that. But if you're asking, you are.***

He responds immediately, and I can't help but grin a little at that. *You still care about me, Jameson Woods*. When I catch the traitorous thought, I shut it down instantly. Because if he cared, if his texted words meant anything, then I wouldn't be here, and he wouldn't be there, and this bullshit four a.m. text conversation wouldn't be happening.

Unknown: ***I'm not asking. Seeing you might change***

everything. But more than that, I need you here with me. My father would want to see you. Come home.

I hate him. I hate him. I hate him!

Me: ***I can't come home. Stop using your father to manipulate me.***

Unknown: ***It's the only play I have. You can come home. I know you can. Are you seeing someone? Before you respond, any answer other than no might kill me right now.***

I growl, not caring if anyone walking by hears. How can he do this to me? How can he be so goddamn selfish? Doesn't he know what he put me through? That I still haven't found my way back after four years? I shouldn't reply. I should just throw my phone away and never look back.

Me: ***No. And you're a bastard.***

Unknown: ***YES. I Am! Please. I am officially begging. Really, Lee. I'm not even bullshitting. I'm a mess. Please. Please. Please!!!!***

Me: **...**

Unknown: ***What does that mean?***

Me: ***It means I'm thinking. Stop!***

My eyes lock on nothing, my mind swirling a mile a minute.

Lee. He called me Lee. That nickname might actually hurt the most. And now he's asking me to come home. Jameson Woods, the man I thought was my forever, is asking me to come home to see him. And for what? To scratch a long-forgotten itch? To assuage some long-abandoned guilt over what he did? Why would I fall for that?

I sigh again because I know why. It's the same reason I never bring men home. It's the same reason I haven't given up this house even though I don't fully live in it anymore and it's far from convenient. It's the same reason I continued this conversation instead of smashing my phone.

Jameson Woods.

The indelible ink on my body. The scar on my soul. The fissure in my heart.

Unknown: **...**

I can't help the small laugh that squeaks out as I lean forward and prop my elbows on the edge of the railing. The cool wind whips through my hair, and I hate that I feel this way. That I'm entertaining him the way I am.

Me: ***What does that mean?***

Unknown: ***It means I'm getting impatient. Please. I need you to come home. I know I'm a bastard. I know I shouldn't be asking you this. But I am.***

Unknown: ***Aren't you at least a little curious?***

YES!

Me: ***NO!!!!!!! And bastard doesn't cover you.***

Unknown: ***Please. It's spinning out of control, and I need to see you. I need to know***.

Me: ***You already know.***

Unknown: ***About you?***

Me: ***Yes, or you wouldn't be texting me at four in the morning.***

Unknown: ***It's seven here***. ***Does that mean you'll come?***

Me: **...**

Unknown: **...**

Me: ***Yes***.

My phone slips from my fingers, clanging to the hard surface of my balcony floor. My phone buzzes again, a little louder now since the sound is reverberating off the ground. I don't pick it up. I don't look down. I don't care if he's thanking me or anything else he comes up with. I don't care. I don't want to know.

Because I'm busy getting my head on straight.

Locking myself down.

I'm worried about his father and I want to see him, want to make sure he's okay with my own two eyes.

I'll go home and I'll see him. I'll see him, and I'll do the one thing I was never able to do before. I'll say goodbye. My eyes close and I allow myself to slip back. To remember every single moment we had together. To indulge in the sweet torture that, if I let it, will rip me apart piece by piece. Because I know what I'm in for, and I know that once I step foot off that airplane, nothing will ever be right again.

Want to know what happens with Lyric and Jameson? Get your copy of Reckless to Love You and fall into this second chance, friends-to-lovers romance today!

Made in the USA
Columbia, SC
01 September 2023

22329282R00167